PENGUIN BOOKS
THE MARGINS

John Wigglesworth is a British national who has been based in Asia for the past ten years. He currently lives in Bangkok.

The Margins

John Wigglesworth

PENGUIN BOOKS

An imprint of Penguin Random House

PENGUIN BOOKS

USA | Canada | UK | Ireland | Australia
New Zealand | India | South Africa | China | Southeast Asia

Penguin Books is part of the Penguin Random House group of companies whose addresses can be found at global.penguinrandomhouse.com

Published by Penguin Random House SEA Pte Ltd
9, Changi South Street 3, Level 08-01,
Singapore 486361

First published in Penguin Books by Penguin Random House SEA 2020

Copyright © John Wigglesworth 2020

All rights reserved

10 9 8 7 6 5 4 3 2 1

This is a work of fiction. Names, characters, places and incidents are either the product of the author's imagination or are used fictitiously, and any resemblance to any actual person, living or dead, events or locales is entirely coincidental.

ISBN 9789814882989

Typeset in Adobe Garamond Pro by Manipal Technologies Limited, Manipal
Printed at Markono Print Media Pte Ltd, Singapore

This book is sold subject to the condition that it shall not, by way of trade or otherwise, be lent, resold, hired out, or otherwise circulated without the publisher's prior consent in any form of binding or cover other than that in which it is published and without a similar condition including this condition being imposed on the subsequent purchaser.

www.penguin.sg

1

JUBBAWY

'One hundred and twenty-seven.'

The policeman speaks slowly, releasing the words one by one, letting them hang in the air. Then he closes his eyes, leans back in his chair, and says nothing more.

I wait, listening to the faint rattle of an air-conditioning unit somewhere behind me. The room is windowless, and there is little to occupy the eye. It is, I reflect, entirely functional. Metal furniture, a mirror set into the far wall, strip lights that hum as they flicker, and white tiles everywhere. The walls are tiled, the floor is tiled. It has been designed to be easy to clean, I reason. You could butcher an animal in here and just hose the waste matter away, down the black drain near the door. My eyes search for a clock—the walls are bare, however. Both men sat across the table are wearing wristwatches, but the faces are angled away from me. I do not want to ask the time because I do not want to precipitate the interview, so I stare at Jubbawy and wait.

It is, I suppose, a rather unusual situation to be in. After all, I am sitting in an interview room with the second-most senior policeman in India, facing several hours of questioning at the very least, and without any legal representation whatsoever. The building to which I have been brought is the Ministry for Home Affairs, and occupies a position not far from the centre of Delhi, just a few minutes' drive from Lutyens' majestic India Gate. I arrived a little over an hour ago, but the events of the night before last relieved me of my wristwatch, and I am thus largely unsure of the time—it is afternoon at least. I am not under arrest, and came here of my own free will. Paradoxically, I had no other choice. Were you somehow able to observe the scene in the claustrophobic room, you could be forgiven for making the assumption that I was reporting a street robbery, or perhaps a serious road accident; after all, neither are particularly uncommon in this part of the world, and my physical appearance suggests a certain level of violence has taken place. You would, however, be misinterpreting the rather limited circumstantial evidence; to do otherwise would be an impossible task.

For me, it is a similarly impossible task to find any kind of rational explanation for what I have done—in fact, I'm not even convinced that there's an explanation to be found. Looking back over the past two-and-a-half years, it seems that I have made so many critical errors of judgement that it is difficult to sieve out one pivotal decision, one key choice, which can be marked as the origin of my downfall. And my god, how far I have fallen. How detached from reality I have become. And here I am—dumped back into the real world, the past yet to catch up with me. It is still slowly ascending, yet to break the surface. It will, of course.

'*One hundred and twenty-seven.*'

Jubbawy's eyes are still closed, although he is frowning now, as if struggling to grasp the enormity of the figure, unable to picture it. A bead of sweat emerges tentatively from the thin black hair above his temple, growing slowly in size until it approaches critical mass and begins to quiver uncertainly, deciding whether or not to succumb to gravity. I try to guess the course it will take when it falls. Initially, straight down and fast, under the tortoiseshell bridge formed by his glasses, but then it will most likely slow as it reaches the rough, frictional pock-marked skin under his cheekbones. Where next? At a slower speed it will be more vulnerable to the contours of his face; perhaps it will attempt to traverse the light stubble towards the path of least resistance, the hairless brown skin by his ear. It isn't far to go, less than half an inch. We always take the path of least resistance, I think to myself. No. There's moisture nestling between the shafts of hair on his cheek. It will seek out these minute rivulets, enveloping them, gaining in size. It wants to grow, exactly like the commune wanted to grow. A small, flat mole, sprouting three wispy hairs may divert it towards the dark mass of his moustache, then down a slight gully formed by a fold of fat that sits like a fleshy bracket around his jowls. Yes. It will end up on his jaw, exactly halfway between his ear and his mouth. I am certain of it.

'One hundred and twenty-seven bodies.' Finally he opens his eyes. They are large, kindly eyes, magnified slightly by the spectacles he wears. 'You were lucky to escape, were you not?'

When I speak, my voice is surprisingly devoid of emotion. 'It depends how you look at it. I'm not so sure . . .'

'Yes, yes, yes,' he says with a dismissive wave of his hand, 'this must be a very difficult time for you. I am sorry to put you through this ordeal so soon after . . . after what happened. It is, however, necessary. And my point is that you seem to be the only one left alive. *Statistically*, doesn't that make you rather fortunate?'

'I suppose it does . . .'

The brows above his eyes are now raised. 'And?'

I shrug. 'It's all rather a blur, I'm afraid. Do you have any cigarettes?'

'You remember nothing?'

'No. Not really.'

Jubbawy produces a handkerchief, wraps it around his forefinger, and carefully dabs the bead of sweat near his temple. I feel a flash of annoyance that I'll never know what path the droplet would have taken. How odd, I think to myself. How odd that such a trivial emotion could emerge through the numbing shock I feel for these events of the past few days.

'Not really,' he repeats. 'I see.'

Again, a long pause. The table rocks slightly as he scribbles something on a pad. It is metal, coated in flaking, grey paint, although in front of me a series of bright silver scars glisten under the strip lights. Someone has tried to scratch graffiti on the surface. The writing is, I guess, Hindi.

'So far,' he continues with a sigh, 'we have identified only a few of the bodies.' A thin, mirthless smile, almost hidden by his moustache. 'I'm sure you'll understand that it's a rather difficult task. I mean, at this hippie commune—if that's what we're calling it—there isn't exactly a register of guests, is there?'

I don't answer, and he eventually looks back down at the pad. On it is a short, handwritten list. I assume that these are the names of the dead. 'One of the victims was the daughter of the Canadian ambassador to India. The others . . .' he shrugs, '. . . people like you.'

'May I see the list, please?'

Director General of Police Jubbawy shakes his head almost imperceptibly. 'No. That will not be possible, I'm afraid. We have only released a handful of names to the press so far.'

'The press?'

'Mr Hicks, a lot of people are dead. They're westerners, not Indians.' He turns his palms to the ceiling. 'World news.'

'World news,' I repeat, uncertainly.

He looks at me, a little puzzled. 'You seem surprised.'

'I just never imagined . . . No one should have died up there.'

'No one? They are *all* dead.' He taps his pen on the table, then looks at me for a moment. 'Apart from you, that is.'

I say nothing.

'So anyway,' he continues, 'Can you tell me what these people were doing on a remote mountainside in Himachal Pradesh? Can you tell me that?'

I get up slowly from the chair and pace over towards the large, rectangular mirror set into the wall. I stare back at myself, absently wondering whether it is two-way. My face looks drawn, the only colour afforded by the yellow and purple bruising around my eye-sockets and cheekbones. They've done a neat job stitching my nose though, I think to myself, examining the tiny rows of black sutures that descend from the corner of my left eye to my mouth like a train-track. 127 stitches, 127 bodies. An odd coincidence, but nothing more. 'Do you have any cigarettes?' I say to my pale reflection.

'Was it a cult? The press are already claiming it was some kind of cult?'

'No, no, not a cult, nothing like that. Look, I could really do with a cigarette . . . They wouldn't let me smoke in the hospital.'

'What was it then?'

I turn back to face the two policemen. A packet of Gold Flake along with an ashtray has appeared on the table. Quid pro quo.

'I don't know . . . a kibbutz, I suppose. Like a collective farm.' I sit back down, and impatiently fumble a cigarette from the carton, pausing as Jubbawy lights it for me. The tobacco tastes sweet.

'Mr Hicks—'

'Ethan's fine.'

'Mr Hicks, I need to know what these people were doing up there. Tell me about this commune . . .'

I take a long drag on the cigarette. 'There were three of us to begin with. Me, Hal and Div—'

'Who were they?'

I slide the ashtray a few inches towards me and sigh. It was a long time ago. 'A couple I met in Delhi. They were Americans.'

2

NEW DELHI, MAY 1986

It was the second time I'd been to Delhi, and the place hadn't changed much in the decade that'd elapsed. The newspapers were saying it was in the midst of an economic boom, and for sure there were more cars, more people, more commerce since I was last there—but the fabric of the city wasn't that different, just a little more frayed from use, perhaps. I didn't have much money myself, and stayed in the old quarter of Delhi, at a rotten, cheap hotel that seemed to attract the very worst kind of traveller. It consisted of a quadrangle of cell-sized rooms and dormitories, surrounding a concrete roof garden that was rendered uninhabitable by the heat in the daylight hours. Below the hotel was a dilapidated Chinese restaurant that was always empty, and for my first few days in India, I sat in there alone, drinking myself into cultural assimilation, watching other travellers come and go from the hotel with their colourful rucksacks.

It was there that Div asked me for a light. That was how we met, a simple, innocuous request that could have amounted to nothing, but which turned out to be the beginning of everything. She offered to join me; I herded the collection of empty beer bottles to one side by way of an acceptance, then offered her a drink, vaguely wondering if she was chatting me up. I wasn't attracted to her—she looked like a junkie going cold-turkey, with strands of sweat-soaked hair pasted to her forehead, pale skin and narrow bloodshot eyes—so it was something of a relief when a skinny, dishevelled man shuffled in and claimed her with a perfunctory kiss. The first words he said to me were: 'Looks like you drink too fucking much. What are you trying to shut out, man?'

There was something slightly odd about Hal. It didn't take too long to figure out: his eyes were far too excited with ordinary life, and he seemed unable to hold a conversation, preferring instead to listen and issue occasional, irrelevant sound bites which were said with gravity but meant nothing. Div later explained he'd been on the hippie circuit for close to fifteen years, just melting his brain and having a good time, but not really doing much else. He was good-looking, I suppose, for someone who'd been on the road for so long; oily, black hair that was distilled into a ponytail halfway down his back, brown eyes framed with laughter lines that gave his face a comforting geniality, and dark, weathered skin. Such was his appearance that when I first saw him walk into the restaurant, before his drawling American accent betrayed his nationality, I thought he was European—Italian maybe. As events would prove, it wasn't to be the last time that I'd make a wrong assumption about Hal.

I stayed with them for a month. We smoked dope, drank beer and constantly flitted between downmarket hotels, trying to make our money last whilst spending it with impunity. Hal and Div occasionally did a bit of harder stuff, mainly opium. Eventually I did too. I think, perhaps, that I was trying to find some kind of identity, and was eager to comply with theirs. Yet, behind the façade of carefree hedonism, their relationship with each other seemed little more than a sham. In the daytime, when the heat leached the toxins from our bodies and forced the three of us into a state of uneasy sobriety, we would skirt around the inevitably turgid conversations, instead immersing ourselves in aimless activities such as playing cards, killing time in cafés or wandering through the bazaars of Chandni Chowk. In truth none of us had much in common.

'You'll like Lorna,' Hal grunted, as we felt the sweat prickle on our skin in the air-conditioned haven of the General Post Office. 'She lives in Delhi.'

I finished thumbing through the pile of poste restante mail on the shelf marked with the letter H. There was nothing from home. 'Who's she?'

'An old friend, dude.' He stared at the letter he was holding for a moment. 'She's an old friend of mine.'

Div started to say something, then seemed to think better of it, instead bunching her ginger dreads into a ponytail which she fastened with a large elastic band. She snapped it into place with a sigh.

'What?' Hal growled, looking up at her.

'Nothing,' she said, rubbing her arms. 'Can we go now? It's freezing in here.'

'She's got her own place not far from our hotel. We'll go and see her,' he continued, looking up at a large electronic calendar on the wall. 'A fortnight. She's out of the country right now, seeing some relative. Back on the twenty-fifth.'

'I thought we were going to hitch down to Kerala?' Div protested.

'I'm not stopping you,' Hal replied easily.

'Oh for Christ's sake . . .' The rest of the words were lost as she put her hand to her mouth and began to walk away. She stopped after a few metres, turned, and snapped impatiently, 'Are you coming or what?'

'Jesus,' he hissed to me under his breath. 'Doesn't she do your head in as well?'

'Shut up, Hal,' I replied.

The fact that time can never be turned back, not even by one second, makes hindsight a virtually meaningless concept—the only purpose it serves is to mark our choices and their consequences, taunting us with the alternative outcomes that could have been but weren't. My choice, the path I took, was to remain with Hal and Div for another fortnight in Delhi. In truth I was already bored with their company, with the constant arguments and resultant toxic binges that seemed to heal the wounds in their relationship until the next sober day, the next fight. For sure I was lonely, in search of company, yet, upon reflection, the way in which I clung to such a false friendship seems sad, wretched even. But I stayed with them, and so it was that the three of us made the noisy journey across the city to meet up with Lorna. There was no way of knowing at the time, but my decision would prove fatal. Lorna was to become the needle that inextricably wove me into the tapestry of events that ended in 127 bodies on a mountainside. She was not only the reason I went to the mountain, but also the reason I stayed. And although she was, in essence, entirely incapable of any wrongdoing, it seems to me that those who are innocent can wreak as much damage as those who are guilty, like the unwitting plague carrier boarding a crowded ferry. Lorna is not to *blame* for what happened, of course. She is no more culpable than the mountain on which so many died; the same cannot be said of me.

'Hal! I can't believe it's you!' Lorna gasped, putting her hands to her face. I detected an accent, Australian or Kiwi.

'Lorna Roberts,' he laughed, hugging her briefly. 'It's been too fucking long, you know?'

The four of us were stood on her colonnaded porch, the floor of which was laid with black and white marble tiles. The house itself was stucco-fronted, with large shuttered windows and colourful baskets of flowers hanging from wrought-iron brackets on the walls. It seemed rather grand, and I was going to comment as such, but a dog started up nearby and Lorna promptly fussed us inside, giving me and Div a weak smile as we passed.

The interior was very dark. At first I thought my eyes had not yet adjusted from being outside, where the sunlight bounces off pavements and walls, making you squint and weep, but it was simply that there was no light, artificial or natural, save for the occasional sputtering candle placed haphazardly on a table or shelf. It smelt musty, like the crypt of a church. From a room somewhere upstairs I could hear music playing, Jimi Hendrix. It made me think briefly of home, of my mother vacuuming in one room while the radio played loud in another. There were no carpets to vacuum here, of course, just cold stone floors with the occasional rug thrown down for comfort or decoration, although the walls were covered in posters of bygone rock stars and psychedelic batiks. The room into which we were shown was large, but somehow managed to look cluttered with out-of-place carvings from various continents, a large antique map of India hanging on the wall, and assorted teak and mahogany furniture which seemed to absorb the little light that struggled through the slats of the shutters. It smelt strongly of incense.

'Lorna, meet Ethan . . .'—we shook hands uncertainly—'. . . and Div.'

'Hi,' we said in unison.

'Great,' Hal beamed. He seemed very pleased, as if Div, Lorna and I were all good friends now that each of us had grunted out a word of greeting.

'It's so wonderful to see you, Hal,' she said, studying his face. 'How long's it been? Five years? More?'

'A long time,' Hal agreed, looking around. 'Too long. Hey, this is a nice place you've got here, you know? Real nice.'

'Thanks. Look, do you guys want a drink? Tea, coffee or anything? I've got some cold beer as well . . .'

'Tea would be nice,' Hal suggested. 'And if you've got any biscuits . . .'

Lorna looked at each of us. 'Four teas, then. I don't think I've got any biscuits, but I'll have a look.' She left the room, jangling the long threads of beads that served as a door on her way.

'So how do you know Lorna, Hal?' I asked after a few moments, adjusting the position of a glass paperweight on her bookshelf. It had a large butterfly embedded in the centre of the orb; the refracted light appeared to give the tiny, fine hairs on its body a strange, ultraviolet hue around their edges.

'I met her in Kathmandu,' he replied slowly, as if uncertain of the memory. 'We go back a long time.'

'Oh,' I replied, vaguely wondering if they'd been an item.

'Yeah, there was a big group of us going right through Asia, just travelling around, meeting people and stuff . . .' A pause, and I heard the flare of a match, shortly followed by the distinctive, acrid smell of cannabis. 'Best times of my life. Don't you sometimes wish you could turn back the clock, go back to how it used to be?'

I flinched at the comment and looked at Div. She had her back to the room, and was stood on tiptoes, peering out at the street through the slats in the shutters.

'Have you been to Nepal, Div?' I asked.

She turned on her heel and looked at me, smiling but saying nothing.

'I just wondered if you'd been there . . .'

She laughed and said softly, 'Thanks, Ethan, but you needn't.'

'Needn't what?' Hal asked without interest, blowing a plume of smoke from his nostrils.

Div remained silent, but held my eye. Eventually the feeling of complicity caused me to look away. I picked up the glass paperweight, rotated it in my fingers, and said absently, 'They say if a butterfly flaps its wings in the Amazonian rainforest, it may cause a hurricane on the other side of the world.'

'Do you believe that?' she asked, sounding thoughtful.

'I don't know, not really. I suppose it's just another way of saying life's complicated, that it's impossible to predict what will happen.'

'Maybe,' she said. 'But you've got to have aims, a purpose to your life, something to work towards . . . haven't you?'

'I guess so,' I said with a shrug.

'It's simple, man,' Hal interjected. 'There are two choices, dude—become a part of the system, give your life to some company, or bum out.'

'That does seem to be about the size of it,' I agreed.

'So what's it gonna be, man? You in or out?'

I was considering my reply when the jangling beads heralded Lorna's return.

'It's condensed milk, so you probably won't need sugar,' she said, gently setting the tray down on a low, black lacquer table. 'I'd have got some proper stuff in, but it's not that often I get visitors.'

The only sound was the delicate clink of cutlery on porcelain as Lorna poured out four cups of tea with studied intent. I sat on the arm of the settee and watched her. Her face was tanned, and she had quite startling cobalt eyes which contrasted with her jet black, almost waist-length hair, which was brushed down over one shoulder, exposing her neck. She was wearing a thin metal chain, adorned with a modest silver cross that swung past her breast with each tiny movement she made over the table. And her skin was perfect. I imagined kissing the back of her neck—for some reason the idea seemed strangely erotic to me.

'So what have you been up to then?' she asked Hal after a time.

'Oh, I don't know. Just bumming around really—my life hasn't changed that much since Nepal. You?'

'Nothing much,' Lorna sighed. She looked around the room as if hoping to find an achievement scrawled on a piece of furniture, then repeated quietly, 'Nothing much at all, to be honest.'

'Still travelling though?' he asked.

'Er . . . no, not for a few years. I suppose I'm getting on a bit for that.'

'You haven't got a job, have you? Don't tell me you're working now?'

She shook her head. 'No, no, I'm not. What would I do, anyway? I've been out of it too long . . . well, I've never been in it, really.'

'Oh, I get it!' Hal proclaimed excitedly. 'You're planning on settling down, aren't you? Kids and all that kind of thing. Who is he then?'

'No one,' she replied, her voice a little hoarse. She once again concerned herself with pouring out the tea, then let the milk jug fall to the tray with a clatter and put her hands to her face.

'Are you okay?' Hal asked.

There was a long silence. I could see a few tears emerge from under her bridged hand, streaking black smudges of mascara down the contours of her face. She seemed to compose herself, momentarily quelling whatever emotion had surfaced, then let out a strangled sob and started to cry uncontrollably.

'I'm sorry . . .' she gasped, shuddering for breath.

Div reached out and put a hand on her back, gently rubbing between her shoulder blades. 'What's wrong, honey?' she whispered.

'We're losers,' Hal muttered, almost to himself. 'That's what's wrong. We're fucking losers.'

I looked at him, surprised by the comment, and began to wonder what I was doing here with these people, thousands of miles from home.

3

JUBBAWY

'Thousands of miles from home,' Jubbawy repeats, thoughtfully. 'Yes, what *were* you doing in India?'

'Not much,' I shrug. He goes to write something in the notepad, then seems to think better of it and instead places the pen back on the table.

'But you must have come here for a reason—a vacation, perhaps?'

I gesture with a nod towards the packet of cigarettes, and take one. I don't light it, just roll the paper cylinder between my finger and thumb. 'I came here for a break—a long break—to get away from my life back home. And why India? Believe it or not, I literally stuck a pin in a map. It landed on India.'

'I see.' He picks up the pen, scrawls a few words on the pad and asks, 'And what did you intend to do on this extended break, might I ask? Go out and see the world? Sit on a beach somewhere and reflect upon things?'

'Ah look,' I say, spreading my hands, 'I didn't really have a plan as such. Just a vague idea that if I got away from the UK, maybe things would become clearer to me—about what I wanted to do in life, I mean. I suppose I was trying to *find myself*, as they say.' I light my cigarette. I cough slightly as I inhale the harsh tobacco; the stitches on my face and nose pull tight from the motion.

'And . . . did you? Find yourself?'

I shrug. 'I guess not.'

Jubbawy says nothing. He puts the pen back to his mouth.

'I certainly didn't figure on this,' I continue.

'Didn't figure on what?' Jubbawy asks. 'Over a hundred people dead?'

The comment seems to strangle the conversation, and the room falls silent except for the tapping of the plastic Bic on Jubbawy's teeth. Tap-tap-tap. Tap-tap-tap. I stare absently at the insignia on his uniform.

'You are bleeding,' he says, eventually.

I look at the floor. There are a few droplets, spread like crimson stars from the impact of their fall on to the white ceramic tiles. I put my hand to my nose, and it comes away wet and warm. I can taste the iron in the back of my mouth, not knowing whether to swallow the blood or spit it out. The floor is so clean that it doesn't seem right to corrupt it with a fat globule of saliva and blood, so I get up and walk towards the drain by the metal door. I spit. It lands with a slap on the small black grill, then disappears all at once, like a lump of jelly.

'Here,' Jubbawy says kindly, holding out his handkerchief. It's the one he used to dab away the droplet of sweat, and as I return to my chair, I take it gratefully, holding it to my nose. It was, I think to myself, impossible to predict. How could I ever have guessed that the droplet of sweat would end up on *my* nose?

'Thanks,' I mumble through the fabric.

'Do you want to stop? Are you okay?'

'I'm fine,' I say. 'It's just a nosebleed.' But the blood slowly spreads from my nose, inching out to the edge of the white cloth. Capillary action, I muse, waiting for it to stop.

'How long did you stay in Delhi?' Jubbawy asks after a time. The words are spoken much more softly than before. His mood has changed; perhaps he pities me.

'A while.' I sigh, and add, 'We were all running out of money, so Hal suggested we ask Lorna if we could stay at hers for a while, to save on hotels. It was out of line, I suppose, but after meeting her that first time... Well, I thought about her quite a bit after that.' I shrug. 'Anyway, I wanted to see her again. I guess that's why I went along with the idea.'

4

NEW DELHI, JUNE 1986

Lorna wasn't in when the three of us arrived at her house, carrying our hastily packed rucksacks. We sat in a dingy café a few hundred metres down the street where we played cards, smoked cheap local cigarettes and sipped Pepsis as we waited for her to return. Hal had managed to convince us that she would be glad of the company, and that to arrive unannounced would simply make for a nice surprise for her.

'You can't all stay here!' Lorna shrieked when she saw us stumbling across the road towards her, stooping under the weight of our baggage as she fumbled with her keys.

'What do you mean?' Hal panted, clearly crestfallen.

'Hal! This isn't a good time for me—I need some space right now . . .'

'Please, Lorna? For old times' sake? Come on, what do you say? What do you say? *Please?*'

'No. Why the hell didn't you phone?' she asked, the exasperation clear from her voice.

'Because you would have said no,' Hal replied, turning his palms to the sky.

The atmosphere seemed to coagulate. Hal appeared reluctant to back down, as if Lorna's refusal to comply with his request amounted to a loss of face for him. His loud protestations were drawing a small crowd of onlookers from the street, and Lorna stood self-consciously on her doorstep, obviously embarrassed by the scene unfolding outside her house but resolute, nonetheless. Div and I, exchanging uneasy glances, shuffled away from her doorstep like school kids walking away from a fight that's about to kick off, dragging our bags in the dust around our feet. I looked around. The street was lined with large, white, colonial, terraced houses, and the black river of asphalt that flowed between them was clogged with people, vehicles and lumbering ox-carts. It seemed impossible that so much noise and bustling activity could be confined to such a small space, and the feeling of claustrophobia was compounded by pavements crowded with makeshift stalls selling fruit, bolts of colourful cloth and cheap, plastic, household goods. Directly across the road, a small group of boys were playing football with an empty plastic bottle. They were not wearing shoes, and were possibly street kids, although in general there seemed to be less poverty in this part of the city—just the occasional beggar sheltering from the sun beneath the awnings of the few converted shops. Most of the pedestrians seemed relatively well-to-do, the men clothed in trousers, shirts and ties, the women in bright saris with detailed, swirling embroidery.

'Hello meester!' shrieked the voice of a child.

I looked for the source. Approaching us was a small, good-looking boy, his hair cut into a perfect pudding-bowl.

'Hello meester!'

'Hello.'

'Hello missy!' he beamed.

'Hello,' Div replied.

'Wanna see my lizard?' He held out his arm, which was adorned with a large green gecko.

'Lovely,' Div smiled.

'You stroke him?'

'Er, no. No, thank you.'

'He like you, see? He smile at you, missy.'

Div peered suspiciously at the reptile.

Everything else seemed to happen with startling rapidity. I remember seeing this green lizard flying through the air towards Div, her screaming as it landed on her shoulders and then scampered down her torso to the ground, the small boy darting between Div's legs and grabbing her day-pack, then running off down the street. I don't know why I bothered to give chase—perhaps I was trying to impress Lorna. Anyway, I managed ten yards before the toe of my flip-flop caught the jagged edge of a pothole in the road. I landed with a thud on the hot, sticky tarmac; my elbows and knees immediately began to sting.

'You better come in and get cleaned up,' Lorna said as the three of them gathered around, looking down at me. 'Those cuts will get infected if you're not careful.'

*

'I can't believe you fell for the lizard trick,' Lorna laughed, examining the raw flesh on my joints.

'Lizard? Seemed more like a small dinosaur from where I was stood,' Div retorted.

'What was in your bag?' I asked.

'Oh, nothing of much value. And Hal's got the passports.'

I winced as Lorna applied an iodine-soaked ball of cotton wool to my elbow, catching her eye. Her gaze lingered for a moment, and she said, 'I think it was very good of you to try and catch him.'

'It was stupid of me to even think I could . . .' Lorna's breast was pushing against my arm now as she bandaged my other elbow, and I could feel the hard seam of her bra pressing into my triceps, the flesh behind it soft and yielding. She would certainly be aware of the contact, but it was hard to know if she was doing it deliberately. I shivered.

'Does it sting?'

'A little.'

She finished winding the bandage around and pinned it into place. 'Right, I'm done. You'll need to change these dressings regularly or they'll stick to the wound, okay?'

'Sure.'

'And you can put your arm down now,' she said forcibly, breaking the eye contact and pulling away.

'Oh. Yes. Sorry.'

'Tea, anyone?' Hal asked from the doorway.

'Er, does anyone want to go out for lunch instead?' Lorna asked with a haste that betrayed her real intentions.

'No, I'm okay, thanks,' Hal replied. 'Those biscuits on the side, can I pinch a couple?'

'Hal, you can't stay here,' she repeated, tiredly.

'Okay,' he replied easily. 'Div, d'you want some lunch?'

Div shook her head. I smiled at Lorna and shrugged. 'I'll come.'

'See you guys later, then,' Hal declared. 'Be good.'

'Come on then,' Lorna sighed, looking at me then jerking her head towards the door.

We ambled around a few side streets for a while, eventually stumbling into an unpleasant looking café selling cheap Tiger beer and serving an array of unappetizing curried dishes from large, well-used metal vats. The contents of every pot looked the same—a thick fatty skin sitting over a collection of anonymous bones that could have been part of a particularly athletic chicken, bulked out with chickpeas or tomatoes or whole eggs. Despite the appearance of the food, we grabbed a table.

The food came quickly. It was served cold, the beer warm. As I toyed dejectedly with a chicken leg, I wondered how many millions of bacteria could breed in a day in this infernal heat, then pushed the unfortunate limb to the side of my plate. Lorna, too, half-heartedly picked at her food.

'I'm really sorry we just turned up like that,' I offered eventually. 'Hal can be kind of persuasive . . .'

Lorna shrugged. 'Yeah. Look, I do need my own space, you know? It was a bit of a shock when you guys turned up. And as for Hal, well, he's always been persuasive.' She nodded to herself and then laughed. 'Actually he used to have quite a following among the hippie community. Back in the day, he was pretty idealistic, wanted to lead some kind of crusade against capitalism. Maybe that's what attracted me to him.' Lorna took a sip of beer, then placed the glass back on the table, swivelling it in her hand.

'Attracted you? You guys dated and stuff?'

Lorna laughed again, loudly this time. 'No, no, no. No, I suppose I was a bit of a follower, that's what I mean. Believe it or not, he was kind of a legend within the scene at that time, an icon—people actually idolized him. You just had to talk to any of the hippies in Goa or Marrakech, wherever, and they'd have heard of Hal Fredericks. He took the most drugs, knew the most people, had been to the most far-out places and done the most far-out things . . .' She laughed again, as if not quite believing it herself. 'Of course, those days are long gone now, although I don't think Hal knows that yet.' She paused for a moment to pour out more beer. 'They were good times, though.'

'Well then, here's to Hal for staying true to it all,' I said, raising my glass.

She didn't reciprocate, and I felt myself flush as I held my beer redundantly in mid-air. Lorna's mind was elsewhere, however.

'I wonder what all those people would think of him now,' she said thoughtfully. 'It would be interesting to see—I mean most of the old hippies are doctors and lawyers and civil servants who had fun for a few years while they could, said how constrictive and pointless capitalism and the rat race was before getting a haircut and joining a merchant bank or something.'

'Not in your case though,' I said, pretending to study the rim of the glass before taking a considered sip.

'No, not in my case, but I suppose I had the advantage of not having to go out and work for a living.'

'Daddy owns an oil well?'

'No, no, no. My parents both passed away a few years back. He was a property developer, back home in New Zealand.'

'I'm sorry.'

She shrugged. 'Yeah, well I inherited a bit, enough for me to get out of the rat race.'

'But why Delhi of all places?'

'Oh, Delhi's not so bad,' she said with a tired sigh. 'For me, the main thing is the cost of living—I've got money, not a huge amount, but here at least it will go that much further. And besides, I've got one or two friends here that I know from my travelling days, although we don't do so much these days except for possibly watching ourselves grow old while wishing we were young again.'

'Isn't that rather sad . . .?' I shook my head. 'Sorry, I didn't mean it like that.'

She dismissed my embarrassment with a nonchalant wave of her hand. 'Don't worry, you're probably right. But put it this way, those two sat over there . . .' Lorna pointed to a couple of backpackers sat playing cards and nursing Pepsis at a table near the bar, '. . . they're our latter-day hippies. They'll spend six months in India, or maybe hop all over the world for a year before getting back and spending the rest of their lives at work, and that's what people do nowadays—it's more of an extended holiday than any kind of ideology. We wanted to stick our finger up at the Establishment, while they just want to pop outside it for a few minutes, have a cigarette and come right back in.'

'You could be right,' I shrugged, 'although I'm not sure I'm qualified to comment, to be honest. I mean, I didn't end up coming to India because of some kind of ideology, you know? Like railing against capitalism or anything like that.'

'So what *does* bring you here,' she asked, a note of curiosity in her voice.

I took a sip of beer, wincing slightly at its warmth. 'Escape, I guess.'

'Escaping what?'

I shrugged, then slowly set the glass down on the table and looked at her. 'Oh I don't know; it just seems to me that life doesn't always work out quite as planned, you know?'

Lorna frowned, but said nothing. As the pause grew longer, I added: 'Hey, it probably sounds stupid, but over the past few years I've had this increasing sense that I've ended up further and further away from where I expected to be . . .' I clicked my tongue in thought for a moment. 'Or maybe further and further away from where others expected me to be.'

'Black sheep of the family?' she prompted.

'Something like that.'

Again Lorna said nothing, so I continued: 'Look, they're just very old-fashioned in their thinking—my family, that is. And with that comes . . . with that comes certain *expectations*, you know? Only particular universities will do, the degree course must be this or that, your career must be banking or law or medicine, you should be earning this kind of money by the time you're twenty-five . . . that kind of thing.' I shrugged. 'Well, university didn't really work out for me, and then I landed myself a dead-end job. So in the end my parents kind of saw me as the failure of the family, I think.' I take another sip of beer, then add: 'Compared to my brother and sister, I guess I was. They're kind of high-flyers, you know? It's not like *they* ever struggle to make ends meet each month.'

'And so here you are . . .' Lorna prompted.

'Right,' I nodded. 'Here I am.'

Lorna laughed, then put her hand to her mouth. 'I'm sorry,' she said. 'I shouldn't laugh. But from what you've just told me, doesn't that mean you're here, er, *railing against capitalism?*'

I looked at her for a moment, then laughed so loudly that the backpackers near the bar swivelled around in their seats and looked over at us. 'Christ, maybe you're right, I hadn't thought of it that way, you know?' I laughed again, then took a long swig of beer before setting the empty glass down. 'Another drink?' I asked.

'No, I think I better get back,' she said. 'I really need to speak to Hal.'

'Yeah, got it.' I looked at her and said, 'Look, Lorna, thanks for coming to lunch with me. And, again, I'm really sorry we imposed . . .' I paused as the waiter noisily clanked the empty bottles from the table.

'You don't need to apologize, Ethan. I know this was Hal's idea. But he's living his life ten years behind schedule, you know? I'm thirty-eight, and I don't have the energy any more. As for Hal . . . well, he'll never slow down.'

'You look a very young thirty-eight,' I said, holding her eye.

'And you are misbehaving,' she replied evenly. Then, to the waiter, 'The bill please.'

5

JUBBAWY

I sigh. The painkillers are starting to wear off, and the bright strip-lights are beginning to hurt my eyes. I ask for a drink of water, and Jubbawy's eyes dart automatically to where the mirror is embedded in the wall. He looks back at me, and frowns. I feel like I have scored some kind of point with him, now that he realizes that I figured out the mirror.

'Of course. It will be here shortly.'

'Thank you.'

We sit in silence, waiting for the water to arrive. I open the packet of Gold Flake and notice that I have already smoked four cigarettes. It is a packet of ten, and I wonder about making them last, rationing myself. They would surely bring me more though, were I to ask. After all, I am here of my own volition, here to help. I am a victim, not a suspect being cross-examined. I take another cigarette and light it. The blue-grey smoke twists slowly to the ceiling; it is almost perfectly vertical, and I realize there are no ceiling fans. It reminds me of the commune; none of the huts we built had fans, of course, and the smoke rose undisturbed. Not like the hotel rooms we stayed in, nor Lorna's house, where the tip glowed from the extra oxygen and the smoke was whisked away, invisible. That's why it's so damn hot in here. There are no ceiling fans, just an air-conditioning unit that sits in the corner, droning away but doing little else.

The water arrives. A woman brings it in; she is dressed like a hospital orderly. She sets it down in front of me, noiselessly. I wonder if it's from the tap, but with my broken ribs and smashed-up face, I'm ill enough for it not to really matter. The water is cool, but tastes slightly metallic. The door clanks shut.

'How long did you stay at Lorna's residence?'

I sigh. 'Oh, long enough. Long enough. A couple of months, I guess.'

'Why *long enough*? You had free accommodation after all . . .'

'Things got out of hand. Me, Hal and Div, we were doing stuff every day, you know? Getting high on opium, I mean. We ended up doing nothing else, to be honest—no sightseeing, no daytrips, nothing. We barely left the house except for food.' I shrug and look at Jubbawy. 'That was all we went out for towards the end—food.'

Jubbawy shrugs. 'You said you were looking for an escape. It is not uncommon to search for such things at the bottom of an opium pipe.'

'Possibly,' I reply, frowning slightly. I trace a finger along the rows of stitches on my face for a moment, considering what he's just said. I hadn't thought of it that way before, but perhaps he's right. I try to think back to when I first arrived in Delhi—a failed life behind me, yet no plan for the future in front of me. Yes, I think to myself, I was pretty lost back then. And how good it felt to float away from that, how good it felt to float away. 'Possibly,' I repeat, chewing on my lip.

The policeman bridges his fingers and looks at me. 'But as I'm sure you're aware, Mr Hicks, that particular method of escape can come with quite a price tag. Both literally and figuratively.'

I look at him and nod slowly. 'Yeah. Yeah, it can. And it's why we left.' I look at him again and shrug. 'At least we had some self-awareness, I suppose. It's why we left. It's why we left for Shadow-Wall.'

Jubbawy raises his eyebrows.

'That's what we called it—the place in Himachal Pradesh—we called it Shadow-Wall.'

Jubbawy stares at me for a moment, then nods his head. 'Ah, yes of course. The mountain is called Shahdawallah. You anglicized it.'

I nod. 'Yeah, look, things were coming to a head at that point in time. Our lives were just disintegrating in Delhi, and we knew it. We were beginning to realize that there had to be some kind of change . . . The idea, the concept—it was born from that realization, I suppose.'

6

NEW DELHI, AUGUST 1986

We were in the lounge. It seemed by then that we were always in the lounge. Hal was slumped in an antique armchair, watching an Indian drama on TV, but although he seemed to be looking at the screen, you could tell he wasn't really seeing much at all. His face was white like alabaster, his eyes bloodshot and his neck seemed barely able to support his lolling head. Div lay motionless on the floor, snoring lightly. Lorna, who always declined the opium we offered, was lying on the chaise-longue, while I sat cross-legged on the floor, reorganizing her bookshelf.

'We must clean up,' Lorna stated for the third or fourth time, staring at the pile of books next to me, a look of pained resignation on her face.

'Yeah, we should.' Hal screwed his face up, looked momentarily around the room and said, 'Ah, shit . . . can you pass that thing . . .' He pointed a trembling hand at the upturned opium pipe on the floor a couple of feet away from him.

'I can't reach,' I said, briefly glancing over at the blackened pipe. Its powdery contents had scorched the rug, and the thought briefly occurred to me that Lorna's parents might have bequeathed it to her. 'We really must get out more,' I commented. 'We've done nothing for days.'

'Huh? Speak for yourself! Man, I've watched some TV, had a bit of a smoke, even made some tea. Been busy actually, man. Yeah,' he nodded to himself contentedly, 'if it's all the same to you, it's been a pretty hectic morning in Delhi.'

The rapping on the door woke everyone, perhaps because the sound was so alien and unexpected. No one moved, but its persistence soon started to grate, like a telephone you don't want to answer that just rings and rings and rings—eventually you pick it up. And so it was in this instance. The sound would seem to go away and the tension in the room dissipate, but then it would start up again, always louder and longer than before, and after we had endured this torture for what seemed like an age, Lorna said: 'Will someone get that?'

No one spoke.

'Hal, will you get that?'

'Dude, it's your house.'

Lorna sighed, and slowly got to her feet. We watched as she carefully navigated the empty mugs, cigarette cartons and takeaway boxes that cluttered the floor, then padded down the corridor.

Hal looked at me. 'Hey dude, we should have a quick pipe to celebrate.'

'Celebrate what exactly?'

'The fact that we didn't have to get up, of course.'

'But Hal, the pipe's over there.'

'So?'

'So someone would have to get up and get it, which kind of defeats the object, don't you think?'

Hal pursed his lips, nodded thoughtfully to himself and sank back down into his chair. Then, the sound of a door slamming, followed by the strains of a conversation that got louder until Lorna appeared in the doorway.

'Guys, I'd like you all to meet Matthew—he's passing through Delhi, and dropped round to say hi.'

Matthew was dark-haired, and strikingly handsome. His skin was deeply tanned, making his grey eyes seem unnaturally bright, and the t-shirt he wore was tight enough to draw attention to an impressive physique. He looked a little scruffy, as if he'd been travelling for a while—several days of stubble growth on his face, a creased and dirty sarong around his waist—but it was hard not to envy his appearance.

'Why are you all staring at me?' He looked uneasy, stood in the doorway fidgeting with his hands.

Hal waved a limp hand at him and said, 'Because you're new.' He shifted up an inch or two in his chair and added, 'I'm Hal.'

'Nice to meet you,' Matthew said, uncertainly.

'Hey man, would you pass me that pipe while you're up? We're not allowed to get up.'

'Why on earth not?'

'Because,' Hal said condescendingly, as if to a child, 'we were going to have a pipe to celebrate not having to get up to answer the door, but if we had to get up to get the pipe it would have defeated the object. You know, like a Catch-22 or something.'

Matthew regarded Hal with a look of puzzlement, shaking his head slowly. Then, with thinly veiled disdain: 'Look at the state of yourselves.'

There was a long, heavy pause. Hal aimed the remote control at the TV, clicked it off, and swivelled round in his chair. He looked at Div, curled up in a ball on the beanbag, then me, then down at his lap which was supporting an ashtray, a pile of cigarette stubs protruding above the rim like a volcanic cone. 'Dude's got a point,' he grunted.

*

'It was a Vipassana meditation retreat,' Matthew enthused, taking a careful sip of tea. 'You see, I'd come to a point in my life where I just felt I needed a new *perspective* on things, to *rebalance* myself. I'd gotten so caught up in work, in the trivial problems of my life, I just felt like I needed to reset myself somehow.' He nodded to himself, as if affirming the decision. 'So yeah, I arranged a one-month sabbatical with work, booked myself a place at the retreat, and made the journey.' Looking at each of us in turn, he added: 'It *changed* me, you know? I honestly feel like a completely different person now.'

'*Meditation?*' Lorna repeated, shaking her head. She looked at Matthew and laughed. 'I just can't imagine you doing something like that.'

'Why, what makes you say that?'

'Oh, Matthew, I don't mean to be rude, but you always seemed so . . . seemed so *career-orientated*.'

Matthew shrugged. 'Well, it's been one of the greatest experiences of my life, actually.'

'Dude, you must have a seriously boring fucking life then,' Hal said.

'I am talking about the *outcome*, Hal,' he replied. 'I mean, look at yourself!'

Hal shifted slightly in his seat, but said nothing.

'Maybe you can't,' Matthew continued. 'Maybe you *can't* see yourself. Look, do you know what Vipassana means? It means to *see things as they really are*. Honestly, I appreciate it's not for everyone, but I really think you'd see things differently if you went, even if it was just for a couple of weeks or something.' He carefully studied Hal, and then looked at me and Div in turn. 'Really, I think you're all in need of a little fresh perspective on yourselves.'

'Fresh perspective on ourselves,' Hal repeated slowly, seeming to toy with the words.

'Hey, it's tough, you know? You have to be up well before dawn, then it's meditation and breathing exercises through to late evening, and just a couple of light meals each day.'

'You can stop right there,' commented Div, flicking through a copy of *Cosmopolitan*. 'I'm not a morning person, Matthew. And as for light meals . . .'

'Ah, you get used to it, Div.' He looked around the room. 'And besides, I'm not sure you've got much to lose.'

'Where's the retreat?' Lorna asked.

'Chennai. But they have these places all over India. Here . . .' Matthew reached into his pocket, withdrew a distressed brown, leather wallet, and shuffled through some cards. 'This is the place. There's a phone number if you're interested.'

Lorna laughed, then slowly placed her hand on Matthew's forearm. 'Oh, I don't think it's really me, Matthew.'

I stared fixedly at her hand as Matthew said: 'I'm sorry—I'm evangelizing too much, aren't I?'

'Perhaps a little,' she giggled.

'It's a bad habit of mine.' He paused, looking around the room for a moment. 'So how are you finding it here, Lorna?'

'You mean Delhi?'

'Yeah, I was just curious about how you're finding it? I've got to admit, when I got to Chennai, it was a bit of a culture shock for me.'

'Oh, I get by,' Lorna replied with a shrug. 'I've been here for over five years now . . .' She paused, then added: 'It was a bit hairy after Indira Gandhi was assassinated a couple of years back—you know, soldiers on the streets and that sort of thing—but other than that, life here's been pretty uneventful for me.' She stared at the back of her hands a moment. 'Yeah, life's pretty uneventful,' she repeated thoughtfully.

'Well,' Matthew said, watching as Div elongated her body in an attempt to pass a reefer to Hal, 'I'm here for another couple of days. Maybe you can give me a tour of the city, Lorna?'

'Oh sure,' she said more brightly. 'I'd love to, Matthew.'

I placed a couple of books on the shelf I'd allocated for the smallest-sized ones and said: 'Pass the reefer, Hal.' He didn't respond, and when I looked up at him, he was staring fixedly at the antique map on Lorna's wall. 'Hal, will you pass the reefer over, please?'

Hal remained both silent and motionless, scanning his eyes across the map. The prolonged silence prompted the others to look at him as well. Then, after half a minute or so had passed, he said carefully: 'Matthew's right you know?'

'What do you mean?' Div asked, a note of caution in her voice. 'I'm not going to some meditation place if that's what you're getting at.'

Hal snorted. 'Nah, look, I'm not into that chanting shit either. But Jesus, man—look at us.'

Nobody spoke, and Hal continued: 'I don't even know what we're doing here in Delhi. I mean, we're too fucked up to even leave the house—in fact the only interaction we have with the outside world is the food delivery man. What does that say to you?'

'We *should* try and get out a little more,' Div agreed.

'What was the word you used?' Hal asked, looking at Matthew. 'Reset? Yeah, that was it. We need to reset, guys.'

'What are you suggesting, Hal?' I asked.

'I dunno,' he said, rubbing his chin. 'You've read that book *Walden*? That dude who lived in a log cabin in the woods or something?'

'You want to live in a log cabin?' Div said, covering her eyes with her hand.

'Well go camping or something, I don't know. Get away from it all. A reset, like Matthew says.' Then Hal got to his feet. We watched as he carefully stepped around the detritus on the floor and slowly made his way to the map on Lorna's wall. He studied it for some minutes before raising a finger and pointing to the top right-hand corner. 'This place up here, Himachal Pradesh, it could be okay,' he said. 'Seems pretty remote, looks like it has mountains and rivers and shit.' He nodded to himself. 'Yeah, some fresh mountain air will do us good.'

'Good on you, Hal,' Matthew chuckled. 'Good on you!'

I looked at Lorna. She was absently plaiting a long lock of black hair, intermittently putting it between her teeth as she tightened the knots. I could feel my circulation rise as I watched her.

'Count me out,' I said. 'I don't think camping's really my thing.'

Matthew shrugged at my comment. 'Well it's up to you, Ethan. Now, look, I'm here for the next few days, so it would be good if you guys can stick around for a bit. I've been eating vegetarian food and drinking lime juice for the last month, so why don't we all have a drink or two of something rather stronger? I've brought some vodka . . .'

*

I woke up with an arm so dead that the pins and needles made me cry out half in pain and half in laughter, and a formidable sore throat. The room, my clothes, my mouth all stank of stale smoke; a couple of empty Smirnoff bottles lay carelessly on the floor, and yet, despite this circumstantial evidence, I still couldn't reconstruct much from the previous night. A few smoky rays distilled through the slats of the shuttered windows—it was daylight at least—but I lacked the energy to get up.

Probably another hour passed before the incessant pain in my bladder finally drove me from the couch. I clambered up the wooden stairs, rubbing the sleep from my eyes, and lurched a little unsteadily down the landing.

'Morning, Ethan,' Matthew said cheerily, emerging from the bathroom clad in a dressing gown.

'Oh, hi,' I exclaimed, slightly surprised. 'Didn't think anyone else would be up yet.'

He smiled, eased past me into the room adjacent to the bathroom and gently closed the door. It was Lorna's room.

The ache in my bladder seemed to dissolve as my addled brain managed to process what I had seen into painful realization, and I began to feel an overwhelming sense of despair. Tiptoeing up to Lorna's bedroom door, I put my ear to it and listened hard. There was a muted giggle, followed by muffled conversation the words of which I couldn't quite make out. My heart was thumping and I could feel the heat in my face. Time passed, perhaps a couple of minutes, and I was beginning to lose interest when Lorna spoke again, her voice slowly rising in volume. I was straining so hard to decipher the words that it wasn't until it was too late that I realized she was actually coming to the door. It swung open.

'Oh. Hello, Ethan!' she gasped, clearly startled at the sight of me stood right outside her bedroom.

'Hi!' I replied cheerily.

She had an expectant look on her face as if she was waiting for me to say something more, but when I remained silent, she asked suspiciously, 'What are you doing?'

'I'm waiting for the bathroom. Hal's in there.' As I said it, I snatched a glance at the bathroom door to check if it was closed. It was.

'Right,' she smiled, looking a little relieved at my plausible lie. 'I'd better join the queue then.'

'Er, I might be a minute or two—I was going to dive in the shower, if that's okay? Shall I give you a knock when I'm done?' I prayed she'd agree.

'Sure.'

My breath hissed out from between my teeth. Then, from down the corridor, came the muffled words: 'I didn't mean it, Div! You know I love you!'

'Then why don't you say it? You never say it any more!'

'I said I was sorry, didn't I? Look, I love you! Okay—are we cool now?'

There was a loud thud, and I heard Hal say 'Ow! That fucking hurt, Div!' before their door flew open and Hal spilled out into the landing, holding his head.

Lorna called over, 'Oh, morning, Hal!' Then, while looking me directly in the eye, she added, 'We were just waiting for you to finish using the bathroom.' With that, she promptly disappeared into her room.

I looked at the ceiling and swore.

7

JUBBAWY

Jubbawy is polishing the lenses of his glasses with the tail of his shirt. He cannot use his handkerchief, because it is sitting on the table, slowly turning brown as the blood from my nose dries. The fabric, I can see, is becoming rigid. It reminds me that I have been in the room for a while, perhaps a couple of hours. I ask the time, and Jubbawy tells me it is six in the evening. Outside it will be getting dark, but we are in our own little world, inside the sprawling ministry building, completely removed from distractions such as the time of day or the weather outside.

'So you left?'

'Of course. I had no friends apart from Hal and Div, and they decided to go up north—so what else could I do? And to be honest, that morning when I realized that Matthew and Lorna had slept together . . .' I pause, tugging briefly at my earlobe. I look at Jubbawy and say, 'I was kind of upset, you know? It might sound weird, but I really felt we had a kind of chemistry, that we might have had something given the chance.' I shrug. 'I thought maybe she was the one. So, I was pretty gutted. Well, very gutted actually.'

'Some things in life are just not meant to be,' Jubbawy offers.

I snort. 'Anyway, Hal's idea, I mean, it was totally crazy, but I didn't exactly have many alternatives . . .' I sigh. 'So yeah, we left and went up north, ended up founding Shadow-Wall.'

He taps his pen but says nothing.

'Anyway,' I continue, 'it was a stupid idea, we didn't really know what we were doing, just this vague notion of going off somewhere, drying out, getting clean, trying to change our lives for the better . . .' I shrug. 'But anyway, that's what we did. We went to Kullu.'

And now, inevitably, my account begins to turn towards events on the mountain. As it does, my thoughts are drawn back to the horror of what happened up there. My god, I reflect, what horror indeed. All those people dead. All those people dead, dozens and dozens and dozens of them. 'My god,' I say out loud to myself, shaking my head.

'Are you all right, Mr Hicks? You've gone very pale.'

My god. The realization of what I've done begins to surface, no matter how hard I try to suppress it. A strange panic begins to grip me, the adrenaline in my body pulses and the panic gets worse, surging through me now as I think about the enormity of what I have done. I realize that I haven't even considered it up until now—not in the air-ambulance that flew me, just me, from the dirt track at the base of the mountain, nor the hospital where they stitched my nose back on to my face and told me that my broken ribs would heal naturally. I really haven't thought about it until now, I haven't thought about the scores upon scores of dead, I haven't thought about what we did up on that mountain. I try to speak in the hope that talking will somehow drown out these thoughts, but the words will not form in my mouth. I feel sick.

'Are you all right Mr Hicks?' he repeats. 'You look rather unwell, if I may say so.'

I am going to throw up. My body is telling me that it is a certainty.

'No. Can we stop?'

'Of course.'

But I am already running to the door, holding my hand over my mouth. The handle is set into the metal, like the door of a squash court, and I fumble hopelessly with it, unable to dig my fingers into the small groove. My body realizes that there is no point holding out, there's not enough time, and I am sick. The smell reminds me of litter rotting in Delhi's heat.

'Sorry,' I say, between gags. 'I'm so sorry.'

*

I feel better today. The table is less bare now, because there are three bottles of pills set down in a neat row. There are painkillers which will also act as an anti-inflammatory, beta-blockers in case I have another panic attack, and antibiotics for my nose, which has become slightly infected. There is also a jug of water with a white plastic lid on it, intended to keep out the dust, although I cannot imagine there being any dust in this sterile room, also a glass, and a fresh packet of Gold Flake. Jubbawy has brought along a packet of twenty today. I have already smoked two, because the same box of matches from yesterday is on the table. There are exactly sixteen matches remaining, so I will chain-smoke four pairs of cigarettes to make the best use of what is available.

'Shall we proceed?' he says, shuffling some papers in front of him.

The policeman is a little more offhand today. I reason that he probably expected the interview to be finished yesterday, yet still knows very little. By the end of the interview, he will know more, but not everything. The small wiry man still sits in a chair slightly behind Jubbawy, saying nothing.

'Right. Sure.'

'Okay. So, you left to go up north. Lorna didn't come with you?'

I shake my head. I can feel the slight centrifugal force as the blood is pushed to my nose, and wonder whether it will start to bleed again.

'No. It was just me, Div and Hal.' I shrug and add: 'Well, to begin with at least.'

8

SHADOW-WALL, SEPTEMBER 1986

Of course we could not second-guess the future, and the three of us felt only nervous excitement as a series of buses conveyed us north from the flat, dry plains of Uttar Pradesh, through to the first uncertain foothills of the Himalayan range in Himachal Pradesh. I remember little else of the journey, although it must have been uncomfortable and hot. Certainly the two days of slow, tedious travel would have provided a good opportunity for reflection, although my time in India had, in truth, provided little to reflect on—I had done practically nothing of consequence since arriving. Perhaps I spent the hours thinking instead of Lorna, of the strange connection I felt to her, of the deep sadness that seemed to consume me as we said farewell on her doorstep. Maybe I let her drift from my mind, concentrating instead on the increasingly vertiginous scenery around me. In all honesty, I cannot remember what thoughts ran through my mind during that bone-jarring journey, and care little for the detail—it holds no significance, given what transpired.

Of course, while the minutiae may be unimportant, I cannot fail to see the layer upon layer of chance that led me to Shadow-Wall. A pin in an atlas took me to India; Hal's finger on the map of the wall at Lorna's house determined that my fate was to travel to Himachal Pradesh. And, finally, a map in Kullu's tourist information centre condemned us to a mountain called Shahdawallah. It appeared to have a col on the western side where a large lake was situated—the presence of water, enabling us to survive there, was the only criterion we used to determine where we would camp. Given the number of souls lost to the mountain, no doubt there is some irony to be found in that. But we weren't to know what would come to pass, of course. And so we bought tents and other supplies in the hillside town and then, weighed down with provisions, we struck out east along the highway; we trekked into increasingly bleak landscape, overnighting in our tents by the roadside. Our intended destination was only about twenty kilometres from Kullu, but remote nonetheless. And the following day, weary and damp from the incessant mist that clung along the valley sides, we finally left the road and made our way up the wooded slopes of the mountain to what was to become our new home.

'Hello-o?'

After the bustle of Delhi, and the raucous whining engines of the various buses we'd taken north, the silence seemed intense.

'Hello-o? Is anybody there?'

Once more, Hal cupped his hands around his mouth. His voice was becoming hoarse. 'Hello-o?'

Just a dull, smothered echo from the forest around us, and the insubstantial patter of rain on foliage.

'Why are you calling out?' Div asked. 'There's no one here, Hal.'

'Just checking we're alone, I guess.' Hal went to shout again, but seemed to think better of it and let his hands fall to his sides with a slap.

'Well,' I said, 'I'm pretty sure there's no one else around.'

'So here we are then,' Div said, lighting a cigarette.

We had stumbled out of the dense undergrowth and emerged into a large glade. Towards the centre of this clearing the long grass had been eroded away, perhaps by grazing animals. In places the ground was churned up, allowing puddles of muddy water to form in the scars. Steep, wooded slopes rolled away high above us where they were greeted by the first semi-transparent strata of cloud, although it was possible to see glimpses of far-off, forbidding dark grey rock where the cumulus was torn by higher winds. There may have been snow on the furthest reaches, but it could just as easily have been a trick of the light—it was impossible to tell. Not far from our clearing, the lake we'd identified on the map in Kullu peered out through an overgrown screen of untidy foliage; it was perhaps 200 metres in length, a little less across. The water looked cloudy, discoloured perhaps by surface run-off; the stretches nearest the grassy banks were cast into shadow—inverted trees and long rushes reflected on the dark surface, shifting slightly with the eddies. A bird, or possibly a monkey, shrieked from a copse of trees that fringed its western edge. The desolate sound seemed to linger in the heavy, moist air.

'I'm cold,' Div said. Her voice sounded oddly detached.

'What are we doing here?' I asked, almost to myself.

'Let's get these tents pitched,' Hal suggested.

'What *are* we doing here?' I repeated, watching my breath condense in front of my face like an empty speech-bubble.

Div just shrugged and wearily dropped her rucksack to the ground.

We pitched our tents in the driest patch of ground we could find, although the dirt gave easily as we pushed in the pegs. Then we stood in the clearing; a long while passed during which nobody spoke. The rain hardened a little, yet none of us moved. The small orange tents, their fabric crackling in the wind, were hardly inviting, although I think it was disbelief that held us mesmerized and ankle-deep in mud, compelled to absorb our surroundings.

'I'm getting *really* cold now,' Div muttered.

The three of us were wearing t-shirts and shorts. I absently noted that my rucksack contained nothing else. 'Shall we light a fire?'

'Fucking hell,' Hal said. His voice had a strange whine to it, like a disappointed child.

'Have you got any cigarettes, Div?' I asked.

Div passed me a cigarette. I lit it, cupped it in my closed palm for warmth, and threw the match to the ground. It landed in a puddle with a gentle hiss.

'The firewood will be soaked,' Hal observed.

'Well we should have bought some fire-lighters in Kullu, then, shouldn't we?' Div snapped.

'Yeah, and that's my fault, is it?'

'Well this whole stupid idea is your fault, Hal.'

'Yeah, well I have plenty of stupid ideas, don't I? Like going out with you, that's a pretty stupid idea of mine.'

'Hal! I can't believe you just said—'

'Oh, shut up you two!' I yelled. 'For Christ's sake, just shut up, will you?'

There was nothing else to do. We'd arrived on a mountainside, and that's all there was to it. Simply nothing to do apart from to arrive.

*

The reefer slowly worked its way round us, its tip smouldering in the partial darkness. A haze of smoke filled the tiny tent, which was damp with condensation, and it was silent apart from the occasional roll of thunder echoing down the valley, and the constant sound of rain beating down on the nylon exterior. All three of us gazed out through the entrance hole, watching the puddles grow ever larger in the clearing outside, shivering slightly with the cold, alone with our thoughts.

'Why are *you* here, Ethan?'

I looked at Hal, raising my eyebrows but not offering a reply.

'We're all here, dude, in India, wasting our lives away,' he continued. 'I mean, do you not find it a little odd that the three of us are sitting in a tent in the middle of fucking nowhere, man? Doesn't that seem a bit strange to you?'

I slowly returned my gaze to the clearing. 'Yeah, I guess.'

'It's fucking bizarre, that's what it is,' Hal declared.

I paused, then said, '*Life* is bizarre, I guess.'

'I guess it is,' Hal agreed. 'And to be honest, if we weren't sitting here, we'd just be stuck in some pointless job somewhere.'

'Yeah, I suppose we would.'

'What did you do for a living?'

'I was a pharmacist's assistant,' I said. 'Much to my parents' everlasting disappointment, I was a pharmacist's assistant.'

'Right, parents are a real pain sometimes,' Hal nodded.

I sighed. 'Yeah, I didn't make it through med school—I guess I wasn't quite smart enough. So anyway, that was the closest I could get to being the doctor they always wanted me to be.' I stared out of the tent again, then added, 'But anyway, talk about mundane, low-paid work.'

'Yeah,' Div agreed. 'And having to talk with all those sick people every day, right? That must suck.'

Hal blew a plume of smoke from his nose but remained silent.

'So, what's that you're reading?' Div asked after a while, perhaps more to break the renewed silence than anything else.

'*War and Peace*,' I said more brightly, thumbing the thick wedge of pages. The paper was already becoming corrugated from the damp. Everything in the tent was damp.

'Is it any good?' Div asked, presumably just making conversation—there was little real interest in her voice.

'Uh, I dunno. I've only just started it. Lorna gave it to me before we left.'

Hal laughed. 'Really? That was nice of her.' He paused, then said, 'I guess she had a bit of a soft-spot for you.'

I looked at him, then shrugged. 'Well, I had a bit of a soft-spot for her if I'm being honest.' I shrugged again and said, 'Actually, I really liked her, you know?'

'Yeah, I know, dude. It was pretty obvious.' He reached out a hand, and gave my shoulder a gentle pat.

'Never mind, Ethan,' Div said kindly. 'You've got us.'

I didn't reply, and the three of us lapsed back into silence. After a time, I took the reefer off Hal and had one last drag, then ducked outside towards my tent. It was getting dark.

9

JUBBAWY

'At first, it was very . . . at first, it was really very bleak. There was this sense of anti-climax—it was meant to be a fresh start for us, a new beginning. In truth, being there was just . . . well, it was kind of depressing. Most of the time in Delhi we'd been high on opium, but we only brought a bit of dope with us to Shadow-Wall. When I had straightened out, well, reality seemed to kick back in. I suppose we had too much time to think about home and stuff, what we were doing with our lives.'

'Why didn't you leave?'

'Oh, I *did* think about it. It rained constantly, we could never seem to get dry, and we had no warm clothes either.' I run my fingernail across the markings on the table. 'I guess it was easier to do nothing. I had nowhere to go to, I was with friends of sorts, and besides, it would've taken a certain amount of impetus to leave.'

'But you mentioned earlier that you considered your friendship with the others as superficial, false.'

'It was, but it was better than nothing, if you like. I felt very isolated. If you travel, there are all these different groups of people—school-leavers, middle-class graduates, travellers, tourists, hippies . . . Usually you fit into one of them because that's the type of person you are too, but I didn't feel like I belonged to any of those. I simply adopted the first identity I came across, but I never felt entirely comfortable with it.'

'And Shadow-Wall? Did you fit in there?'

'Perhaps.' I nod and add, 'Yeah, maybe I did, eventually.'

'Eventually?'

'Yes.' I shrug. 'Look, we went there to force a stop to the kind of life we were leading in Delhi, but yeah, over time we came to realize we'd inadvertently created something.' I click my tongue for a moment, then say slowly: 'Something quite special, actually. We ended up creating a new society, call it what you will. The manifestation of an ideal, maybe.' I pause, then add: 'Then again, ideals can change, it would seem.'

'How so?'

'An ideal, a belief, it can be redefined, or even discarded.' I snort. 'I guess in our case it was the latter. We chose a different god to worship by the end.'

10

SHADOW-WALL, OCTOBER 1986

We survived on chilgoza seeds and unripe gooseberries and jujubes that we scavenged from the surrounding woodland, and drank water from the lake. Despite our best efforts to boil it over the reluctant fires Hal built, all three of us fell ill and spent most of our time smoking in our tents, wondering when the rain would stop, making small talk. I tried to continue with *War and Peace*, despite the fact that Hal had used the first quarter of the book to light the fire; the other two just sat about watching. Time passed, the weather slowly deteriorated, the three of us killed time. The subdued atmosphere worsened when Hal and Div had a tremendous row one afternoon. It started as a trivial argument over whose turn it was to collect water from the lake, then morphed into a screaming match followed by a long period of icy détente. Hal was at fault; he seemed to almost enjoy fighting with Div, but I considered the friction to be generally indicative of the fragility of their relationship. Not wanting to favour either side, I was forced into uneasy solitude.

There was, of course, very little to do. And without the company of others to distract me, my thoughts inevitably turned to home. It wasn't that I was in any way homesick—there were too few happy memories to draw on, too much disappointment to look back on from that chapter of my life. In truth, I didn't even miss my family—and perhaps they didn't miss me. My father seemed utterly indifferent when I told him I was leaving for India, and neither he nor my mother came to the airport to see me off, despite it being just a twenty-five-minute drive from their home in Berkshire. I suppose I did feel a few pangs of sadness as I said my farewells on the doorstep of their house, the taxi idling on the gravel drive outside. But looking back, it seems that the sorrow I felt was no more than an inherent reaction to the impending separation, like the child who cries when they see blood on their arm from a painless scratch. Just a few days later, all thoughts of home had faded away like the image on an old photo.

No, I wasn't homesick, and I didn't miss my family. Back home, I had resoundingly failed to establish a successful, conventional, happy life. So I was right to leave, I reasoned. But here I was, on some mountain in the Himalayas, lying on a foam sleeping mat in an orange tent, dragging on a half-smoked joint from the night before and swigging on cheap local whisky. Was I not simply laying failure upon failure?

'Well, whatever, it won't matter much longer,' I muttered to myself, taking another sip of whisky. And it was true—the failure that was our brief time at Shadow-Wall was about to come to an end anyway. The provisions we'd brought up from Kullu were starting to run low—there was barely a dozen cupfuls of rice remaining in the sack we'd carried up so laboriously, and we'd long ago consumed the salted fish and dried meats that were intended to provide some kind of protein; the unripe fruit that now dominated our diets had left me with permanent stomach cramps, presumably from the acidity. Perhaps we're slowly withering to death up here, I thought to myself—I felt exhausted and empty from lack of sleep, the nights disturbed by a combination of the sharp pains in my stomach and the crackling of the plastic tent from the wind. Feeling a sudden urge to see my face, I stared at the glass surface of the bottle, trying to discern my reflection. It was pointless; it merely reflected an orange glow from the light filtering through the tent. I sighed to myself. A mirror was really of no consequence, I reasoned. There were so many other things we lacked that we'd failed to have the foresight to bring—toilet roll, utensils with which to cook, tools for cutting wood, warm clothing. I shook my head, then took another long swig of whisky, listening to the soft patter of rain on the tent. Eventually, I set the bottle down on the damp floor and ducked outside to find the others.

'Guys, this isn't really working out,' I started. Hal was trying to goad more life from the campfire with a long, gnarled stick; the damp logs and branches hissed with the release of water vapour. 'We don't know what we're doing.'

'Leave then,' Hal grunted. 'No one's stopping you, dude.'

I looked at him for a moment, surprised by the abruptness. There remained palpable tension between Div and Hal—the warmth between the two of them was no more notable than that of the spluttering fire around which they sat—but now his anger seemed to be overflowing towards me.

'You should see yourself, Hal,' I said eventually. 'You must have lost, what, five kilos? And now we're *really* running low on food.' I gave another shrug. 'We can't live on fruit.'

Hal hawked, then spat into the centre of the fire. He cupped his head in his hands, resting his elbows on his knees, and stared into the glowing embers. He said nothing for some time.

'What are you suggesting?' Div asked finally. 'Where would you go?'

I sighed but said nothing. The three of us sat in silence, listening to the low crackling of the campfire and the ubiquitous muffled patter of soft rain on foliage.

'How much money have you got left?' Hal asked after a time. He didn't look at me as he spoke.

'About $200 in cash, I guess. A couple of thousand more in traveller's cheques, but that's everything.' I turned my palms to the grey sky and added, 'I pissed most of it away in Delhi. And I need to keep some back.'

'For what?' Hal asked.

I laughed, although the sound was hollow. He was just being awkward. 'When my money runs out, that's it for me. Time to go home. And it's not exactly like I've done very much in India so far.'

'Go take a look at the Taj Mahal or something then,' he said.

I felt a flash of annoyance, but said nothing else.

'Give me your $200,' he said eventually. 'I'll put in $400 for me and Div.'

'Why?' I asked.

'I'll hike into town,' he replied. 'Get us the stuff we need up here. Do it properly this time.'

'Hey, we can all go,' Div offered.

Hal looked at her for a moment, then said evenly: 'I am going alone, Div.'

I scraped my foot on the ground, carving a small furrow in the soft mud. Perhaps because I could think of nothing to say, I grunted: 'Sure, whatever, Hal.'

11

JUBBAWY

'Div and I, we weren't even sure if he'd come back. He was gone days, you know?'

Jubbawy simply shrugs.

'Anyway, there I was, stuck up on this mountain with his girlfriend, and that was pretty weird. We kind of kept ourselves to ourselves, but we had a few conversations the contents of which sort of gnawed away at me for many weeks after.'

'Gnawed away at you?'

'Yeah,' I say slowly. 'You see, she talked a lot about Hal while he was gone. They'd been dating years, so she knew his background, his history.' I pause, then shake my head, trying to arrange my thoughts. 'I don't think *duplicitous* is the right word, but maybe I started to think he was a bit of a fake, a bit phoney?'

'How so?'

'Well, it turns out he was a trust-fund kid. His dad owned some huge construction company in the US.' I sigh and look at Jubbawy. 'Don't misunderstand me, there's nothing wrong with that. And in fairness, Div said he'd pretty much blown it all by the time I'd first met them, by the time we went to Shadow-Wall. But to me it was a bit surprising to learn, that's all.'

'Surprising because of his persona?'

'Yeah . . . right,' I agree. 'So Hal, the legendary hippie, was actually some rich kid. At the very least, it seemed a bit paradoxical. At worst . . .' I shrug. 'Well, it didn't sit easily with me. So yeah, a bit duplicitous, perhaps.'

'Perhaps,' Jubbawy says, a note of tiredness in his voice. He looks at me for a moment. 'Now, while I do find your ruminations about your friend's integrity quite interesting, I am not wholly convinced they are really of relevance to the purpose of this interview?'

Not relevant? I am not so sure he's right actually, although I cannot be sure. But the sequence is odd. The trust fund finally frittered away, crashing at Lorna's to save money, the decision to go to Shadow-Wall, the direction that it then took, even the final outcome . . . I am uncertain whether it was all by design or simply happenstance. The only thing that *is* clear to me is that I will never know for sure.

'Well,' I say, 'I am sorry for my *ruminations*.'

'I'm sorry, Mr Hicks,' he says, a slight note of contrition in his voice, 'but you must understand, I do not have the luxury of limitless time.' He shuffles the notes in front of him for a moment, then shrugs. 'So anyway, my assumption would be that he *did* come back from Kullu. Otherwise it would seem unlikely that you and I would be sitting across this table from one another right now, would it not?'

I stare down at the table. The plastic water jug glows and fades every half-second or so as the strip-light above my head blinks off and then on. 'He came back all right. He came back with others.'

Jubbawy leans forward. 'Others?'

I shrug. 'Hal was quite gregarious, people were attracted to him.'

'People such as yourself.'

I consider his comment for some moments, wondering whether it was intended to be derogatory. I take another cigarette, and light it. 'Yeah, people such as myself.'

12

SHADOW-WALL, DECEMBER 1986

Div and I had been sitting in the clearing, watching the drizzling rain in uncomfortable silence, when we first heard their voices. The sound carried up from the trail long before they emerged from the treeline below us. Three figures, all stooped under the weight of heavy loads, the bright colours of their rucksacks contrasting with the dark edges of the forest. Without speaking, we watched them trudge up the slope, the resolution of their features sharpening as they drew closer. One of Hal's new companions had long black hair, worn in a ponytail, and an assortment of tattoos on his thick arms. The other looked younger, and had a handsome face crowned by blonde hair.

'Hey, dudes,' Hal called over as they approached the clearing, his voice a little breathless. 'Found us a couple more losers in Kullu.'

'I'm Miles,' said the more thickset of the two, dumping his rucksack in the centre of the muddy clearing and then rubbing his tattooed arms against the cold. He gave us each a nod of greeting, then pointedly looked around. He turned to Hal, and added: 'It's not exactly how you described it.'

Hal pursed his lips. 'We can make this place awesome, Miles. You'll see.'

Miles slowly shook his head, wiped a droplet of water from his nose and then looked at the sky as if he'd only just realized it was raining. 'This weather . . .' he grunted. 'Is it always like this?'

Hal shrugged. 'Yeah. Most of the time.'

'There's nothing here,' he said, looking around again. 'You said there were huts?'

'I said there *will* be huts,' Hal replied slowly.

'And I'm Scott, by the way,' Miles' companion grinned, holding out his hand, which we each shook in turn. His appearance was in marked contrast to that of Miles—close cropped blonde hair, a wiry, athletic build of the type I'd managed to drink away over the last couple of years, and eyes that seemed unnaturally blue.

'So here we are,' Miles said. He looked around at the clearing and asked, 'So what's the plan?'

'First we eat,' replied Hal. 'I'm fucking starving.'

Div and I watched in fascination as the three of them emptied their rucksacks on to a parcel of dry ground next to the fire, which was still producing a half-hearted plume of yellow smoke. They'd bought a few tools—a small axe, a hammer, a bow-saw, a couple of those compact army spades one sometimes sees strapped to the back of Jeeps, and also some warmer clothing for me and Div. But mostly food. Unidentified silver tins, bags of rice, shrink-wrapped noodles, foil-wrapped cartons and small cardboard packages soon littered the ground as if someone had tipped over a supermarket trolley. Hal had also carried up a crude wooden cage containing two live chickens that were noisily protesting against the cloud of smoke which occasionally shifted direction in the wind, temporarily obscuring them from sight.

'Chickens,' explained Hal, a little unnecessarily. 'I've decided to call them Agnes and Zelda.'

'How shall we kill them?' I asked. 'I don't mind plucking—'

'They're here to lay eggs,' Hal interrupted, with a shake of his head.

'Oh.'

'We've got noodles, though,' he offered.

'These?' I started picking up the assortment of unlabelled packets, closely examining each before throwing them back on to the pile.

'Scott, did you remember to buy those biscuits?' Hal asked suddenly. 'I'd really like a biscuit.'

'Yeah, I think so.'

'What sort did you buy?' he demanded.

'Er, crackers.'

'Crackers? Have you nothing else? Oreos or something nice like that?'

Scott shrugged as he started to extract a tent from its blue plastic sheath. 'Nope, no Oreos. I guess we're all going to get used to a few sacrifices.'

'Tell me about it,' Hal said.

13

JUBBAWY

'It was dumb really. I mean our vision was this idea of subsistence living, surviving off the land with no need for money, that kind of thing. It just didn't work out like that.'

'Why not?'

'We tried. I mean, we tried to make the place liveable. We built some half-decent huts, that took nearly a month, and Hal planted rice and maize on a stretch of land down by the lake.' I shrug. 'He didn't know what he was doing, none of us did really. I mean it was winter by then and crops never took of course, so once or twice a month someone would have to hitch to Kullu and buy food. We weren't even subsisting, just deluding ourselves that we were. Eventually the last of the money we had started to run out, then that was it. We went back to eating fruit and berries and stuff again, and although we had bought enough rice to keep us going for a while, it wasn't sustainable. We were going to pack up and leave, the weather was getting colder and colder you know, but then a solution just landed in our lap.'

'Oh? What kind of solution?'

'A financial one, I suppose. Hal and I discovered these bamboo copses when we were scavenging for fruit. We hacked off some of the thicker stuff to try and use as pipes to irrigate the rice, you know, running water down from the lake. It didn't work of course, but we discovered Scott had a bit of a hidden talent.'

*

As we sit amongst the leftover clutter of another tasteless meal, Scott picks up one of the sections of bamboo which have been lying about redundantly for days, and gently strikes the palm of his hand with it, gauging the weight. He unfolds a wicked looking jagged blade from a Swiss army knife that he takes from his pocket, and then studies the thick cane intently for a few moments before gently starting to saw around two thirds of the way down its length above a knot. We all watch as the blade slices into the wood, scattering specks of sawdust over his thigh, collecting on the hairs of his leg, the tiny mounds growing in size until they are disturbed by the slight movement of the sawing, and start to cascade to the ground in miniature clouds. The uncut section slowly grows thinner, the blade inching closer to the bare flesh of his leg—only the thinnest sliver of bamboo is left, and the shiny silver blade continues back and forth with dazzling speed, millimetres from his skin. Back and forth, back and forth—I can see the blade begin to snag his hairs as it wheezes gradually through the wood, and imagine how easily the serrated metal could slice into his skin. Scott's head jerks up suddenly.

'Why are you all watching?' The smaller third of the cane falls to the ground with a thud.

'Jesus,' I gulp.

His eyes dart around the ground until he spies a thin stick that hasn't quite made it on to the fire. Like a midshipman cleaning a cannon, he rams the stick into the soft, honeycombed flesh inside the cane. It bursts out in an explosive cloud of chaff at the other end.

'Wow, you made a tube,' Hal declares, his voice heavy with sarcasm.

Scott smiles, his teeth highlighted for a second by the orange glare of the fire, and folds the saw blade away into its maroon plastic housing. With a click, he exchanges it for a knife and carefully makes a number of incisions at equal intervals around the rim of one end, cutting out four long v-shaped slivers of wood. The remaining section folds in on itself, forming a kind of elongated pyramid, which he binds tightly with a long stem of grass plucked from the ground by the log on which he sits. We watch him swap a knife for a gimlet which he uses to puncture the casing, producing a neat row of five holes along the length of the tube.

'There!' he announces after a further couple of minutes spent cleaning and scraping. 'Now, listen to this.'

He puts the miniature recorder to his mouth and blows tentatively. A low-pitched note emerges that seems to float on the air. It is a simple sound, but pleasant nonetheless. He nods to himself, and then starts to experiment with the different notes, eventually synergizing them into a tune that is reminiscent of the snake charmers we occasionally saw on street corners in Delhi. He plays for around five minutes, and no one speaks; the strains of sound that drift around the crackling fire are really quite hypnotic.

'Christ, man!' Hal says after a considerable pause, his eyes wide with amazement. 'You should go into business making these! Tourists would love them!'

*

'I don't understand . . .' Nor care, from his expression.

'Well that's exactly what we did. We chopped more bamboo and Scott carved a dozen or so of these flutes, then we took them into Kullu to trade. Thought some tourist shop might buy them from us. We called them Krapi-Krapis.'

Jubbawy lurches with surprise, then looks at me, his face momentarily suspended in disbelief. 'Krapi-Krapi? As in . . . as in *the* Krapi-Krapi?'

I nod.

'I bought my daughter one for her birthday. She told me all her friends had them.' Jubbawy's demeanour transforms rapidly from surprise to irritation. 'Continue.'

*

We enter the shop, the fifth or sixth we've been to that afternoon. A bell above the door rings shrilly as we pass inside. The interior is dark, and smells of mildew. There is no sign of the shopkeeper amongst the plethora of goods for sale—unstable piles of carpets that almost reach the low ceiling, marble artefacts haphazardly displayed on low wooden tables, chess boards, figurines, ornamental daggers, wooden backgammon boards—all the stuff you get hawked to buy in every city in India, nothing new. In one corner is a giant carving of a tiger about to leap at some imaginary prey, its lips drawn back in a fearsome snarl that reveals long white teeth that contrast against the dark, grainy wood. I guess they are either real tiger teeth or carved from ivory. A white tag, tied to one of its ears, bears the red lettering: 'Not for Sale'.

'Are you liking?' a voice behind me says. Both Scott and I spin round. There is no one there. 'Are you liking?' I look down to where the voice is coming from. There stands a tiny old man, no more than four and a half feet high, with his hands on his hips. 'My grandfather was carving this for twenty-seven years. It was his hobby,' the shopkeeper declares, puffing out his birdlike chest. He looks a bit like a miniature Gandhi, I think to myself—wire-rimmed spectacles, a bald head and dark brown skin that glistens with perspiration.

'Yes, I do,' Scott says, nodding slowly to himself. 'I like it very much.'

The old man beams at the compliment. 'My name is Hemen. So how can I be helping you? Are you looking for a carpet perhaps? I am owning a very great selection indeed. Here . . .' He strides over to the highest pile, and I wonder how he can possibly take a carpet off the top, but the little man simply clambers up the swaying column and starts throwing rugs down to the floor around us.

'Er . . .' I cough at the ceiling, for he is out of sight on his minaret. 'We don't really want to buy anything.'

The procession of carpets flying through the air stops abruptly. Half a dozen or more lie on the floor around us. The shopkeeper's head appears over the edge of the pile, then he scuttles back down in reverse, tutting loudly, picks up a carpet and climbs back up. 'So what *are* you wanting?' he asks, slapping it on the pile.

'We have something we would like to sell to you.'

'I am thinking this is crappy,' the shopkeeper says, shaking his head sadly at one of the flutes Scott has presented him with. 'Very crappy crappy, indeed.'

'But listen to the sound it makes . . .' I argue, playing a few discordant notes.

'Yes, well I am not selling sounds in my shop, am I? I am selling rugs and carvings and marble, not noises.' He shakes his head again at the flute. 'No, no, no. This is simply being awful.'

'Look, I'm a tourist. I know what tourists like, and they'll love these. Snap them up like hot cakes!'

'Hot cakes? What are you talking about? I am not seeing hot cakes, only the most crappy piece of bamboo wood.'

'So you don't want to buy these then?' Scott cut in. 'I have a dozen—of course, it's up to you.'

'No, I am not buying your things.' With a heavy sigh, he pushes the instrument across a glass counter filled with garish, painted plates. He nods at them and says, 'Perhaps I can be interesting you in one of these? Only Rs 300—special price!'

'No, thank you.' I turn to walk out.

'I am making you special daytime discount—Rs 250!'

'No, thank you.'

'Well,' Scott says, turning around to the shopkeeper as he reaches the door. 'Take them anyway, and next time we're in town, we'll look you up. If you do sell any . . .'

Hemen laughs. 'I am agreeing, but these pipes will still be here when you are returning. They may be a little dustier, but they will be here.' He laughs once again, and shakes his head.

The door clanks shut behind us as we spill out on to the street, empty-handed.

*

'The next time we went back, he had sold most of them—nine, I think. We didn't make much—about Rs 1,000—but it was a start. Scott taught us how to carve them, it was pretty easy to be honest, and we were soon knocking out a dozen or so a week between us. It covered our food, and we had a little left over for other things like cigarettes and alcohol and stuff.' I pause. 'That was the start of it, really. We never looked back once the money started trickling in, just smiled at what we thought was our good fortune.' I look at Jubbawy and shrug. 'I suppose it was, at the time.'

14

SHADOW-WALL, JANUARY 1987

That transaction marked the beginning of our slow descent into capitalism. Of course, we didn't know it then, but once that particular genie was released, there was no way of returning it to the bottle. While hardly in keeping with the concept of a kibbutz, we justified it by telling ourselves it was just an indirect way of living off the land, and maybe, at first, there was some truth in that. Yet the first trappings of the money we made quickly manifested themselves; we bought mosquito nets, mesh grilles for the windows and doors of the huts we had built, alcohol, toothpaste, soap. We even splashed out on a few luxury items—Hal purchased a Persian rug off Hemen, and I bought a set of storage boxes for my hut. Time continued to pass slowly, but at least life was more comfortable for us.

'Hey, I've got a couple of bits of news,' Hal proclaimed as the five of us sat around the fire that evening upon our return from our second trip to Kullu. We'd sold twenty flutes to Hemen, and were sharing a bottle of cheap whisky to celebrate. 'First up, my visa officially expired today.' He spat into the fire, then looked at the sky. 'So how the hell will I ever get out of this damn country?'

'Thinking of leaving us?' I asked, enjoying the burn of the liquor in my stomach as I carved a Krapi-Krapi.

'No, not really. But I haven't seen my mom in three years,' he continued. 'Haven't spoken to her in six months or something. Might be dead for all I know.'

The comment strangled the conversation, and we sat in silence for a while, listening to the damp wood crackling and hissing in the fire. Perhaps we were all thinking of home. It seemed such a remote concept, so dissociated from our own circumstances that it didn't usually figure in our everyday thoughts.

'If we save enough money, we can bribe an official,' Div offered, eventually.

'Yeah,' Hal said thoughtfully. 'Yeah, you're probably right.'

I threw my finished Krapi-Krapi on the pile, then folded the blade of the Swiss army knife away with a snap.

'How many's that you've carved today, Ethan?' Div asked.

'Four,' I said, pausing for a moment as I considered whether to knock out one more before turning in. 'It's funny, don't you think,' I ventured, 'that we're in India so as not to work, and yet here I am—working.'

'Don't get a job—get a life!' Hal proclaimed. It was one of his favourite sayings.

'Hardly work,' Div said brightly. 'I mean, it's more of a hobby, don't you think?'

'Well, I wouldn't be doing it if we weren't able to sell the damn things.'

'No. No, okay, but it's not a *bad* job, a few hours a week spent carving. I mean it's like when I picked zucchinis in Australia—you do it to support your way of life. Ours happens to be very cheap, so we don't need to do so much work.' She laughed. 'Kind of perfect, if you think about it.'

'Yeah,' I nodded. Then I turned to Hal. 'What was the second development, by the way?'

He smiled, then kicked my leg gently with his foot. 'Looks like your girlfriend might be coming to visit, Ethan. When I checked poste restante, there was a letter from Lorna, she wants to come up in the springtime to see this place. I wrote back telling her to let us know when she's got firm dates so we can hook up with her in Kullu.' He grinned and said, 'I guess love might be in the air pretty soon, dude.'

'She's not my girlfriend, Hal,' I said.

'Why are you blushing then?' he laughed. 'Bet your heart's going boomity-boom right now.'

'I'm not blushing,' I hissed back. 'It's probably just the whisky—I haven't drunk in a while.'

'Anyway,' Hal continued with a shrug, 'let's just hope she doesn't bring that prig of a cousin of hers. I'm not sure I could take another of his fucking lectures, although I guess he's gone back to Hong Kong by—'

'What do you mean *cousin?*' I blurted, unable to suppress the shock in my voice.

'Huh?' Hal grunted. 'What are you talking about, dude?'

'Matthew's her . . .? *Matthew's her cousin?*'

'Yeah, man. She did say.' He gave another shrug. 'I guess you weren't in the room at the time or something.'

'But they . . . but they . . .' I shook my head at Hal. 'But they *slept together!*'

Hal looked at me for a moment, then laughed. 'Dude, are you a complete fucking idiot? They shared a room, sure—where else would he sleep with your inebriated carcass on the sofa?' He chuckled to himself. 'Man, Lorna even got me to put the camp bed up in her room—she did ask you, but you'd passed out by then.'

'But I thought they—'

Hal raised his eyebrows. 'Ethan, cousins don't sleep with each other.' He paused, then scratched at his head. 'Well, except in Iowa. Anyway, dude,' he said, getting to his feet, 'I'm off to bed.'

'Me too,' Scott agreed with a yawn, throwing a Krapi-Krapi on to the pile. 'See you guys in the morning.'

'Yeah, I'll join you,' Miles agreed.

Div flicked her cigarette at the fire. 'Yeah, I might turn in myself.'

The two couples dusted themselves down, then trudged towards their huts. Alone in the clearing, I stared into the fire, still giddy with elation from what Hal had said, but also wondering if Lorna really would come to Shadow-Wall.

*

Of the four others at the commune at that time, I perhaps identified most strongly with Scott. While I felt that my life certainly hadn't turned out as planned, the starting hand Scott had been dealt seemed a hell of a lot worse than mine. From what he told me, he came from a pretty poor background, and was orphaned before his tenth birthday after his parents both overdosed in the space of a few months. From there on, it was care-home after care-home. He spoke about it all with what seemed like indifference, but you could see from his eyes that his past contained little except pain for him. He had nothing, really, except Miles. Of course, unlike the rest of us he'd never really had a place he could call home, and I think that goes some way to explaining his energy in transforming Shadow-Wall into something much more than a handful of rundown huts in a glade on the mountainside. He built a chicken coop, then renovated all the huts so that the floors were raised from the ground, supported by low stilts hewn from a storm-felled tree. He also made a covered storage facility for the flutes, which slowly filled as the weeks passed. While Scott clearly wanted to improve Shadow-Wall, the rest of us were largely indifferent, and rather idle when it came to making improvements to the place. It was, perhaps, because none of us expected to stay very long.

As time drew on, the clouds, which had for so long cloaked the valley, gradually became thinner until finally the skies cleared completely, revealing the winter sun. It was a sign, perhaps, that spring was on its way. Yet although there was now little rain, it was still bitterly cold, with frequent overnight frosts coating the branches of the trees and rhododendrons around us with glittering ice crystals. Some nights, the frost was hard enough to produce a thin layer of ice across the lake—we'd sometimes skim pebbles across the surface the following morning. And the days remained short—with no electricity, it was completely dark by six o'clock, and impossible to cook by the feeble light of the fire. We ate early, and spent the evenings huddled in our sleeping bags, playing cards or drinking cheap whisky. It was a simple existence for sure, but life had become quite relaxed and carefree, the small income from the flutes providing more than enough to cover our costs. I even began to feel content with the strange path I had chosen.

15

JUBBAWY

'Life was kind of okay. For those few months, it really was—I think I might even have been happy, looking back. Anyway, it all changed.' I pause, and say thoughtfully, 'I suppose that's nature's way—it just can't leave things as they are; has to meddle.'

'Would you like some coffee?' Jubbawy asks. 'I would like some coffee.'

'Yes, thanks. That would be good.' I light a cigarette in anticipation. I have smoked so many that my throat is sore, and I close my eyes, imagining the soothing effect the hot, sweet coffee will have.

A minute passes, and the water-woman brings the coffee in on a tray. Jubbawy pours three cups, and I help myself to milk and sugar. The milk is fresh, not condensed.

'We drank so much tea and coffee that winter to keep warm,' I reflect, stirring my drink. 'It was bitterly, bitterly cold overnight. That first cup of coffee in the morning was one of the things we looked forward to most, you know?'

'You said it changed,' he says. 'You said life was good, and then it all changed. How?'

'Oh. We'd run out of bamboo, and Scott had gone up the hillside to cut some more. He'd been gone a while, but no one was really worried or anything.'

*

Div sees him first, realizes straight away that something's wrong. All four of us look up at her frantic prompting. Scott is stumbling towards us as if his legs are about to buckle, clutching his throat with both hands like he's trying to strangle himself. Perhaps he is. His face is a weird shade of blue, and his eyes are bulging. It looks like he's wearing some sort of ghastly, coloured mask. A dozen yards from us, he collapses.

'Christ.'

We are knelt around him; his face is turning a deeper shade of blue with each passing second, and his throat is swollen on one side, a huge protrusion of puffy white flesh bisected by the straining collar of his sweatshirt. Hal tries to tear it off, but the material refuses to rend.

'Get a knife.'

He can't talk although everyone's shouting at him, asking him what happened. The poor bastard is imploring us with his eyes, but he can't make a sound.

'He can't breathe.'

Of course he can't breathe, but it still takes us thirty seconds to deduce the obvious.

'He's been stung by something,' Miles rasps. 'He's got this allergy.'

Hal returns with a Swiss army knife, and the sweatshirt pings away from his neck as if it was made from elastic.

'What do you need for that?' Div asks.

'I don't know, but it's anaphylactic shock.'

'Adrenaline,' I snap. I try to stick my fingers down his throat, hoping to let some air into his lungs, but I can't really feel much, just a wedge of mushy flesh. 'Someone check his rucksack, he needs an adrenaline shot. He must carry something.'

I am aware of Hal sprinting off again. There is little we can do in the meantime, and the three of us just stare at Scott in silence. He is shaking his head from side to side, clawing at his throat. His mouth is open, he's trying to gulp down breath, but there is no sound of air flowing—just the scrapes and thuds as his thrashing feet kick up small clods of earth.

'It's okay, man,' Miles says softly. 'It's going to be okay.' He takes Scott's hands, restraining him. 'It's gonna be okay, man.'

I hiss, 'Where the hell's Hal?'

Div goes to find him, and then it's just me, Scott and Miles.

'It's gonna be okay, man, they've gone to get your . . . your medicine.'

The two of them return, Scott is starting to struggle less. Hal throws down several blister packs of tablets. Aspirin, chloroquine, imodium, paludrine. Nothing.

'Fuck.'

'What? What?' Div shouts.

I shake my head, and say, 'These are no good. Was there nothing like a needle or something? He needs an injection.'

Hal shrugs. 'It's all I could find,' he pants.

'Oh shit, man,' Miles cries out. 'What are we going to do?'

'Jesus,' Div wails. 'He's going to fucking die.'

I shout, 'Get me a tube, a pen or something.'

Hal goes again.

'Fucking hell, he's blue,' Miles states, his voice numb. And he really is. Blue, like the sky above us. It gives me an odd sense of detachment, the thought of us crowded around a dying man, and he is dying, on the side of a mountain in the middle of nowhere. Five tiny figures under a massive sky.

I continue poking around his throat, achieving nothing, waiting for Hal to get back. Scott has started to go into a fit, his legs and arms twitching in the dirt. His throat is making an odd clicking noise, and his eyes are beginning to roll like a shark's.

'He's going to fucking die,' Div shrieks again. 'Can't you fucking do something?'

It's something I saw once on TV—one of those programmes where they re-enact real-life emergency situations. Same story, anaphylactic shock from a wasp sting or something. They had no adrenaline either.

'Here,' Hal rasps.

'Not a fucking pencil, you stupid shit! A *tube*, a fucking Bic or something.'

This time Miles goes.

He's shaking less as the seconds pass, and I wonder if it's too late. The pupils in his eyes are no longer visible—just the whites show, webbed with thin red blood vessels. His neck is now as thick as my thigh, and I start to run my fingers down the flesh beneath his Adam's apple, looking for a horizontal ridge in the cartilage, for that is where I'll need to cut.

Miles returns, squats down next to me, and pulls the nib and stem of ink out of the pen with his teeth, holding out the empty plastic tube to me.

I can feel the ridge of cartilage, I think. Actually, I can feel three, and the deepest one is higher than I remember from the television programme. It's also the wrong side of his Adam's apple. No one says a word, they have all assumed I know what I'm doing. Their helplessness has made them unquestioning.

'I'm not sure where to cut,' I whisper, almost to myself, holding the shiny steel blade above his throat. My hand is shaking like a jackhammer.

Still no one speaks, not even a word of encouragement. I select the middle ridge, the first one I can find below his Adam's apple, and push the knife in.

'Shit.' There shouldn't be any blood. There was none on the TV.

'You've cut a fucking artery,' someone says. I'm not even sure who, because I'm just staring at Scott's neck, which is now pumping blood out over my hands and forearms. I grab the tube from Miles, and fumble around looking for the hole. There is so much blood that I can't find the incision. A few seconds pass while I try repeatedly jabbing the pen at his throat, hoping it will miraculously slide into place. Of course, it doesn't; so I use his sweatshirt to try and wipe the blood from his neck, and then it's obvious where the incision is, because a weak spray of blood is issuing forth from it. In fact, it's not so much an incision as a gash. Still, I push the pen in.

'What now?' A female voice. Div.

I'm not too sure myself, because I've fucked it up, but I try blowing into the pen, hoping the air will reach his lungs. Instead there is a gurgling noise, and bubbles of blood appear either side of the tube; the air is simply coming back out because the slit is far too wide. The pen, too, is filling with blood. There's so much of the stuff that it's collecting in a dark pool around his shoulders.

'You've cut a fucking artery,' the voice says again. I can hear someone else being sick.

I push the pen in further, hoping to get it down into his lungs, and blow again. My lips are practically on his neck now. There is a slightly deeper gurgling noise, but the bubbles are still frothing around my mouth, and he's perfectly motionless, not even twitching. I'm not even sure whether I should try and get air into his lungs or try and staunch the blood. There is an unbelievable amount; the frozen ground is unable to absorb it, and it runs away in long lines, crimson rivers.

'Someone stop the bleeding.' But the words stick in my mouth, my dry tongue unable to form the sentence properly. 'Someone stop the bleeding.'

No one comes to help. I realize they are looking at Scott, staring at him. Hal's head is cocked slightly to one side, a look of puzzlement on his face. Miles is shaking his head, saying something, although I can't seem to absorb the sound of his voice. Div is crying, wiping vomit from her chin. I look down at Scott, at the blood, at his throat. He is dead.

*

'We buried him in the woods.'

'You buried him in the woods,' Jubbawy repeats slowly, shaking his head. He looks at me. 'Where in the woods? Exactly, please.'

'I'd need to show you on a map or something,' I reply.

'A map?'

'Yeah, the body is in the woodland to the west of the commune. I can show you on a map, if you have one. It's kind of hard to describe the location.'

Jubbawy scribbles something on a pad, tears the sheet off, and hands it to the wiry man who gets to his feet and then leaves the room.

'I didn't mean to kill him.'

'That must be a comforting thought for you.'

'Do you think what I did was wrong?' I ask.

'Do *you* think so? Is that why you're asking me?'

I sigh and say nothing.

'Anyway, I'm not here to give you some kind of moral absolution.'

'I was trying to save his life.'

'Yes, so you said.'
'He would have died anyway.'
'So you keep saying.'
'I don't *keep saying*. I'm just telling you.'
'Yes, and I am listening. I'm just making the point that in the light of what you have told me, there will have to be an investigation. Someone is dead, in quite different circumstances to the others. We have to look into these things—it is standard procedure, even if there has been no crime as such.'

No crime as such? The passage of time tends to filter out emotions, leaving only physical recollections, but I can still remember the guilt. Anyone there would have known we had to try something, but the thought offers only limited solace. I still screwed up, and the wound is yet to heal entirely. Instead it festers, as wounds so often do in this part of the world.

I look up sharply. Jubbawy is talking to me.

'I'm sorry?'

'And after this, you all *stayed*?'

'No, no,' I say. 'Miles left of course, he was heartbroken, devastated. We walked down the mountain with him the day after we'd buried Scott.' I pause, then add, 'I think he was in shock, to be honest. We probably could have done a bit more for him, but after . . . after what happened to Scott, none of us were thinking straight really.'

Jubbawy shakes his head slowly. 'But you, Hal and Div. You stayed?'

I nod.

'You stayed like nothing had happened?'

'Not like nothing had happened, it affected us all,' I shrug. 'But yeah, in the end we decided to stay.'

16

SHADOW-WALL, FEBRUARY 1987

I picked up the whisky bottle and tipped the last half-inch of amber liquid into my mouth, feeling the burn of the alcohol on the back of my throat. Four empty bottles of imported Scotch lay on the ash-speckled ground by the fire, the reflected flames dancing like forked orange tongues on the curved surface of the glass. I felt very drunk. It was all we had done since leaving Miles stood alone and sobbing on the winding valley road into Kullu.

'I wonder if that's what Hell looks like,' I said aloud, poking one of the bottles with my foot.

'D'you believe in that shit?' Hal asked. He was on the opposite side of the fire to me, and the heat waves, flecked with crackling sparks, distorted his face so that his features seemed to shimmer.

'No, not really.'

'No,' Hal sighed. 'No, nor do I.'

I shot Div a sidelong glance, reluctant to engage in eye contact. Her face was blotchy from crying, the eyelids puffy and swollen. The faint orange glow from the fire illuminated the wet streaks that had not yet dried on her cheeks. 'What about you, Div?'

A shrug. 'Do I believe in God? No, it's all just nature, isn't it? We all die sometime—all of us. It's simply a matter of timing.' She scraped up some dirt, then let it slide slowly through her cupped fingers. 'I mean, one day all of our bodies will bleed into the soil—they'll rot and become part of this.' She paused, and looked at the stars. 'The reality's pretty far removed from Heaven or Hell, if you ask me.'

'Yeah,' Hal grunted in agreement.

There was a long pause, punctuated only by the occasional, angry crack from the fire.

'I've ruined everything,' I offered eventually.

'Hey, no one's blaming you, man. You did what you could. At least you tried, instead of just watching.'

'I *took* his life.'

'Not deliberately. No one thinks that. And you haven't *ruined* anything, it's just a setback, that's all.'

Div snorted.

'Aw,' Hal said, 'I didn't mean it like that. I just don't think it should have to necessarily derail this project; I don't think that's what Scott would have wanted.' He nodded to himself, as if pleased with the line of reasoning he'd stumbled across. 'Yeah, we should continue this place in honour of Scott.'

So we stayed, and tried to deal with it. It was hard, but what else could we do? I couldn't sleep, of course, regardless of how much I drank. An event like that sticks in your mind, like the image of a flashbulb burned on your retina long after the photo's been taken. Instead I sat by the fire, not far from where I'd inadvertently slit Scott's throat, huddled in my sleeping bag, trying to capture the little heat offered by the smouldering embers. The stars, as always, were bright—pinpricks in a vast, black canvas. I watched them until the first rays of dawn began to dissolve away the darkness.

It was an ordinary sunrise, accompanied by the distant caw of birds. One by one the huts emerged from the gloom, then the forest behind them, finally the mountain. As the air around me warmed slightly, I scraped the fire out with my foot and wandered down to the lake. A few dragonflies buzzed in noisy circles over the water, and though a thin sheet of mist still clung to the surface, I could still make out tiny ripples around the pond-skaters. I shattered the glassy surface with a pebble, watching the orange orb that played upon the surface break into a million parts, then lay down in the grass by the bank, letting the winter sun warm my face.

Three weeks had passed since Miles' departure, and they had been marked by uncertainty. We'd half-expected the police to come—there was a very great chance that Miles would have reported Scott's death, although time would show that he never did—and we had relapsed into a kind of cataplexy, spending the days getting drunk and replaying those strange fifteen minutes over and over again, analysing every aspect of our actions until we finally managed to convince ourselves that there was nothing that could have been done to prevent his death. I slept little. When I lay alone in my hut at night, my mind would endlessly replay the death scene of Scott. The thoughts came back like video, variously shown in widescreen, or grainy shaking camcorder footage, or black-and-white, or slow-motion.

It was a difficult time. And our dark moods, and the resultant lethargy, would perhaps have lasted indefinitely were it not for the basic demands of commune life that made prolonged inactivity impossible. We needed to forage for food, cook, wash our clothes, gather wood for the fire. Yet we could find little fruit in the surrounding forest even though winter was turning to spring, and our stock of food was once again running low.

*

'Dude, we need to get some more supplies,' Hal called out from the clearing as I lay in my hut one morning, head throbbing from another night of whisky on an empty stomach.

I reluctantly pulled myself to my feet, and opened the door. The bright sunlight hurt my eyes. 'How many flutes have we got?' I asked, rubbing my hand over my face. 'It's not like we've carved much this past month.'

'Yeah, not so many, eighty or so.'

'Well anyway, I need to get out of this place for a bit,' I said. 'And, yeah. We really need to get some food in.'

'Right, dude. Well put some clothes on, and we'll start loading up. Div's got diarrhoea again, so she's gonna stay put. It's just the two of us.'

'Just the two of us,' I repeated.

By mid-morning, we were struggling down the mountainside, bowed by our loads, tripping over roots and fallen branches. It took three hours to make the descent, and once we stumbled on to the road, as was often the case, we had to wait another couple of hours before a vehicle passed in the right direction. This time it was a battered, yellow Toyota pick-up truck. We rode all the way into town, neither of us speaking much, just smoking and watching the mountains inch by. We were two days in Kullu. Two long days, as it turned out. Hemen only bought thirty-six Krapi-Krapis from us, and we ended up trying to sell the remaining ones to other shops in town.

We bought food, whisky, cigarettes, and any special items that had been requested. It didn't matter that Hal wanted a new torch, and that Div wanted a waterproof mascara—our motto was 'sharing is caring' and irrespective of the number of flutes each of us had personally carved that month, we always considered the cash we earned to be part of a communal fund. But none of us failed to notice that the money went a lot further than usual that month once we'd split it out.

17

JUBBAWY

The room seems much warmer now. Perhaps it is noon, or thereabouts. Or maybe it feels warmer because of the hot coffee we have just finished. Whatever the reason, two dark stains are spreading slowly from Jubbawy's armpits; soon they will meet one another in the middle of his chest. One of them looks remarkably like the outline of Africa, except that Madagascar is missing. I try to impose a continent on the other, but give up. It is just a sweat stain. Strangely, the other man does not seem to be perspiring at all. Not even his brow is moist.

'Something preoccupies you?' Jubbawy asks brusquely.

'Continental drift . . .' I say absently, the question catching me off guard. 'Er, sorry, nothing really.'

Jubbawy regards me, then slowly looks down at his shirt. He returns his gaze to me and snorts. He is a smart man, I muse.

'Is there any more coffee?' I say to divert the conversation, picking up the silver flask and shaking it. It is empty.

'No,' Jubbawy states flatly, not a little annoyed. He doesn't offer to order any more. 'How much money were you making on these monthly trips?'

'Oh, that particular one was . . .' I try to make the calculation in my head, but the flickering strip-light spoils my concentration, and I eventually just guess. 'Not a lot. A few thousand rupees—it all went on food and stuff. Overheads, if you like.'

'I see. Was that the norm?'

'Not really. The following month—March I think it was—Hal and I made the same trip, and the majority of Krapi-Krapis had been sold. I remember that figure—Rs 6,440—a couple of hundred dollars.'

'Very precise.'

'Yeah. Well after we bought supplies and stuff, there was enough left over to get a headstone for the grave. Div had insisted we get one. That's why I remember. Our first substantial profit.'

'Ah.'

I look at Jubbawy, and add slowly, 'That trip was the one where we'd arranged to meet up with Lorna. She'd been delayed by something or other, so we ended up staying a couple of days longer in some rundown guesthouse waiting for her to arrive.' I pause. 'I got pretty drunk those two days, I was so nervous about seeing her again, of her learning about what happened with Scott. I was also a bit worried we might bump into Miles; I figured he might still be in town or something. I was pretty fucking stressed, to be honest.' I look at the policeman. 'Sorry.'

He shrugs to say the obscenity doesn't matter. 'So you told her?'

'Yeah, we kind of alluded to it on the journey back to Shadow-Wall, but the first time we really talked about it was after we arrived. Straight away, she went to put flowers on the grave. Wildflowers from the woods, gladioli and bluebells and stuff.' I take another cigarette and light it, dragging too early; the sulphur from the match stings my throat. 'That was just the kind of person she was—she'd never even met Scott, of course. Hal and I . . . well it didn't even occur to us to put flowers on there.'

*

She is kneeling by the graveside, shaded from the warm spring sunshine by the leafy branches of a poplar. In her hand is a penknife, which she uses to break up the clods of earth left from the burial. She has tilled nearly a third of the surface—the soil is still dark from moisture—and to her left is a small pile of stones that she has removed. Next to them is a selection of wildflowers, carefully chosen for their compatibility with one another—yellows, blues, mauves, a smattering of whites.

'How are you doing, Ethan?'

'I'm okay.'

'I'm glad to hear that.' She is looking at me strangely. There is a tension between us that I know we both sense. I wonder if it's because of what she knows, or perhaps what she feels.

'You?'

'Yes. Fine. Thank you.'

'We sound like a conversation out of *Mansfield Park*,' I say, not smiling.

'I haven't read it,' she replies. Then she looks at me, her head tilted slightly. 'What have you *done*, Ethan?'

'I don't know what I've done. Everyone keeps telling me I did the right thing trying to save him. But it doesn't quite feel like that.'

She turns away from me, scrapes a hole in the earth, and then places down a bluebell. 'I am sorry.'

'Sorry for what?'

Lorna focuses her attention on planting the flower, scooping soil into the hole before gently pressing it down with her fingertips. 'I'm sorry for what happened,' she says finally.

'Yeah.'

'We should go back to Kullu and tell the authorities,' she says, still not turning to face me.

I sigh. 'He had no family, Lorna. Nothing.' I shrug. 'This he told me. Miles was the only person on this planet who cared for him.'

'That's very sad,' she says, softly, still talking to the ground.

'Hal thinks we should just let it be, and maybe he's right. I'm just not sure what would be achieved bringing the police into this, given the circumstances.' I pause, then add, 'And to be honest, I'm a bit worried they might, like, kind of like charge me with something. I mean this is India, the police here have something of a reputation, you know?'

Lorna finally stops attending to the soil, and looks at me. She sighs. 'Yes, you have a point.'

I shrug. 'This is really hard for me, you know? About what happened, well, I think of little else.'

'Give it time.'

'That is the one thing I have in abundance.' I kneel down next to her, examining the flowers she has planted. Then look at her. Mud cakes the white dress she is wearing, and her hands are covered in soil. 'Would you like a hand? With the flowers?'

'No. I rather like the solitude, actually.'

'Well, I'll go back then.'

'Yes, okay,' she murmurs softly.

I get up, turn and leave.

*

'Why *did* she come to Kullu? You never said. A vacation?'

'Oh, I don't know. I think Delhi was pretty lonely for her.' I pause. 'You know, although she was a bit pissed off with us for crashing at her house, well . . . after we'd gone—and after Matthew went back to Hong Kong—I guess she missed having people around. She kind of said as much to me at Shadow-Wall one time.'

'I see.'

'Anyway, she arrived and kind of fell in love with Shadow-Wall, I guess. Not just being around people, but the place itself too—it was springtime when she came, it was really beautiful up there at that time of year . . . everything was bursting into flower, the rhododendrons and stuff.'

'Himachal Pradesh is a lovely part of the world,' Jubbawy agrees.

'Yeah,' I nod. 'You know, I taught her to carve Krapi-Krapis under this blue pine near the clearing, she got really good at it. And when it was just the four of us . . . well, we just all got on really well, it was great having her there, she really improved the dynamic, if you know what I mean? Those couple of months—before the others came in summer—it was like living in paradise.'

Jubbawy is silent for a moment. 'Paradise?' he asks slowly, curling his lip.

'Yeah, well,' I grunt, 'Nothing worked out in the end, did it?' I look down at my hands and shrug. 'Nothing.'

He sighs, then takes a cigarette from the packet, feeds it between his lips, lights it. I can't help gaping at him.

'I didn't know—'

Jubbawy shrugs. 'It's been almost a fortnight since I quit, and then you come into my interview room, chain-smoking in front of me. And that is fine, of course, I want to make you feel as comfortable as possible after what . . . after what happened. But it's driving me to distraction, to be honest. So I will join you for one cigarette, although my wife will most certainly admonish me if she finds out.' He takes a drag, and blows smoke towards the ceiling. 'Perhaps I will buy some peppermints on the way home,' he says, absently.

I also take a cigarette from the packet, slide the matches back over to my side of the table and light it. We sit opposite one another, smoking. I wonder briefly whether Jubbawy's comment about him going home was designed to needle me, to highlight my own plight.

'Actually yes, let's get some more coffee,' Jubbawy says good-naturedly after some time has passed.

'Yeah, that would be good,' I agree.

'Okay. Well, why don't we take a break for a few minutes?'

'I could use the toilet actually . . . if we're taking a break?'

'Of course. Inspector Shah will show you the way.'

*

When I return, Jubbawy is in his seat. A replenished tray sits on the table, my coffee already prepared. I take an antibiotic and a painkiller with my first sip, scalding my mouth slightly.

'You should get that strip-light fixed, you know?' I say to Jubbawy, gesturing towards the ceiling with my hands.

'Yes.' He looks briefly at the flickering light as if seeing it for the first time, and says without interest, 'I'm sure someone will see to it.' Then he takes a considered drink of coffee and says slowly: 'Now, I have to give a press conference this evening, and it would be immensely helpful if I can add a few details to the somewhat sparse information we have thus far. So let us move on, if we may.' He looks at his notes for a moment. 'Ah yes, you mentioned that others were about to arrive. Do continue, please.'

18

SHADOW-WALL, MAY 1987

The arrival of summer had transformed Shadow-Wall into something quite unrecognizable from the windswept and rain-lashed glade we'd stumbled into all those many months ago. Now, all around the clearing, the dark green walls of rhododendrons were speckled with mauve and white blossoms; bees and butterflies droned lazily from flower to flower, making the air around us hum with sound. We also shared the mountain with monkeys, the occasional deer and all manner of exotic birds, a constant reminder of our close proximity to nature. The warm waters of the lake had taken on an almost turquoise hue, and high above us the snow-capped peaks of the Himalayas were finally free from any cloud, the dark granite rock of their lower reaches contrasting starkly with the azure sky.

Our physical appearance changed too as summer established itself. Our hair was bleached to variously lighter hues by the sun, our bodies hardened from labouring on tasks such as improving the huts and digging new latrines, and our skin coloured a deep brown. Yet little altered in our everyday lives. When we weren't carving, we'd sit around talking or playing cards, or go swimming in the lake, or take long meandering walks along the cool pine-scented paths of the forest. Life felt good, and financially we were secure—we managed to make around a hundred Krapi-Krapis a month, and demand for the flutes was maintained by a steady flow of tourists into Kullu during those summer months. Even after overheads, each of us collected a small brick of rupees each month. Life was both idyllic and carefree, and if the gods had left us in peace, perhaps it would have remained so. But change was coming—and it was marked by the arrival of a couple that Hal had met on one of our increasingly regular trips into town.

Jed and Annabel were hard-core stoners. They were probably in their mid-forties, but it was hard to tell. Their skin had endured too much sun exposure and looked like the bark of a tree, and their often nonsensical utterances provided little clue as to their life-stage—they both spoke with a slowness that suggested many years of substance abuse. I suppose they were harmless enough, and we simply accepted these dread-locked new arrivals into our commune in much the same way as we were to welcome everyone else who subsequently passed through. Yet their lethargy soon began to grate. They barely moved from the hammocks they'd slung between some trees in a shady copse on the edge of the clearing, and seemed to spend almost all of their time smoking dope, sleeping or simply staring into space. Indeed, the only time they joined us as a group was at mealtimes; yet even then we'd sit as far as possible from them to try and avoid the rancid odour of their unwashed bodies and hair.

'What do they see in this place?' I asked Lorna as we watched them examining the hut Hal was constructing for them. We were sunbathing by the lake, side by side in the long grass. She wore a bikini, I a pair of shorts that the sun had faded from blue to mauve. If Lorna had noticed my propensity to sunbathe at the same time as her, she had not let on. 'They don't *do* anything.'

'I saw Jed washing in the lake yesterday,' she commented. 'I suppose that's a good thing, but I kind of feel the water's contaminated now, you know?'

I laughed. 'Do you mind that Hal brought them here?'

'Well it's nice having new people around, you know? But they are rather . . . rather idle.'

'Yeah, I wish they'd help with carving,' I agreed, stretching out so as to allow my foot to wander a couple of inches to my right. It rested there, lightly touching Lorna's ankle. 'It's kind of unfair on everyone else, you know?'

'Right,' she replied, dreamily. Her ankle remained where it was. She must have been aware of the contact, surely. I would have felt a hot coal no less strongly. 'Well, they probably won't stay very long I suppose.'

I paused, then asked: 'And what about you, Lorna?'

She raised her head off the ground for a moment to look at me. 'What about me?'

'Are you going to stay? Through the summer?'

'I don't know,' she replied thoughtfully. 'I'm really not sure. I mean the place is quite quaint, isn't it? The thing is, I don't really know where my life's going at the moment. I feel a bit like I'm in limbo.'

'Well what do you want from life?' I asked, after a pause.

'Oh . . .' she turned on her side and faced me, the contact broken. 'Happiness, I suppose. Yes—happiness.'

'Yeah, but that's what everyone wants.' I paused, then said slowly, 'Okay, how do you envisage *finding* happiness?'

'I really don't know—there are so many different factors, wouldn't you agree? Relationships, health, friendships, financial circumstances, environment. Some can be influenced, controlled even, others not.'

'And of those you can influence? Relationships, for example?'

She laughed. 'Is it an example? It seems a little coincidental that you chose that particular one?'

I didn't answer, and the only sound was the gentle slopping of water against the bank, and the drone of insects.

'But seeing as you asked me,' she continued slowly, 'I think that we have so little time here that to make a wrong choice would be . . . well it would be a dreadful waste. It's very easy to start a relationship, but sometimes very hard to leave one, even when it is the time to do so.' She paused and added, 'Whatever the reason may be.'

'Yes, but with so little time, doesn't that present the danger that relationships, love even, will pass you by altogether? After all, if you wait too long for the fruit to ripen, you might return to the tree to find it bare.'

She smiled, and shading her eyes from the sun said, 'So you would have me eat unripe fruit, Ethan?'

'No, I simply do not wish to see you starve.'

Lorna laughed. 'And what about you?'

'Me? I appear to have been fasting for some time now.'

'I'm sorry to hear that,' she said with a laugh.

We both watched a brightly coloured butterfly land tentatively on a dandelion, then flit away, disturbed perhaps by the slight breeze. After a thoughtful silence, Lorna said, not a little mischievously, 'And what fruit shall you try next, Ethan?'

I thought for a moment. 'I hear Kiwis are nice.'

Lorna giggled, and flopped back on the ground, burying her head in her arms. 'Some fruit are not so easy to peel, Ethan. Especially Kiwis.'

I lit a cigarette and smiled to myself.

*

We took exactly one hundred and fifty Krapi-Krapis into Kullu that month. Although Jed and Annabel had contributed nothing, it was our largest consignment to date. Our trip was marked by other milestones too; it was the first time Lorna joined us, and thus the first time she met Hemen. And, when we finally arrived at his shop, it was the first time he'd sold all of the previous months' consignment of flutes.

Yet despite those significant events, it is the journey into Kullu that I recall with most clarity. The four of us had managed to flag down some kind of minibus, a small Hyundai van that the owner had apparently converted so that it might carry passengers. There were two benches that had been screwed into the floor of the vehicle but, even so, with the four of us and our bulky cargo of flutes, it was very cramped. And I sat next to Lorna. The driver, a young smiling Indian man who was barely out of his teens, drove fast along the winding roads so that we skidded and veered around the many sharp corners. Rock music blared out from the sound system. Then at one point, as we felt the wheels spinning on gravel as we hurtled around a particularly sharp corner, Lorna held my hand. The contact was brief, but not fleeting—perhaps thirty seconds or so. It wasn't until some time after we'd safely navigated the bend in the road that she let go. It was, I admit, a small thing—almost inconsequential. Yet, to me at least, it seemed anything but.

*

'Welcome, welcome, my good friends! And who, might I ask, is this most delightful young lady you have brought along today to grace my humble outlet?'

'Lorna, this is Hemen,' I said, looking around his shop. Many of the carpets and cushions he'd previously had on display were gone, replaced instead by large wooden display cabinets.

The diminutive Indian clasped her hand and kissed it, then bowed away with a flourish. 'Enchanted,' he said with a broad smile. 'Enchanted.'

'Well,' interrupted Hal, a note of impatience in his voice, 'shall we get down to business?'

Hemen wrung his hands, and then looked towards the pile of black bags by the door of his shop. 'Indeed, we shall, my dear Hal,' he smiled. 'Indeed, we shall. So, pray tell, how many of your fine instruments do we have this month?'

'150,' declared Hal, a hint of pride creeping into his voice.

There was a long pause. 'So few?' asked Hemen, shaking his head. 'So very, very few?' He turned away, pointing to the empty display cabinets. 'Observe and then reflect, my friends. Observe and reflect. These cabinets were constructed by my cousin, who is a very fine carpenter indeed. But apart from the most excellent craftsmanship, which I must confess to finding rather pleasing, what is it about these cabinets that you find most notable?'

'Well, the fact they are empty,' Div offered with a sigh.

Hemen clapped his hands together. 'Indeed, madam. Indeed. We have been blessed this past month with a significant upturn in sales of your fine musical objects.' He pursed his lips. 'So much so, I would add, that a most unfortunate scenario developed, a most unfortunate scenario indeed.' Hemen gave a shrug of his shoulders. 'You see, I was sold out a number of days before the middle of the month fell.'

'Wow,' I exclaimed, examining myself in an ornate mirror on sale in the far corner of the shop. My hair had grown long, almost to my shoulders. And my face was lean and brown. 'That's great news,' I continued absently, trying to work out if my new appearance was better or worse than before.

'Is it?' Hemen asked, his eyebrows raised high above his wire-frame spectacles. 'I must be sharing with you the fact that for someone such as myself operating in the retail trade, empty shelves are *never* good news.'

He wagged his finger towards me. 'It is a sign of a weak supply chain, Mr Ethan. It is a sign of a weak supply chain.'

'Well,' Hal interjected, 'you have more stock now, so we're all good, right?'

Hemen gave a long sigh, then turned on his heel and walked behind his counter. He then disappeared from sight as he knelt down. We heard a series of clicks, then the loud thud of heavy bolts being slid back. After a minute or so, he reappeared with several bundles of rupees, each neatly bound with a yellow elastic band.

'Here,' he said, sliding the money across the glass counter.

Div walked over and thumbed through the banknotes, before turning and giving Hal a nod. We muttered our thanks to Hemen, then opened the door on to the street. As we walked out into the afternoon sun, the bell on the doorframe jangling behind us, he shouted: 'Bring me 200 next month, my dearest friends. Bring me 200 next month.'

*

'Over a $170,' Div panted as we slowly ascended the path up to Shadow-Wall. All four of us were bowed by our loads of food and other supplies.

'And we'll make even more than that next month,' I said, pausing to both catch my breath and adjust the straps on the rucksack I was carrying, which were starting to dig into my shoulders. I'd drawn the short straw at the base of the trail, and thus had by far the heaviest load—tins of tuna fish and canned vegetables, as well as roll upon roll of trash bags.

'Yeah,' Hal agreed. 'But I think it's time we had a little chat with our dread-locked friends, you know?'

*

It ended abruptly for them when we finally made it up the trail after a gruelling five-hour climb. As we slowly walked into the clearing, still struggling with our heavy loads, Jed gave a slow wave of his hand by way of greeting. He was lying on his side on the ground, a blue and purple daypack wedged under his head like a pillow. A reefer hung from his thick, dry lips. Annabel lay at a right angle to him, her head nestled on his hip.

'Hey, guys,' he said, as we dropped our bags near the fire, which had been allowed to go out.

'Hello, Jed,' Hal grunted.

'Good trip?' Jed asked.

'Well Hemen had sold everything, and wants 200 flutes next month, so yeah, a pretty good trip,' Hal replied, a little tightly. 'So I've been thinking. From now on, you guys need to start pulling your weight, you know? You didn't make one Krapi-Krapi last month.'

Jed slowly hauled himself to a sitting position and laughed. 'Hal, we've discussed this already. Me and Annabel did *try* carving, you know? It's just that neither of us are much good.' He chuckled to himself, then slumped back down. 'Leave it to the experts, I say.'

Hal held out his upturned palms—like all of ours, the skin was heavily calloused from the repeated actions required to carve. 'Well that leaves you with a problem then,' he snapped.

Jed reluctantly sat up again. 'Huh?'

'All this food,' Hal said, gesturing at the piles of tins and packages that now littered the clearing, 'was bought with the money we made from the Krapi-Krapis. And if you're not going to carve any flutes, you're certainly not going to share in the proceeds. So, if you want to stay, that's up to you. But go find your own fucking food, okay?'

'But it's a *commune*!' Jed protested, the sentence seeming to take a full ten seconds to complete. 'It's like, er, *communal?*'

'Yeah,' Annabel added, slowly turning her head to us. 'What happened to *sharing is caring?*'

'Not any more,' Hal proclaimed. 'Now we all carve or starve, man! Now we all carve or starve.'

19

JUBBAWY

'Anyway, when they left it was all rather acrimonious, I'm afraid. They started saying all this stuff about how we'd regret kicking them out, that they'd ruin our commune. We thought they were just letting off steam, you know?'

'I see.'

'Once they headed back to Kullu, well, that was to be the last time it was just the four of us. It all changed after that, of course.'

'Yes.'

'Still, we were kind of glad when they'd gone.' I pause. 'And maybe we were lucky that they left when they did.'

'Why so?'

I look at Jubbawy, then emit a long sigh. 'I suppose it was the last event of consequence—before the others came, that is.'

'Go on.'

I take a drag on my cigarette. 'It's rather bleak, I'm afraid. Hal and I were scavenging for apples in the woods, some way southwest of the camp. We'd collected dozens actually, not just apples, but apricots and chilgoza seeds too. Anyway, we used these black bin liners we'd got in Kullu—Hal's had split, and I'd made a makeshift bag with my t-shirt for him.' I laugh. 'Isn't that weird?'

'What?'

'That I can remember every detail, every last damn detail. Don't you think that's weird, how it's the bad memories that stick the most?'

'Yes,' Jubbawy says slowly. 'Ironic.'

'We were scrambling down this steep slope, and I'd scratched my arm on a lantana bush, nothing too bad, but a thorn had pushed right into one of my veins, so it was bleeding pretty badly. Anyway, we stopped so I could wrap something around it; of course my t-shirt was being used as a bag, so we used Hal's bandanna, he often wore one. Then we heard this humming noise.'

He raises one eyebrow. 'A humming noise?'

'Yeah, like electricity going through cables or something. We'd been there nine months or so, and all the sounds you hear in the forest—you know, monkeys and stuff—were pretty familiar. This wasn't.' I tap a long cylinder of ash from my cigarette. 'So we went to have a look. It was hard to pinpoint, I mean the sound seemed to come from every direction, but we knew we were close just from the volume. Jesus, it was so loud. Then Hal says to me, "What's that?" or something along those lines, and he's looking at this thing down by the base of a cedar tree, quite far away, about twenty yards or so.' I laugh, without any mirth.

'What?'

'Well, I really thought it was this black sheepskin rug my parents used to have in front of their fire—I even thought I could make out the tufts of wool moving in the breeze. You know when it's . . . like . . . completely impossible that you're seeing what you think you're seeing, but you're utterly convinced it is?'

'I don't think I've experienced that particular feeling, no.'

'Oh. Well anyway, we moved a little closer, and there was this smell, and this incessant buzzing, and Hal just says, "Flies, dude." Then it's obvious, we're looking at a carcass, a bit bigger than a deer, and there's this great black cloud of flies on it.'

'I see.'

'And we must've made a noise, maybe one of us said something . . . No, I retched from the smell, that was it. Yeah, I retched, and the noise must have disturbed this crow or rook because it squawked away, then this great big cloud of flies just lifted off the carcass from the sudden movement.' I pause, visualizing the scene. 'You know, the noise they made was bizarre, like you could hear each individual fly, yet you took in the whole sound.' I can still hear it now, like a dark symphony. 'We both just puked. It was Scott.'

'Scott?'

'Yes.'

'How did it come to pass that his body was no longer in the grave?'

'I've no idea. We guessed a bear or something.'

'A bear. Yes, that's possible, I suppose.'

'It was hideous finding him. Just hideous.' I pause. 'I'll never forget it, you know? There were maggots crawling from his eye-sockets, from where his nose used to be, everywhere.'

'I imagine that was a very unpleasant experience.'

I realize that the cigarette that I'm holding has burnt right down to the filter. The hairs on my knuckle are starting to curl, and I can smell the stench as they blacken. I grind the cigarette into the ashtray, and the smell of frazzled hair is joined by the smell of burnt filter. I am already thinking about lighting another. 'Yeah. Well anyway, that's why his body will be kind of hard to find. It was deep in the woods. We left him there, you know? We left him there to rot.'

*

'Do you think we can just leave him?' Hal asks.

'No,' I reply, but say nothing more. The smell of the corpse seems to still linger in my nostrils, and I gag involuntarily.

'So . . . ?'

'What?' I snap.

'What are we going to do?'

'I don't know.'

'Well we can't send the girls, dude.'

Lorna remains silent, but Div, perhaps confident that she is now exonerated from the task, says, 'It can't be *that* bad.'

'It's very fucking bad,' I hiss. 'Oh Jesus, I mean he's . . . he's rotten. Just mush!'

Hal nods his agreement. 'Yeah, the dude's right. He's pretty far gone, if you know what I mean.'

An image enters my head of me gripping Scott's arm, the fingers of my hand sinking into the putrid flesh until it gives way to hard bone. The flies that cake his body like black armour lift, the decaying body is exposed, the smell of rotting organs are set free. 'I can't,' I state flatly. 'I'm sorry, really I am, but I just can't do it.'

Hal spits into the grey embers of the fire. 'Well I can't do it on my own, so I guess we leave him, then.'

Div lights a cigarette and is silent for a few moments. Then she says, 'To be honest, there's nothing wrong with leaving him to nature, is there? I mean, I read about this American Indian tribe that bury their dead at the base of trees and stuff, the nutrients from their bodies become part of the trunk and the leaves, so they are kind of reborn or something. I saw it in *National Geographic*.'

'So that's settled then,' Hal says, more brightly. He nods to himself. 'So that's settled.'

*

'Anyway,' I sigh, 'whether it was a bear or something else, the four of us were a lot more cautious after that when we went to forage for fruit in the woods.'

'Of course.'

'It became part of the orientation process for new arrivals,' I add. 'Briefing them about the dangers of bears.'

'Orientation process,' Jubbawy repeats, removing his glasses and rubbing his eyes.

'Yes,' I say. 'It was around that time that others started to come. Many others.'

20

SHADOW-WALL, JUNE 1987

'Is this the place? Shadow-Wall?'

I stared at the tall stranger who had, without warning, emerged from the treeline at the head of the trail with his two female companions, and then strode confidently into the clearing. 'Who are you? What are you talking about?'

'The *hippie commune*,' he said, his voice a strong American drawl. 'The one advertised in the flyers that were being handed out in Kullu.' He looked around, then waved a piece of paper towards me. 'Is this the place?'

'Let me see that!' I snatched the white A4 sheet from his hand, looked at it, then scornfully passed it to Lorna. On it was a reasonably accurate hand-drawn map of the route up to Shadow-Wall, with a prominent headline of 'Welcome to Paradise'. Underneath it was a long paragraph extolling the virtues of life at our commune.

'I guess Jed and Annabel produced this,' I said slowly.

'I guess so,' Lorna agreed with a shrug. She read slowly from the paragraph below the map: 'Free food and accommodation in the gorgeous foothills of the Himalayas. Be at one with nature. Live the dream.'

'Amazing,' I said, shaking my head. 'They didn't have the energy to carve or help with anything while they were here, but they must've gone to quite a lot of trouble getting these made.' I looked at the American, 'These were being handed out in the street in Kullu, you say?'

He grunted an affirmation.

'By a couple? With dreadlocks, dark skin, real stoners?'

'Yeah, that would be them,' the American nodded.

'I see.' I looked at Lorna, but she said nothing.

'So, this *is* the place,' the American said, more to himself than anyone else.

'Hey, look,' I said, 'this may be the place, as you say, but really, it's nothing like what that stupid flyer says, okay? I mean it's a pretty basic way of living here, you know? And it's certainly not paradise.'

'Oh basic living sounds so cool,' the taller of his two female companions piped up. 'I think this place is great, you know? The scenery is just so stunning!'

'Right,' I agreed, not quite sure how I felt about having more new arrivals to Shadow-Wall, especially after our experience with Jed and Annabel.

Then Lorna said, 'I'm Lorna, this is Ethan, you'll get to meet the others later. They're off gathering fruit right now.'

The group dropped their gear haphazardly on the ground, and as I attempted to make the pile a little more orderly, I noted how heavy their rucksacks were—it must have taken some effort to get up the trail, I mused, remembering what a struggle it was bringing up the last consignment of food.

'I'm James, this is Pippa—'

'Hello,' the tall girl said warmly.

'And this is Rachel.'

'Hello.'

After spending a few more moments rearranging their baggage, I put out a hand and said, 'Welcome to Shadow-Wall then, I guess. But you guys should understand there are a few . . . a few ground rules that we have in place here.'

'Oh?'

'If you're staying a while, well, you'll have to earn your keep. We, er . . . we carve things.'

'*Things?*'

'Well, musical instruments. Flutes, to be exact.'

'Why on earth do you do that?'

'We sell them in Kullu—it pays for our food and stuff.'

The three of them started to protest, but Lorna cut them short.

'Don't worry, it's really easy once you get the hang of it. Ethan will teach you, won't you?'

'Well yes, someone will, yes.'

'Then we take them into Kullu to sell. We each carve thirty or forty flutes a month to cover food and essential supplies.'

'Oh, I see. Can I have a look at one of the flutes?'

'You're standing by them,' Lorna replied, nodding at a small pile of perhaps a dozen flutes next to James.

'These? We saw some like that on sale in Shimla! I nearly bought one!'

'No, no, you mean Kullu,' I laughed. 'You can buy them in one of the tourist shops in Kullu.'

'No, I'm sure it was Shimla where we saw them.'

'Hemen must be spreading his wings,' Lorna said slowly.

'Yes, it certainly looks like it.'

'Oh this is going to be so much fun,' Pippa giggled excitedly, examining the flute carefully before looking around once more at the commune.

'You guys will need to share a hut for the time being, I'm afraid,' Lorna added, waving a hand at Jed and Annabel's now vacant structure. The she turned to me. 'Ethan, you and Hal can start work on building another, can't you?'

'Sure,' I agreed without enthusiasm, conscious of the amount of work it would involve.

'Awesome!' Pippa grinned.

Lorna and I watched as the three of them gaily skipped off towards their hut.

'And then there were seven,' I said.

'There'll be more, I guess,' Lorna said, almost to herself.

'You think?' I said, brushing the hair from my eyes. 'Seems a bit of a leap of faith, coming all the way out here on the basis of some flyer.'

'We'll see.'

We stood in comfortable silence for a few minutes, watching the new arrivals carefully inspect their new home.

'I need to sort my hair out,' I said eventually, brushing the fringe from my eyes. 'It's driving me mad; I really need to get it cut.'

'Really? I prefer it long, actually,' Lorna replied. 'Why don't you wear it in a ponytail?'

'It's not long enough.'

'No, I suppose not.' There was a pause, and Lorna said: 'If you wanted to grow it and keep it out of your face, I could plait beads into it.'

'Sure,' I said, appalled by the idea.

'Come on then,' she laughed, pulling me by my arm towards her hut.

'You, er . . . you have beads, then?'

'I have an old necklace which will do. I'll use that.'

We ducked inside her hut. It somehow seemed warmer than outside, and perspiration began to roll down my back and sides. I wanted to take off my t-shirt, but for some reason I thought it rather inappropriate.

'It's hot,' I offered instead, looking out of the door at the shimmering landscape.

'You're very observant,' she replied dryly. 'Sit here.'

I flopped down on the floor between her knees. 'You're not going to make me look too ridiculous, are you?'

'Would I?' she said reproachfully, taking the first handful of hair and running it through her fingers. 'You've got nice hair actually.'

'Thanks.' There was a lazy pause, and I said, 'How long do think this will this take?'

'I don't know—half an hour?'

Good. I closed my eyes, and let my mind drift as Lorna began to gently plait my hair, softly clicking her tongue as her hands twisted the tresses. 'Is half an hour long enough for you to tell me your life story?' I asked.

'My life story? Why would you want to know that?'

'Sorry,' I said hurriedly, alarmed by the defensive note that had crept into her voice. 'I'm just prying. Look, if you don't want to tell me—'

'No, it's not that . . .' she trailed off, then added, 'it's just that you may regret asking me, that's all.'

'I doubt that,' I responded softly.

She paused, briefly resting her fingers on the back of my neck. 'Okay. Okay, well I was born in Wellington, no brothers or sisters, went to school there until I was twelve or thirteen, then my parents moved to Auckland with work. My dad—'

'What were you like when you were at school? Did you have a burning ambition to be a ballet dancer or an astronaut or something?'

'Pretty normal, I think. I actually wanted to do what my dad did, build skyscrapers. I thought that would be the most amazing job, to leave your mark on a whole city, to look at a building and say, "I put that there."'

'That would be pretty cool,' I agreed.

'But after we moved to Auckland, well, you know what teenagers are like, I hated my parents for making me leave my friends and my school. I think I actually sulked for about two years, until they despaired enough to buy me a horse. I must have driven them mad.'

I laughed. 'Blackmail.'

'Yes, I suppose it was. But they got me the horse in the end, and I rode every weekend: that's one of my happiest memories of home. New Zealand's got some of the most amazing scenery, and I used to trek for hours and hours, just me and Anagram. There was this place I used to go, Roe Island, a few miles north of Auckland. You could only reach it at low tide—there was this sand bar that connected it to the mainland—and I'd stop there, just watch the surf breaking over the reef, listening to the sound of the waves. It was the most beautiful, beautiful place, especially at dawn. The early sunlight actually turned the whitecaps this kind of golden colour . . . The best thing was, no one ever went there.' She paused, and continued, 'I've always liked solitude, I suppose.'

'Don't you get lonely?'

'Yes, but one gets used to it.'

'But I get used to the mosquito bites—it doesn't mean I like them.'

'It gives you an awful lot of freedom, Ethan. There *are* benefits.'

'Yes, I suppose there are.'

'Anyway, I left school, travelled for a year and then—'

'Where did you travel?'

'Australia, Indonesia, Malaysia, Thailand, Vietnam—the usual. Didn't get as far as India, mind you. Not on that occasion, anyway. Then I went back to New Zealand for university, to Wellington.' She paused. 'I was in my second year, studying architecture, when my mother phoned me to say dad was ill. He had cancer, it was all terribly quick, which I suppose is a good thing these days. My mum followed a year later, same damn disease, different part of the body. Unfortunately for her it was all rather drawn out.'

'I'm sorry,' I said, meaning it.

'Yeah, it was a rough time. Neither of them reached sixty. Anyway, I flunked my third year. My university was actually really good to me; said I could come back and re-sit after the summer holidays. I never made it back.'

I waited, not wanting to prompt her.

Eventually, 'You see, I had quite a bit of money left to me. I bought this small two-bedroom flat in Wellington, let out the other room to this student called Lee. I'm obviously not much of a judge of character, because it turned out he was a dealer.'

I could feel her hands tighten around my hair, and I winced slightly with the pain. Then she relaxed her grip and said, 'I was lonely, depressed. By the middle of summer, he was paying his rent in heroin, and by the time I was due to restart my third year, I was . . . well, completely hooked of course. It was a very, very bad time for me. I burned through an awful lot of cash. Anyway, I suppose it all struck home that Christmas—I was still in the flat; Lee had gone back to Christchurch to see his parents; and there I was with just the TV for company, getting high. I think it was on Boxing Day—yes, it must have been—I had this kind of breakdown. I was in the bathroom, brushing my teeth, and I got on the scales, just for something to do more than anything else.' She paused, then said, 'I weighed six stone . . .' Lorna trailed off, and we sat in silence, listening to the familiar creaking of the hut as the bamboo walls slowly expanded from the heat.

Through the open door I could see James and Pippa shaking hands and laughing with Div, snatches of their conversation carrying on the light breeze. Beyond them, Hal was slowly walking up from the lake, his features blurred by the caloric waves of heat that rose from the clearing. Perhaps thirty seconds passed before he finally reached the group; Hal hugged each of the new arrivals, chattering excitedly. Then he made an expansive gesture with his hands—I could clearly make out the words as he loudly proclaimed, 'Look at this place—it's paradise, man!' James grinned, punched his fist into the air and let out a whoop of joy that seemed to echo around the valley. Hal slapped him on the back, got a bear hug in return, and then the two of them started to play-fight, falling to the ground in an explosion of dust as the others looked on in amusement. I felt a vague flash of annoyance; how could two complete strangers behave as if they were life-long friends simply because they happened to be compatriots? I'd known Hal for over a year, and yet as I watched them thrash around in the dirt, wrestling with each other, our friendship suddenly struck me as rather tepid in comparison.

'*I was a junkie*, Ethan.'

I swivelled around to face Lorna. She looked nervous, clearly uncertain as to what my reaction would be. 'Doesn't matter, does it?' I offered, shrugging. 'Not now.'

She lowered her eyes and returned her attention to my hair. 'I wanted to tell you. I thought you might see me differently.'

I returned my gaze outside. James was beating the dust from his clothes with a baseball cap. Why was she being so candid? Was it simply as a friend wanting to confide? It seemed unlikely—after all, she said she was worried that I might see her differently. Was it not more probable that she was somehow ashamed of her past, and wanted to get it out in the open before . . . before *us*?

'Lorna—' I started.

The word was lost as she continued: 'Anyway, that was my awakening, I suppose. The turning point. I wasn't eating, wasn't going out, I hadn't even got any friends—my life was nothing.'

'These things happen,' I offered, my heart rate increasing slightly with my hopeful thoughts.

'Yeah, maybe,' she sighed. 'Anyway, I phoned a travel agent, bought a one-way ticket to Bangkok, turned the flat over to an estate agent to rent out. I've never been back to New Zealand since.'

I wanted to grab her hands, pull her to me and whisper urgently, 'Tell me what you feel towards me!' Yet I procrastinated, feeling that the right moment had passed. Instead I said, 'So how come you ended up in Delhi? Apart from it being cheap, I mean.'

'Oh, I travelled for nearly a decade on the hippie circuit before I got fed up with living out of a rucksack. I couldn't face New Zealand, too many painful memories. Anyway, my dad used to do quite a bit of contract work in Delhi, and I knew a lot of people. I came to visit and just kind of decided to stay. I've been there six years now. And that's my story really.'

The conversation died, and I felt a surge of anger with myself for not thanking her for her candour, or at least offering a few words of sympathy in the light of what she'd told me. But my mind was preoccupied with the thought of directly asking her what she felt towards me, trying to think of an appropriate way to couch the question. But wouldn't that be foolhardy, a rash act doomed to embarrassing failure? More than likely, I thought to myself. Instead, after a few moments' consideration, I decided upon a compromise, an approach that might not only provide me with some evidence for my optimistic hypothesis, but also an opportunity for escape if it were to prove wrong. So, an apology already prepared, I rested my head against Lorna's naked thigh.

She didn't flinch. Heavy silence, just the occasional clink as a bead was slid into place. Her skin was smooth, the soft flesh warm on my face. Then, a fingernail scraped gently down the back of my neck. Just the once, an ambiguous action, enough to leave me uncertain. I briefly thought about reciprocating, perhaps running my finger down her calf, but I couldn't quite find the confidence required for the risk. Instead, I stared at her feet, vaguely trying to think of something to say. No one bothered with footwear at Shadow-Wall and, like mine, there was a dirty tidemark around the curve of her soles. Her toes were small and the nails, flecked blue with varnish, were scratched and worn from walking barefoot. Her ankles were delicate, bony, and I could make out deltas of thin blue veins that spread down from them, along the sides of her feet, eventually disappearing along the length of the dirt Plimsoll line.

'You've got a tattoo.' God that's lame, I thought.

Her toes twitched in acknowledgement. 'Oh, it's very small. Most people don't notice it.'

'What's it meant to be?' It looked like a yellow smudge, just above her right ankle. I wanted to kiss it.

'I got it in some rather dodgy backstreet place in Vietnam. It's meant to be the sun.'

'It looks more like a pineapple,' I offered, tilting my head slightly so it pressed more firmly against her thigh.

'Shut up, you. It wasn't always that bad.'

I winced as she tugged hard on my hair. 'How's it coming along?'

'I think I'm done,' she said after a time. 'Turn 'round and look at me.'

I swivelled around, my head level with her bare navel. Rivulets of perspiration glistened on her abdomen like condensation on the skin of a glass, and the top of her sarong, tied loosely above her hips, was damp. 'Well?'

Lorna giggled, then burst out laughing and put her hand over her mouth.

'Well?' I repeated, running my fingers through my hair, feeling the tufts of plaited hair that dotted my scalp.

Lorna giggled again, and held out a small mirror set into her compact.

'I look bloody ridiculous!'

'Who looks like a pineapple now?' she laughed.

'Take it out!' I demanded.

Lorna kissed me affectionately on the top of my head, then gently pushed me away. 'I like it, actually. I just think you need to let it grow a bit.' She looked me in the eye. The humour had left her voice when she said, 'Yes, give it a few months. If you still feel the same way about it, let me know, and maybe we can do something about it.'

*

Lorna was right; there were others. Greg was first, a hippie from South Africa who had seen one of Jed and Annabel's flyers on the corkboard of the guesthouse where he'd been staying. He was probably in his sixties, judging from his sallow face that was framed by long silver hair, tinged yellow from the roll-ups that always hung from his lips. His legs were very thin and mottled with red spots, and the outline of his ribcage was visible through the distressed t-shirts he wore. When I first saw him, his appearance conjured some half-remembered quote, of a man not looking like the ruins of his youth, but rather the ruins of those ruins. Greg was ailing too. Each time he laughed or sighed, his chest would rattle as if it were made of wood and contained marbles, and he had a pronounced lazy eye. But the most outwardly obvious of his maladies was his missing hand—about a quarter of his right arm, from the middle of his forearm down, had been removed. There was no hook or prosthetic limb in its place, just a smooth pink ball of flesh.

'One of those things,' he said, when Pippa enquired as to the cause. 'Happened in Peru, I was trekking out west with just a few provisions lashed to the back of a llama. Stopped one night, pitched my tent, dotted up a few sugar cubes with some good acid, and decided to brew up some tea. Anyway, I went off to gather some damn firewood to boil the water and when I get back, this bloody llama's in the tent, foraging through my gear. I said, "What have you been doing, Llamy?" and he gives me this kind of reproachful look, so I go to take him by the bit and the damn animal sinks his teeth into my forearm. Have you seen a llama on acid? They're vicious damn animals at the best of times. So anyway, I'm a three-day trek from the nearest town, and by the time I make it there my arm's stinking like an old fish, even the flies were staying away, it was so rotten. Doc cut it off in the end. Gangrene, so he said.' Greg hawked and spat a glob of brown saliva into the fire. 'Yep, been fifteen years since I've been able to give someone a round of applause, so don't you be expecting me to be doing any of that damn carving stuff you get up to, Ethan. Just ain't possible.'

'That's quite all right,' I replied quickly. 'You just do your own thing.'

'Good on ya, Ethan.' He coughed loudly again, then hawked and once more spat the phlegm towards the fire. He wiped his mouth with the stump of his arm and added, 'Hal tells me I'm gonna be sharing your hut, man. So I guess we're gonna be room buddies until you guys put another one up. Isn't that great?'

'Yes, Greg,' I muttered. 'That's just great.'

*

The trickle of arrivals gradually became a stream, Shadow-Wall grew. They were hippies, university dropouts, drifters. Our commune seemed to be some kind of magnet that attracted only the most dysfunctional of travellers, a sieve that could not capture the fine matter, collecting only the coarse. And just a few days after Greg had arrived, the commune began to fill with people, with no sign of the stream of new visitors to our commune abating. Some came with tents, others without; the huts were becoming like dormitories, with four, five or even six people in each. Constructing each new hut was slow as we had limited tools available; very soon we were overflowing.

Oh how it grew. And I am not proud of the fact that, because of that growth, I don't recall many of their names. I am not proud of the fact that most of the dead on that mountain are as anonymous and remote to me as they are to someone watching the recoveries of the bodies on cable news, or reading the long, long list of the deceased in the papers. Yet, without wishing to seem aloof, or callous even, it should be remembered that Shadow-Wall generally attracted the transient, those without roots—people would come and go from our commune all the time. And so I felt that investing my emotional capital in building some kind of bond with any of the hippies and backpackers that passed through would probably have offered scant return.

However, some people's names stuck. We got to know the first dozen or so newcomers pretty well. And I do recall the names of some of the later arrivals, although if I am being honest it was more because of their function, their utility, than because of any kind of emotional connection to them. There was Hideki, a punkish Japanese school-leaver whose parents were pushing him to join the family furniture business when he returned home. He became our official carpenter—his ability to construct the wooden huts in days rather than weeks would become invaluable as our numbers swelled. There was Bella, the farmer's daughter from Missouri who finally managed to find at least some success planting crops of wheat and rice, reducing our reliance on buying in food from Kullu. There was Jamie, the vegan chef from Scotland who markedly improved the quality of our evening meals, and identified new ingredients we could use from the woodlands around us. But those were exceptions: for most of the newcomers, their names elude me. Of course, they are dead now, and I do feel a little sorrow that I never took the time to get to know them, or at least to learn their names. Yet, at the time, what mattered to me was not names or friendships—what mattered to me was the bigger picture for Shadow-Wall, the fact that its future seemed secure. With the revenue from the flutes, we had finally created a sustainable project—there was a feeling of permanence about the commune. To me, that was far more fulfilling than getting to know individual inhabitants, many of whom came and went like the clouds over the valley.

21

JUBBAWY

'It was working,' I reflect.

'Working?' Jubbawy asks, absently.

'Yeah. I mean we had built something sustainable, something that could go on in perpetuity, I guess.'

'Judging by the capacity problems currently being experienced at the mortuary in Kullu, I am not entirely sure the word *perpetuity* is appropriate, is it, Mr Hicks?'

I say nothing.

'And you say you only knew the names of what, a dozen or so people at Shadow-Wall?' Jubbawy slides his glasses slowly down his nose, and stares at me over the dark tortoiseshell rims. 'From over *a hundred dead*?'

'Yeah, look, like I said—we didn't form strong bonds with the people passing through.'

'So you barely knew the names of the people living at your commune. But let me ask you this, then. When people started to arrive at your commune, Mr Hicks, did you feel a *responsibility* towards them? I mean, you founded Shadow-Wall, right? So does that not mean you also have some responsibility of care for the people who came to your commune?'

'I don't know. What are you getting at? Sure we *founded* it, yes, but we'd hardly invited the others to come.' I fold my arms and stare at him

'Surely the causation there was not me or Hal or Div or Lorna, it was Jed and Annabel.' I shake my head and shrug. 'So why don't you go interview them, then?'

Jubbawy bridges his fingers together. 'I see. So you are saying that because the *mechanism* by which they came to Shadow-Wall had nothing to do with you, you are thus abrogated from all responsibility for their welfare. Is that a fair summary?'

I shrug. 'I really don't see the point of the question.'

'Did you keep medical supplies, in case people got sick?'

'They'd made their choice to come, it was nothing to do with us.'

'And in terms of what ultimately happened—do you feel any responsibility for that?'

'In what sense? I'm not sure I understand?'

'Well it's a rather straightforward question, is it not? But perhaps I might paraphrase. Almost 130 people are dead, and they are dead because they were living in an illegal commune, a commune that you have already told me that you founded with your friends. So, Mr Hicks, I will ask you again—do you not feel any *responsibility* for the fact that these people are now dead?'

'Why should I?' I retort. 'What happened at the end, it was an act of God! Do you not believe in God?'

'What *I* think is not important.'

'It was an act of God,' I repeat, reaching for the cigarettes. Curiously, he puts his hand over the red and gold packet, and draws it away from me.

'Do you not see, Mr Hicks? *You* were the reason that these people were on the mountainside!' He slams his fist on the table. '*You*! You are the reason they are dead!'

Jubbawy will probably never realize quite how close to the truth he really is. Like an absent-minded lottery player, the prize is his to claim but he doesn't even know he has it. I look at him, then say softly, 'You know, everyone is dead. *Everyone.* Nearly everything I ever cared about is sitting under a million tons of mud, and I have to deal with that. But please don't try and infer that it was somehow my responsibility.' I shake my head. 'It's not. It's not. I'm not to blame for this and you know it.'

Jubbawy regards me at length. I note with surprise that there are tears welling in my eyes. How very odd, I muse—I'm actually starting to believe my own lies.

'*I'm not to blame,*' Jubbawy repeats thoughtfully, scratching at the light stubble around his throat. 'I'm not to blame, I'm not to blame. No one is ever to blame, are they Mr Hicks?'

I lower my gaze, say nothing. The room is silent save for the air-con unit, rattling away in the corner of the room.

Eventually my interviewer sighs, then removes his glasses and gets to his feet. I watch as he slowly paces to the door, seeming to study the rivets that run around its edge. Then, without turning to face me, he says, 'My wife is an entomologist, works at the Zoological Gardens in Purana Qila. Did you know she can identify the species of a spider just by examining the web it has spun?'

'*What?*'

'You have to know what patterns to look for of course,' he continues, as if not hearing. 'Same goes for people, as it happens.'

I snort and look away from Jubbawy, staring instead at the smooth grey surface of the table. In my peripheral vision, I see the policeman turning to face me.

'I am not to blame,' he calls over with a mirthless laugh. 'Do you know how many times I've heard those five words?'

'I don't understand what you're insinuating,' I say softly.

'Hundreds and hundreds of times. That's what's worrying me, Mr Hicks.' He starts to move back to the table, talking as he walks. 'The people who say those words are almost always the guilty.' Jubbawy is halfway across the floor now, barking each syllable so they seem to ricochet from the hard walls. 'The murderers, thieves, pickpockets and wife-beaters, they're never to blame! Same words as you use, Mr Hicks.' He reaches the table, stands over me, and says quietly, 'And the same patterns. You might not have known all of their names, Mr Hicks, you may not have necessarily . . . what was it you said? Ah yes, that's it . . . you may not have necessarily "*formed strong bonds with them*", but tell me Mr Hicks, why is it that you have not once asked me about how the rescue operation is progressing?'

'Rescue operation? Everybody's dead for Christ's sake!' I protest.

'Are they? How do you know we haven't found any survivors?'

'I don't, I just assumed—' I pause, and say hoarsely, 'have you? Have you found any survivors?'

'The guilty never ask about their victims, Mr Hicks. They are too busy thinking how to save themselves to even think about anyone else!'

'What are you implying?' I snap. 'That I've . . . what . . . murdered these people?' I laugh, although the sound seems more like a strangled bark. 'That's ridiculous! There was a landslide, I'm a victim!'

'I'm implying nothing, Mr Hicks. I'm simply trying to do what my wife does so well, looking at the web in the hope that I might identify the type of spider. It's just that the pattern of yours is rarely spun by an innocent man.'

I am conscious of my pulse quickening, though not as much, perhaps, as the insinuation warrants. If I can remain this calm throughout, keep it together, perhaps he will find no weakness in the wall of deceit that surrounds the truth. That is my hope at least. It is all I have left.

I shake my head slowly and say, 'It was a landslide—no one can control nature, sir.'

22

SHADOW-WALL, JULY 1987

I don't know why they came—in truth, Shadow-Wall was little more than an aggregation of societal misfits, living in basic huts that were randomly located in some remote part of the Himalayan plateau. But they did. They crawled from their youth hostels and cheap hotels and run-down guesthouses, like iron filings drawn to a magnet. I remember some of the stories from the earliest arrivals. The Spanish couple, Carlo and Isabelle, bouncing around in the cheap bus from Kanpur. Anne-Marie watching the Indian landscape slip past on the Lahore-Chandigarh railroad. Alex hitching down from Islamabad in a battered lorry carrying tractor components. I can picture it now, like I can somehow observe the entire sub-continent, the dust trails of dozens of dropouts, travellers and hippies meandering slowly across the sun-baked land, converging on a single point in India, like pilgrims coming to pay homage to the fake God we had created.

Of course, it was the ideology that they all found so appealing. The flyer that Jed and Annabel had created may have ignited the fire, but rumours and gossip fed the subsequent blaze. Like some kind of mortal epidemic that was spread by word-of-mouth, travellers would mention Shadow-Wall in conversation with their contemporaries in the bars and the eateries in Kullu, Manali, Shimla, Mandi and beyond. The concept would draw many in, intoxicated by the idea of a commune that could provide everything for its inhabitants, whilst rejecting capitalism as a philosophy. Yet the concept does not always match the reality, as so many would come to learn.

'Flush, dude. Beats three of a kind,' Hal laughed, taking a swig of Johnnie Walker Red.

I looked at the pile of dollar bills that were piled up on the floor of my hut, and said, 'I'm broke.'

'Lucky it's only pretend then,' Hal chuckled. He leaned forward and began to sweep up the piles of dollar bills. 'You know, we're starting to make quite a bit of money off these stupid carvings?'

'Right,' I agreed, momentarily distracted by a honey-coloured ring of whisky the bottle had left on the floor.

Hal fanned out the banknotes like they were playing cards. '$1,500. That's a lot of money for a few flutes.'

'Not really,' I said absently, looking around the hut for some toilet roll. 'What do you Americans say—do the math?'

Hal looked at me blankly. 'Huh? What the fuck are you talking about man? What *math*? $1,500 is $1,500, dude.'

'Yeah, and last month we grew from four to thirty. So, we're producing more, sure, but when we divide it out it's only fifty bucks each. Nothing to get excited about.'

'What? Why would we share the money out?'

'Huh? Oh . . .' I looked at Hal questioningly. 'Well we can't keep it. It belongs to everyone.' I pushed my hands into my pockets to see if I could find a tissue and said, 'they all carve as many flutes as we do. It's only fair, right?'

Hal sighed and lit a cigarette, staring blankly at the glowing tip. 'Ethan, I've been thinking. This place, our humble little commune, Shadow-Wall, it has changed, yeah? If we carry on growing in size like this, we'll be producing thousands of carvings each month, and that means thousands of dollars in revenue. Before . . . Well I never realized we'd make money from it. Even with feeding these people, building new huts, buying the tools and provisions and whatever—we're still making a decent profit each month, and it's only going to get bigger and bigger over time.' He finally took a drag, exhaling lazily towards the roof. 'This place could make a lot of money, dude, you'll see. The question is, how do we *manage* that?'

'I know what you're saying,' I nodded. 'But we came here with ideals, right? This is a commune, everyone contributes equally, and everyone is entitled to their share.'

Hal shrugged his shoulders. 'Are you so sure of that? See, I've been thinking this through, you know? Actually, I figure it would be *wrong* to share it.'

I laughed. 'Nice, Hal. And how did you arrive at that conclusion?'

Hal didn't smile back. Instead he spread his hands in thought, then said slowly: 'Look, Ethan, I'm serious. This place, Shadow-Wall, it appeals to people because of what it is *not*. And what it is *not* is a capitalist entity. Look, do you think all of these folk would have come here if they heard there was a factory that made carvings, and that the factory would pay them each month?'

I shrugged in agreement. 'No, probably not.'

'No, man, they wouldn't,' he continued. 'They like the *ideal* of the place, a carefree existence and all of that hippie shit. If we effectively start paying them, then boom!' he clapped his hands together to emphasize the point, 'we'll destroy this place—what it stands for—in an instant.'

'Right.'

'I see it as a personal sacrifice,' Hal continued, his face entirely serious. 'As leaders of this place, we need to start facing up to the fact that the time has come to sacrifice *our own ideals* for the greater good. We cannot pollute this commune with money and materialism.' He waved a hand towards the commune outside, 'I mean, have you heard what these guys talk about all day?'

'Go on . . .?'

'All they talk about is how *wonderful* this place is, how *great* it is to be so close to nature, all that kind of crap. That's what they want—they're not after a roll of banknotes at the end of the month. It's not why they're here, dude. It's not what this place is about.'

'Yeah, I understand exactly what you're saying, but—'

'There *is* no "but", man. I *know* it would be wrong to share the money out. That leaves us with a big dilemma, man, because you, me, Lorna, Div, we need to decide what *we* do with it. Now, we can all have a conversation about what we do with the money—perhaps give it to charity at the end of each month, you know, helping little Indian kids get an education, that sort of thing. Or we may decide otherwise. But,' he said, shaking his head firmly, 'what we cannot do is to be as selfish as to share it out with the others.'

23

JUBBAWY

'That was the beginning, I suppose.'

'The beginning? The beginning of what, exactly?'

I clasp my head in my hands, feeling the rough stubble on my palms. There is a foul taste of stale tobacco in my mouth, and I suddenly feel an overwhelming craving for a Coca-Cola—an image of a can being poured into a tall glass, filled with cubes of ice and wedges of lemon, persists in my mind. I can imagine the gentle fizzing and spitting on the surface of the liquid, the cracking of the ice-cubes as they fracture, the bitter tang of the lemon cutting through my furred mouth.

'Do you have—'

'You said it was the beginning, Mr Hicks?'

'Yeah.'

'Well?'

I sigh and continue, 'You could call it the beginning of the end, if you wanted. It wouldn't be so very far removed from the truth, I suppose. Look, is there a vending machine or something here? I'd really like a soda or something.'

Jubbawy snorts and makes a show of exaggeratedly peering around the empty interview room. He returns his gaze to me and arches his eyebrows. 'This is not a restaurant, Mr Hicks—why don't you have some water?'

'Yes.' I take a gulp from the glass. The liquid is tepid.

'So why was it the beginning of the end?'

'That conversation . . . it was the first manifestation of our greed, I suppose. Of course we kept the money to ourselves, and when another twenty or so people showed up the next month, and about the same the following month, it was pretty clear that Hal was right—it seemed like Shadow-Wall really could generate significant quantities of cash.'

'And you were comfortable keeping the proceeds? Morally, I mean?'

'Look, Hal was a pretty clever guy, actually. Underneath all of the hippie stuff, he was quite smart. Read all of the philosophers, Descartes and Plato and Mill. He'd read of lot of Mill actually, and that's when he started talking a lot about utilitarianism, about the greater good. He seemed to genuinely believe this idea that keeping the commune's profits was some kind of philanthropic sacrifice on our part. And to answer your question? Yeah, I bought into it, too, I guess.'

*

'They look like they're having a good time,' Hal smiles, fanning himself languidly with a large poplar leaf.

'Yeah.'

About forty or so people are doing the conga through the narrow avenues between the huts, whooping and cheering into the night. Around the fire perhaps half a dozen others are lying on the ground passed out, nestling amongst a mound of empty beer cans. Midnight is still an hour or so away.

We sit in silence for a few minutes, watching the moon come and go as occasional clouds venture slowly across the sky. I feel drunk, and light a cigarette in the hope it will settle the swirling sensation I feel in my head.

Someone yells over, 'Hey, Ethan, fancy a dance?'

The head of the conga has returned to the clearing, and everyone starts dancing to the strains of 'Brown-Eyed Girl' which is blaring out of the sound system we've recently bought. The batteries are fading though—the volume ebbs and flows through the night air.

'Come and dance, Ethan!' I don't recall the name of the girl—she is pretty, though, and wearing just a sarong and a bikini top—the light from the fire gives her skin a radiant, orange glow. And all she seems to be is skin—bare arms, bare shoulders, bare feet, bare legs.

'Not now,' I say simply. I turn back and stare into the fire.

'What's up with you, dude?' Hal asks, prodding me with his foot.

'Nothing much. Just tired, I guess.' There is a loud shriek of laughter. I can see Lorna with Hideki and a few others trying to squeeze under a limbo pole made from the ubiquitous bamboo that not only surrounds our commune, but also provides it with the means to exist. Someone falls, and there is more laughter and clapping.

'See dude—everyone's happy. Why aren't you?'

There is a pause. I close my eyes, heavy from drink, and say slowly, 'Because I'm the only one looking to the future, I guess. Just rams it home when everyone's so happy. I mean, every party has to end sometime, doesn't it?'

'Live for now, man.'

'Yeah, but what's next?' I wave my arms at the commune. 'Where will all this lead us?' I take a final drag on the cigarette, even though it is down to the filter. 'Where will all this lead us?' I repeat softly.

'You're right, dude.' Hal, too, waves a hand at the mass of people dancing, laughing, chattering away to one another. 'This is just going to be a chapter of our lives one day, a memory.' He spits into the fire. 'Nothing much is permanent in life, is it?'

'Nope. Nothing much at all, I guess.'

Another pause. An ash-clad branch cracks loudly, dropping further into the fire with a shower of sparks.

'Yeah, life's fucking weird,' he continues. 'You spend it trying to find some kind of meaning, some purpose or whatever, something that makes you happy, then when you do find it . . .' he pauses, 'I fell in love once, you know? *Really* in love. Some girl from the States I met, and boom!' Hal claps his hands together, the sudden noise making me start slightly. 'Boom, and I'm so in love, I'm so happy I'm starting to believe there's a God, right? We go out six months, then a year. This is great, life is fucking fantastic, right? So then another six months go by, and you know how things change . . . We go out to a bar, and we know everything there is to know about each other, so what do you talk about? D'you want another beer?'

I nod. Hal picks up two bottles, feeling them briefly with the back of his hand. 'Man, we left these ones a bit too close to the fire,' he grunts, and proceeds to prise them open with a plastic cigarette lighter.

'Thanks,' I say, grimacing as I take a swig.

'So, what do you talk about?' he continues. 'There's nothing left to say, so all of a sudden you realize it's kind of boring talking to your girlfriend, and when you're out with friends and stuff you start talking to their girlfriends instead, and every last thing they say seems interesting in comparison . . . I mean, jeez . . .' Hal takes a swig of beer, then leans over to look at me squarely in the face, 'and you're sleeping with her every night, you're so *used* to her being there that she's more like your fucking sister than your lover, and it's really already over at this point, although you don't actually know it yet. All of a sudden you realize that Jim's girlfriend is prettier, and Al's has got this really sexy look about her, and Jason's is really intelligent or something. You know why?'

I shrug.

'It's just nature. Like I said, nothing's permanent in life.'

'But what about you and Div? You've been going out years.'

'And why not? Look, I've never really *loved* Div. But what the hell? I like her as a friend, we get on most of the time, so all I'm really doing by going out with her is missing out the "being-in-love" part. The end result is just the same, though.'

'No, you're wrong,' I mutter, almost to myself.

'Aw, you can't have been there to say that,' Hal snorts with a dismissive wave of his hand. 'How many times have you been in love, dude?'

I reply a little more hotly than I intended, 'Does that really matter?'

Hal shrugs. 'Look, I'm just making a general point.'

I don't reply, and light another cigarette instead.

'So your question still stands—where's all this going to lead? Shadow-Wall, I mean.'

'Right.'

'And the answer, my friend, is quite simple.' Hal takes a swig of beer. 'Nowhere, most likely. But if it keeps growing like it is, then we could make a fair bit of cash before this place gets found out and closed down by the police, or whatever fate awaits it. So yeah, let's see what we can milk from this place while we have the chance.'

*

'You must think me pathetic,' I say quietly. 'How we changed.'

'Mr Hicks, I'm not here to hold opinions. You do realize that, don't you?'

'One minute we're hippies or something, the next minute we're . . .' I shrug, not bothering to complete the sentence. 'How very fickle of me.'

Jubbawy shrugs, but says nothing.

'Anyway, I thought I'd found my direction in life—with the commune, with Lorna. Then a little bit of money started coming in, and it all started to change,' I wave my hand and add, 'it all started to change after that.'

'I see.'

'But, you know . . .?' I pick up the glass of water, take a sip.

'What?'

'Well, Hal was right in a way. If we had shared out the money each month, Shadow-Wall would just have become materialistic, would have turned into what would basically amount to a business. So, I guess, Hal had a point, actually.'

'A rather convenient point. For you, that is.'

'Perhaps.'

'Perhaps,' he repeats, toying with the word.

'I don't know,' I add with a sigh. 'Maybe it was our way of justifying what we were doing. Anyway, the greed started to take hold, either way.'

'Do please elucidate?'

'Well, we were making a bit of money, but we knew we could make more. We just had to increase the number of Krapi-Krapis we produced each month—the demand was there. Hemen was starting to ask for more and more flutes each month.'

'I see,' Jubbawy says.

'So,' I continue, with a resigned wave of my hand, 'it was around that time that we imposed quotas.'

'Quotas?'

'Yes,' I state, 'quotas.'

'What kind of "quotas"?'

'We asked everyone to produce a minimum of three flutes a day to cover costs. It was no big deal really—carving a few Krapi-Krapis a day was hardly much effort, it only took an hour or so to knock out each one. Besides, we decided that Saturdays and Sundays should be like a conventional weekend where no one has to work, and the kids didn't have to carve of course. Anyway, it meant we were suddenly producing something like 3,000 to 3,500 carvings a month.'

'*What?*'

'I know it sounds a lot, but really—'

Jubbawy shakes his head. 'No, no, not that! You said *kids*?'

I hadn't meant to say that; it was a foolish slip. I bite into my lip in annoyance.

'Are you saying there were *children* on the hillside?' he continues.

'Of course,' I shrug. 'It was a commune. What were you expecting—a minimum age?'

'No, you misunderstand. We have not recovered the bodies of any children from the mountain, Mr Hicks.'

I look down at the table, and say nothing. My interviewer, too, remains silent. Eventually I add, 'There was a woman, Felicity, a new age traveller from England. She had two children, Sol and Star. Towards the end, others came—other people with kids, I mean. I don't remember their names though . . .' I trail off.

My interviewer doesn't speak. I, too, say nothing because I know what he is thinking—he is considering the fact that there are not 127 bodies. He is considering the fact that there are more. And there are. My god, there are. Many, many, many more. He has no fucking idea how many more. It's why he's not asking. He thinks that 127 bodies is close to the upper limit of what they are going to find up on that mountain. He is so wrong. I stare at the water jug to occupy my thoughts.

Finally the suffocating silence is broken. 'My god. Children.'

'Yes,' I say quietly, 'it is a very great pity.'

'Your remorse is touching.'

'People died, some of them were children,' I say simply.

Jubbawy looks at me, biting his lip in thought.

24

SHADOW-WALL, SEPTEMBER 1987

'Can I ask you something?' I asked Div over breakfast in the clearing one morning, after a sleepless night spent thinking about Lorna.

'Of course you can, Ethan.'

'Um, do you think . . . well, look, you're a girl, so I wanted to get your opinion on something. From a female perspective.'

'Go on.'

'Well, er, do you think . . . there's any way Lorna might . . . like me?'

Div let a slight smile cross her lips. '*Like you?*'

'Yeah, you know. *Like* me. As in . . . well, you know what I mean. *Like* me.'

'Why don't you ask her?'

'Because it's . . . it's such a small place that, well, if I made a fool out of myself, it would be really awkward. Seeing her all the time and stuff.'

'Oh right, yes, I can see that might be difficult.' Div paused and seemed to consider her response. 'Well, you certainly seem to spend a lot of time together.'

'Yes, but I spend a lot of time with you.'

'Not as much.'

'No, I suppose not.' I paused, then asked: 'So has she ever mentioned anything to you, hinted even? We always have these totally ambiguous conversations, and I don't know if I'm just misinterpreting them.'

Div stared down towards the lake for a moment. 'No, I can't say that she has. Sorry, I'm not being much help, am I?'

'No, I'm just being stupid really.'

'Look, do you want me to try and find out? Have a chat with her or something?'

'Would you? I'd be eternally grateful, really.'

'Of course I will, if that's what you want.' She paused. 'So you really like her then?'

'Yeah, even when I first met her in Delhi. And spending all that time with you and Hal, you know . . . well, being with couples kind of rubs it in when you're single.'

'The grass is always greener,' she said thoughtfully, scraping at the dirt with her foot.

'You'd rather be single?'

Div looked up at me. 'Sometimes, I guess.'

'But you and Hal—you've been going out for years.'

'What's that got to do with anything?'

'Well, you must have something good to be together that long?'

'You'd think so, wouldn't you?' she replied, her expression thoughtful.

We stopped talking for a while, and the silence grew in length until Div said, 'I need to go.' With that, she got up and started to walk over to her hut. 'I'll ask Lorna when I see her,' she called back to me.

'Don't make it too obvious,' I replied anxiously, receiving a wave of acknowledgement.

Beyond Div's hut I noticed some of the more recent arrivals, a French trio whose names I did not know, emerging from the tree line. They were jabbering away to one another after an afternoon spent exploring the surrounding woodland, laughing and shrieking excitedly. For some reason their carefree happiness darkened my mood. Feeling a sudden urge to be alone, I picked up a packet of cigarettes and a bottle of Red Label. Wandering north out of the commune, I followed a winding track—presumably a wildlife trail—for perhaps a kilometre or so. As I gained in altitude, the path suddenly forked. I followed it round to the west, passing dense thickets of bamboo, until I emerged on to a large granite plateau overlooking the commune.

It was a place I'd end up coming to many times in the months ahead. Often I went there for the solitude, to think about the future. Ironically, it's where everything came to an end. But at that time, it came to be my favourite place in Shadow-Wall. The plateau was small, half a dozen square metres perhaps, and its dark grey granite surface was almost completely flat, save for a few boulders. Dotted here and there were clumps of flowers and shrubs where soil had collected in the cracks and life had taken hold and grown. The rock itself was warm from the sun, the latent heat noticeably warming the air around me. And the view was quite something. Elevated a few hundred metres above the commune, it was possible to look down and see the dozens of huts we'd built; in the clearing they surrounded, there were perhaps thirty or forty inhabitants sat carving. But for the real view, one had to look south-east across the valley. From this high up, it was possible to see over and beyond the tree-lined crest of the valley that formed the horizon a little lower down the mountain at Shadow-Wall. And reaching into the distance were perhaps a hundred snow-capped peaks of the Himalayas. As the sun began its descent, one by one they turned to amber; red-flecked cirrus stretched away above them endlessly.

And there was no sound, save for the occasional snatch of birdsong. In the commune, even at night, there were the constant sounds of humanity—doors being closed, voices, laughter, coughing, footsteps. Here there was nothing but virtual silence, an endless view, and a gentle evening breeze that lazily stirred the leaves of the Himalayan cedars and rhododendrons that fringed the plateau.

And that late afternoon, as I took slow swigs from the whisky bottle and stared out over the mountains, I tried to disentangle my thoughts. Deep inside me there remained a conflict. On the one hand, it seemed that we really had created something genuinely special with Shadow-Wall, however inadvertently. All of the inhabitants of the commune seemed happy—that was evident to see from just walking about the place. We had made a sanctuary, a place far removed from the everyday burdens that the capitalist world presented—we'd created a cashless society that was content, thriving and in want of nothing. Yet ironically, like tailings from a mine, Shadow-Wall was beginning to produce a pollutant, and that pollutant was money. And while I understood—and probably agreed with—Hal's philosophy that sharing it out would somehow taint our commune, his increasing obsession with the idea of maximizing profit through concepts like quotas did not sit easily with me.

Yet idealism is rarely the master of pragmatism, I reflected. I was close to broke, and if I left Shadow-Wall, I'd barely have enough money to stay more than a few months in Delhi. After that, returning home would be my only option. Hal's idea—of staying in Shadow-Wall for as long as it lasted and accruing as much money as possible in the meantime—seemed to provide me with an almost indefinite stay of execution. And, just as importantly, it also provided me with an almost indefinite opportunity to spend time with Lorna.

I slowly drained the last remaining whisky, and carefully screwed the lid back on the bottle. Then I looked down at the commune, which was slowing melting into the dusk. Yes, I thought to myself. It might not feel quite right, but it was the only way.

25

JUBBAWY

'It's strange, you know? I said earlier that I came to India to find myself. Well perhaps that point in time was the closest I came.'

'How do you mean?' the policeman asks.

'Well my life was pretty much . . . it was pretty much *binary* by then, you know? There were only two things of any importance to me—Shadow-Wall and Lorna. And Shadow-Wall was really working, it was growing and people were happy there, it was even starting to provide me with some financial security. And as for Lorna? Well, while I fretted a lot about what her feelings were towards me, I think deep down I knew she liked me.'

'I see.'

'And so, yeah, I felt very happy with the direction my life had taken. I started to feel *hope*, you know? I'd never really had that before.'

'Hope that you and Lorna might get together, that you might work out as a couple?'

'Right,' I agree. I slowly run my finger along a small scab on my wrist. It's from where they inserted the cannula when they put me on a drip, I reflect. Around it, I can still see small deposits of glue that remain from the tape used to hold it in place.

'Yes, your attachment to Lorna is very plain to see,' he ventures after some time. 'You cared for her a lot—or so it seems.'

I put my hand to my face, and rub the stubble on my chin for a few moments. Then I move my fingers slowly up to the stitches around my nose. The skin is tender and swollen from the infection still. '*Care* for her,' I correct.

'Indeed. *Care*.'

We sit across the table, not speaking. It is possible to hear the sound of voices from a distant room somewhere, and the occasional screech of a chair. I wonder how many other people like me are being interviewed, or held, in this building.

After perhaps five minutes has passed, Jubbawy gets to his feet and unfolds his arms above his head, stretching. He walks over to the far wall, which is entirely featureless. I get the impression he regrets the fact that there isn't a window to look out of. He just stares, expressionless, at the white tiles.

'Yes, you seem to *care* for her a lot,' he calls over without moving. A pause, then: 'Mr Hicks, I know already from what you have said that you still have parents.'

'Yes.'

He turns around. 'Would you like to speak to them?'

'Not really,' I say.

'And your brother and sister? Would you like to speak to either of them?'

'No,' I say. 'I'm really not very close to my family, you know?'

He clicks his tongue in thought. 'When were you last in touch with your parents, might I ask?'

I pause, then look at the floor. 'Not since I came to India,' I say quietly.

'Two and a half years? Two and a half years!? Mr Hicks, whatever feelings you may harbour towards your parents, does it not occur to you that they might be concerned about your wellbeing? I mean, my god, two and a half years? They might very well think you're dead by now, I'd have thought.'

I say nothing.

'Did you not feel at least some duty of care to them, maybe a letter or two to let them know you were okay?' he prompts.

'They never wrote to me when I was in Delhi,' I mutter. 'Anyway, what's your point?'

He places his hands on his hips and looks at me, 'It just seems odd.' He pauses, then adds, 'Lorna seems to be the only person you care for.'

'Perhaps,' I shrug.

'And even then, Mr Hicks,' he continues, 'I wonder if you do really *care* for her, like you say. Given the lack of empathy you seem to exhibit to everyone around you—your family, the people on the mountain, the *children* on the mountain even—I wonder if you do indeed care for her, or whether it's something else entirely. Perhaps you care for what *she brings you*, for example?'

I regard Jubbawy for some time. 'No,' I say finally.

'We often covet things,' he continues. 'Things we desire that make us feel good about ourselves. An expensive car, a nice house—'

'No,' I repeat.

'Love—or obsession over something we desire for ourselves—often these feelings are quite similar in nature, and thus very easy to confuse.'

'No,' I repeat. Then, very firmly, 'No.'

'Let's move on then,' he says with an indifferent shrug.

26

SHADOW-WALL, OCTOBER 1987

There were clear signs that summer was drawing to an end as the four of us made the descent from the mountain to the Kullu road once more. The path down was heavily carpeted with leaf-fall from the deciduous trees that lined it, and there was a slight edge to the morning breeze. Progress was slow, partly because the fallen leaves obscured roots and protruding stones that made us trip and stumble, but also from the sheer bulk of the Krapi-Krapis which we carried down in black plastic bin liners—each of us had four or five sacks slung over our shoulders. Not only was our passage down the trail torturously slow, but when we did finally get to the road, hitchhiking was all but impossible—no one would stop for a group of westerners with twenty or so bulging trash bags strewn on the road next to them. After three or four unsuccessful hours spent trying to flag down passing vehicles, we were forced to start waving handfuls of rupees at the passing vehicles. It worked, although the first pick-up truck that stopped wasn't large enough to accommodate the four of us and our bags of flutes, so Lorna and I had to wait another hour or so while Hal and Div went on ahead without us.

'3,200 flutes,' Hal said cautiously as we reconvened in Hemen's shop. He scratched at the stubble on his face nervously, then added, 'look, I know you might not want to buy *all* of them off us, but we thought we'd bring the lot down, you know?'

'No, no, fear not, my dearest Hal. Fear not!' Hemen rubbed his hands together, then smiled at each of us in turn. 'Indeed, I do believe you are underestimating my considerable business acumen, if I am not very much mistaken. Which I do believe I am not. You see, my friends, I am wanting many more of these. Many, many more.'

'How many more?' Lorna asked, her voice curious.

Hemen tutted. 'What you have brought me today is certainly a good amount, dear lady. But yes, I am wanting more. You see, we are selling elsewhere now, in Delhi and Jaipur and Agra and Jodhpur. Anywhere that tourists are visiting, we are selling.'

'Yes, but how many more?' I repeated, adjusting the pieces on a marble chess-set that sat on his glass counter.

'If you can be giving me 8,000 a month, I can be selling quite easily.'

'8,000? That's more than double what we produced last month!'

'Well then, I am thinking you should be working harder, my friend. I am having a large family to support, and we are still going hungry through your laziness. I have been talking to a friend in Goa, and another in Calcutta—they are wanting to be buying, but I have to be telling them no!'

'Look, we'll see what we can do, okay? We might manage 5,000, at a push.'

Hemen shook his head dejectedly. 'That would be an improvement of course, but I must be telling you, I am feeling very most disappointed by your rank idleness. We could be selling many more.' He slid two bricks of rupees across the glass display cabinet.

'I thought we agreed that you'd pay us in dollars from now on,' Hal protested.

'The bank is closed today,' Hemen replied. 'It is Sunday.'

'Is it? Oh. Well I'm going to have to count all this, man.'

'We'll meet you in the café across the road,' I volunteered, as Hal began slowly thumbing through the dirty, crumpled bank notes.

'Later, dude,' he nodded, not looking up.

*

'I spoke with her,' Div whispered as Lorna ordered coffees from the bar.

'What did she say?'

'She thinks you're nice.'

'*Nice?*'

'That's what she said.'

'Oh. So what else did she say?' I snatched a look at the bar. Lorna had only just got served.

'She thinks you're kind-hearted.'

'That's good I suppose,' I said slowly. 'Anything else?'

The Indian woman behind the bar slid over a pot of coffee and three cups.

'Well, yeah, I guess she *likes* you, yes,' Div shrugged.

I grabbed Div's head, and planted a kiss on her forehead. 'Thanks, Div. I owe you.'

She didn't return my smile.

*

'It's a little under $4,000, man,' Hal smiled, as we deposited the wads of Indian banknotes in a cavity under the floor of his hut. 'Not bad.'

I nodded in agreement. 'A good month all right.'

'Yeah.' Hal carefully placed the floorboards back and rolled the large Persian rug into place. 'Ethan, here's a question. How much money do you think someone needs to never work again?'

'Wow, I don't know,' I replied. 'Never thought about it.'

'A million US dollars?'

'I'm really not sure. It depends what kind of life you want to lead, I suppose.' I thought for a moment. 'Even with a million bucks, I guess you'd need to live pretty frugally, right? Say forty years, that's only twenty-five grand a year, right? Then you've got inflation eating away at it, even with interest and stuff.'

Hal emitted a low whistle. 'Shit, yeah, you're right. Two million, I guess.'

'Why do you ask? We're never going to make that kind of money here if we're earning 3,000 or 4,000 bucks a month.'

'No reason,' he replied, stretching out his arms and legs like a cat. 'Just making conversation, really.'

*

While Div had provided me with at least some self-assurance during our conversation in the café, I still felt a surge of adrenaline as I wandered down to the lake with the intention of asking Lorna about her feelings towards me one warm October afternoon. It seemed to me that I was being entirely unrealistic, that I was deluding myself by thinking that someone as flawless as her could see something in me. And, as I approached her, I felt the little confidence that I had dissipate like morning mist in summer. She was wearing a new bikini bought in town only a few days ago, a simple white affair that complimented her dark skin, along with a disconcerting pair of Ray-Bans that were smoked deeply enough for me to be unable to make eye-contact. She looked beautiful.

'Hi!' I said, sitting cross-legged on the warm ground beside her. There was a slight breeze, and parallel ripples sloped diagonally across the lake until they dispersed amongst clumps of bulrushes a little way from the bank.

'Oh, hi, Ethan.' A smile. 'You okay?'

'Yeah.' I stripped off my damp t-shirt. 'Jesus it's been hot today—I thought it was meant to start getting cooler at this time of year?'

'Yes, winter is not so far away, I suppose.'

'I don't know why we still bother sunbathing—look at us!' I held out an arm, the skin the colour of teak.

'Yeah. Just routine, I suppose.'

The sound of laughter drifted down from the clearing, and we both looked up to its source. Bella and Jamie were both giving Felicity's kids piggyback rides.

'What are you thinking?' Lorna asked. 'You look miles away.'

'Nothing.' I stretched out my legs, resting my feet against Lorna's. I pursed my lips and said, 'Lorna . . .'

'Yeah?'

'Lorna, you know what we talked about all that time ago, you know, about my hair?'

'What about it?'

'Um, it was a metaphor, right?'

'I'm not sure I'm following you?'

I wished she would remove her sunglasses so that I could see her eyes. 'Well anyway, you said I should come to you if I still felt the same way.' I stared at the back of my hands before looking at her again. 'I do.'

'Oh?' she said nonchalantly. 'Do you still want to change it?'

'It plays constantly upon my mind.'

A smile. 'I'm sorry that it's affected you so deeply.'

'Will you help me remedy it?'

She removed her sunglasses, cocked her head to one side and regarded my hair. A slight frown crossed her brow.

'Are you certain that you wish for a remedy? I mean, if we were to change it, there is little chance that we could recreate what we have now . . .'

'I'm positive that it would be an improvement.'

'Yes,' she replied slowly. 'In the short-term at least.'

'I cannot foresee myself wanting to revert to how it is now,' I smiled, running my fingers through my hair, 'however it might grow.'

'Some things are impossible to foresee, Ethan.'

'Yes, yes they are. And some things are . . . inevitable.'

Lorna self-consciously played with her earlobe. Her voice was tense. 'Such as? What is inevitable?'

'That . . . that you and me . . .?'

Lorna looked at the ground and tore out a clump of long grass, throwing it to the wind. 'I wouldn't say it was inevitable. *Possible*, yes, but not inevitable . . .' She smiled to herself, and regarded me. 'The metaphor has, I think, reached its expiry date.'

'It certainly seems a little tired.'

'Yes. It does.'

There was an awkward pause, and though my mind was racing with a million thoughts and questions, I couldn't think of anything to say. The longer the silence lasted, the more difficult it seemed to break.

'Will you go out with me?' I blurted, eventually, but the words just seemed to clatter to the ground. 'I can't believe I just said that,' I said quickly. The concept was, of course, ridiculous—there was nowhere *to* go out. Perhaps it was just easier to fall back on familiar language when taking such an unfamiliar risk.

'You're very sweet,' Lorna laughed.

'You've called me that before—I'm still uncertain whether it's a compliment.'

Lorna drew a little closer, arching her back slightly. 'It is.'

I lifted my hand and stroked a long strand of black hair away from her face. Her eyes were fixed on mine, the pupils a little dilated. 'May I?'

A smile, nothing more.

'Lorna?'

Her lips parted slightly, as if she were uncertain of what to say. Eventually, another smile. 'Yes Ethan. You may.' Her voice quivered slightly as she spoke.

I drew myself forward, then wrapped my arms around her waist. I gently kissed her neck, then her lips, pulling away after a moment. 'No more metaphors, Lorna.'

'No more metaphors,' she agreed, running her hands over my back before kissing me once again.

27

JUBBAWY

I stare at the grey, graffiti-scarred table, picturing Lorna's face in my mind. God, what pain these memories inflict. What was it Dante said—that there was no greater sorrow than looking back at a time of happiness in misery? For me, the memories of Lorna that flood back, that thin sliver of my life when I actually found happiness, seem only to anaesthetize me with a grieving numbness. The misery is, of course, knowing that we will never again experience those happy moments together. Too much has passed for that. I am a little too cynical with life now to hope I will ever see the walls of that elegant house in Connaught Place again, or hold her, or kiss her, or talk idly with her about inconsequential things. Although my mind is not quite ready to commit me to despair, something inside me tells me that it is the truth, my fate. I will not see her again.

    I start to cry. I wipe my nose with my bare arm. The tears have mingled with a little blood, leaving pink watery streaks on the skin of my forearm. I look at Jubbawy and say with a humourless laugh, 'You asked me before if I really loved her . . .' I grind my cigarette into the ashtray until the curls of smoke dissolve, and wave a hand at my tear-streaked face. 'I really do. More than anything else in this world.'

    'I pity you.'

It is an interesting choice of words, I reflect, smudging away more tears. Totally ambiguous, and thus totally without any real meaning. Of course, that is precisely the reason that he chose the phrase. I notice my right hand is shaking, so I place it on my lap instead.

'Are you all right?' Jubbawy asks. The tone of the question makes it clear he is not asking out of concern. He simply wants the answer to an entirely empirical question.

'Yes.' I wipe my face with my forearm. 'I need some more painkillers.'

He slides the plastic container across the table. The policeman watches me detachedly as I try to open the bottle. The cap is childproof, and I struggle for a minute or so, eventually managing to prise it off. I tip out two of the small white pills into my palm, then put them in my mouth and take a long drink of water. I am close to retching. My interviewer still says nothing—he just stares at my shaking hand. I place it back on my lap. I hold the plastic bottle of tablets in my other hand, rotating it slowly as we sit in silence. I can still taste the salty tears on my lips.

'Do continue,' he says, after a time.

I shrug. 'Things were about to change,' I say. 'Winter was on its way, and soon enough the weather began to turn. By late October the temperature couldn't have been more than ten or twelve degrees centigrade, even during the day. Unfortunately, quite a few people started to leave.'

Jubbawy furrows his brow. '"Unfortunately" you say? But Mr Hicks, I would have assumed you didn't give a damn if these travellers, these hippies, these—' he pauses, and flips through his notes for a moment, perhaps for effect, 'ah yes—these *dropouts*, surely you didn't give a damn if they stayed or not, right? After all, I believe we've already established that you had little or no emotional attachment to them?'

I emit a slight snort. How tenaciously he has latched on to that, I muse. 'It was beginning to create a problem for us,' I reply slowly. 'You see, the demand from Hemen was already starting to outstrip what we could produce. And things were about to get a lot worse in that regard. Me, Div, Lorna and Hal, we took a shipment in to Kullu in the late fall. We were producing a good volume still; we'd even had to make bamboo sleds to bring the Krapi-Krapis down the hillside as we could no longer carry them. You see, we're talking *thousands upon thousands* of flutes by this stage. But Hemen . . . well, the cup he was wanting to fill, it had no bottom, you know?'

*

'I have recently been undertaking some most interesting marketing activities, my friends! Most interesting indeed. Suffice to say, I do believe we have hit the potjack, as you westerners like to say.'

'Sorry?' Lorna asks guardedly. 'You mean jackpot?'

'Yes indeed, madam, yes indeed. We have hit the potjack squarely in the bullseye, and I do believe we are going to be being very rich indeed, madam, very, very rich indeed. Yes, quite possibly very rich.'

'And why is that?'

Hemen rubs his hands together, a broad grin splitting his face. 'Well, madam, due to a peculiar convergence of good luck, fortunate timing, a touch of mendacity by my good self, and what can only be described as utterly abject editorial standards from a certain well-known publication, we now have exposure to the global marketplace, and it is all for free! This is really very good news for us all, we will quite possibly become very rich indeed!'

'I'm not sure I'm following you?'

'*Lonely Planet*, madam, *Lonely Planet*! Many, many months ago a young woman from the venerable publication came into my shop and asked me about the carvings that I sold. I was spinning very greatly to her. I think your expression is *hook, line and sinker*?' He claps his hands together in delight. 'I thought nothing of it at the time, so completely and utterly preposterous was my story. Yet it would appear that the seeds I sowed managed to take hold in the fertile soil upon which they were cast.'

'What are you talking about?' I ask suspiciously.

'The woman was wishing to know where the flutes were originating from . . . she was writing an article about hill-tribe handicrafts, and I thought it only being fair to be telling her what she was wanting to hear.'

'Hill tribes?'

'Oh so very fashionable, Mr Ethan, so very fashionable these days.'

'Well I suppose we *do* live on a hill,' Hal offers.

'And in many ways we *are* a tribe,' Div adds. 'Kind of.'

'It is not being so very far from the truth, I am agreeing,' Hemen nods. 'Only a very minor embellishment, if one is thinking about it quite hard. But the consequences for us are going to be very significant.'

'What consequences?' Lorna asks cautiously.

'Demand, madam, demand.' Hemen walks to his counter, and returns holding a book in his trembling hands. He thumbs excitedly through the *Lonely Planet* until he finds what he's looking for. He holds out the book, and the four of us stand side by side in his shop, reading the text in silence.

MUSICAL INSTRUMENTS (CONTINUED): THE KRAPI-KRAPI

Few travellers to India will fail to notice the small bamboo flutes, known locally as 'Krapi-Krapis' that are sold in bazaars, shops and by vociferous street hawkers in virtually every town and city on the subcontinent. The instrument is thought to originate from the north-eastern state of Himachal Pradesh, carved from local bamboo by a small hill tribe, the Shadwallians, who live in the forested foothills of the Himalayas near the Tibetan border.

Until recently, little was known of the Shadwallians, and there is still a considerable debate raging within the anthropological community as to their origin. However, the general consensus is that these gentle folk fled west across the border in the 1950's as the army of the People's Republic of China rolled into Tibet. Various estimates of the tribe's size have been made, ranging from only a hundred or less to several thousand, but the fact that no recorded sightings have been made of these elusive nomads suggests that the former may be closer to the truth.

The instrument itself usually measures no more than twelve inches in length, and consists of a hollowed bamboo tube, tapered at one end and bound with reeds. However, its simple form belies the importance of the Krapi-Krapi to the Shadwallian culture, where religion and music are closely entwined. The tribe believes that the five notes that can be played represent the voices of each of the five cosmic Buddhas—Vairocana, Aksobhya, Ratnasambhava, Amitabha and Amoghasiddhi—and that playing the instrument brings the individual closer to spiritual enlightenment. The actual sound is not dissimilar to that of a low-pitched recorder, but the great attraction of this instrument to the traveller is the ease with which it can be played. Expect to pay between Rs 200 and Rs 250 for a Krapi-Krapi, although those experienced at haggling may be able to pick one up a little cheaper. If you are visiting northern India, you may consider waiting until you reach this region before buying your flute—intricately carved examples can sometimes be found in the shops of Kullu and Shimla, but expect to pay around Rs 500 for these rarities.

*

Hemen closes the book with a theatrical clap. The four of us look at one another in stunned silence.

'Now, my friends,' he continues, 'might I suggest you take a moment to admire the rather fetching photographic work they have used on the front cover?'

I take the book from Hemen and turn it in my hands. 'Now that *is* weird,' is all I can think to say. On the front of the guidebook is a colour picture of a small Indian boy. He is stood in the middle of a busy street lined with stalls selling colourful ground spices piled high in plastic containers. In his hands is a large wooden tray; stacked on it are a dozen or so Krapi-Krapis.

'Does anyone else feel a certain . . .' Hal looks around the shop, searching for the right words, 'does anyone else feel a certain sense of *pride*?'

'Mr Hal,' Hemen interjects, 'this is no time for your vainglory, I'm afraid. Please be thinking instead of the *implications*. This new edition has been out almost two weeks, and already my network of Krapi-Krapi vendors are complaining their stock has run dry.' His expression changes in an instant, all signs of joviality instantly expunged from his countenance. 'I need more stock, my friends. I need more stock, and I need it fast.'

*

'The Krapi-Krapis were everywhere by now, all over India—everywhere. But you know, getting our product on the front cover of *Lonely Planet*, it was crazy, and we were one of the lead items in the arts and handicrafts section.' I am about to continue, but Jubbawy holds up a hand, then engages in conversation with Inspector Shah for several minutes. Presently the policeman nods, looks at his watch and turns to me.

'Do you want something to eat? I think we need to take a short break.'

'No, I'm fine.' I haven't eaten since breakfast in the holding cell at the ministry, but the thought of food somehow turns my stomach.

'As you wish. Will you excuse us for an hour or so?'

'Er, yes, of course,' I reply, a little surprised. I thought they were in a hurry to get this over and done with too.

Both policemen get to their feet, and leave the room, immersed in conversation. I watch them close the door behind them, noting the sound of bolts sliding home. I look at the table. On it sits a thin blue folder, also the hand-written notes that Jubbawy has been making on an A4 pad, and the list of the dead. It seems a strange oversight to leave them there, in front of me. I light a cigarette and sigh. I settle back into my chair, put my fingertips to my temples, and begin to think. I start to consider what to tell this smart, smart policeman next. Jubbawy knows pretty much everything about our first year in Shadow-Wall. There was nothing much to hide. The second year, our last, is a different matter entirely. Quite how we managed such a rapid moral descent in such a short period of time still baffles me. But that is not important. What is of consequence is the sizeable kernel of incriminating fact I need to obscure when they return. There are only a very few, slender strands of truth with which I can work. It remains to be seen whether I can weave them cleverly enough to conceal what happened up on that mountain.

*

Sometime later the door swings open. Lost in thought, I realize with a start that I am running my finger along the edge of the pile of paperwork. I snatch my hand back across the table, and look at the two policemen. Jubbawy is finishing the remains of a samosa, just a small corner is left between his thumb and forefinger. Inspector Shah is talking animatedly, moving his arms apart as if trying to convey some measure of size.

'Sorry to keep you, Mr Hicks,' Jubbawy says brightly, still chewing. 'I cannot do this sort of thing on an empty stomach, I'm afraid.'

I do not reply, instead staring fixedly at the half-full ashtray. Jubbawy sits down, looks at me briefly, and says, 'So.' He rummages through his notes, and continues, 'ah yes, you were saying about the guidebook . . .' he looks once again at his notes, then at me, '*Lonely Planet?*'

I decide to take another cigarette, although my decision is driven more by a sense of neatness than a desire to smoke. I have just counted nine stubs in the ashtray and wish to add another. 'Yeah, look, we were absolutely chuffed that our product got into *Lonely Planet*, I think we all felt a huge sense of achievement. But we also realized it could be something of a mixed blessing—'

'Mixed blessing?'

'Well, we were already struggling with our output—the onset of winter meant we were losing a lot of our workforce. So the idea of having to suddenly produce *more* was kind of worrying.' I pause, then add, '*really* worrying. We weren't sure if we could deliver anything above what we were already producing, to be honest.'

'Workforce,' he repeats.

I jolt slightly in my chair. My use of the word was unintentional. I press my right arm into my broken ribs. It is an instant way to summon pain, and it helps me to concentrate. 'Population,' I say.

'Go on,' he says after a time.

I shrug. 'It wasn't like we could suddenly increase production among those who remained over winter to compensate for those who left, you know? We had to strike a balance at Shadow-Wall—people came to our commune for the way of life, for the philosophy or concept of it, I guess. They certainly didn't come there to work, and we knew we couldn't push them too hard or they'd just leave. And that would have made the situation even worse.'

Jubbawy shrugs. Then he looks down at his hand and a thin smile breaks on his lips. He's forgotten he still has the little corner of his samosa remaining. He regards it for a moment, then pops it in his mouth and breathes a contented sigh. What simple, inconsequential things can bring pleasure in times of normality, I think to myself. But when will I next smile? It is very hard to foresee. Jubbawy proceeds to slap his hands together to rid them of any remaining crumbs, then folds his arms, reclines in his chair, and returns to watching my face with his usual studied intentness. I place my shaking hand on my lap, away from his gaze, and continue.

28

SHADOW-WALL, NOVEMBER 1987

'It's beautiful,' I commented to Lorna as we cradled one another, taking in the last dying moments of dusk. The wispy cirrus that streaked the sky was coloured pink and mauve, and the low orange sun seemed much larger than usual as we watched it plummet rapidly towards the horizon, briefly impaling itself upon a jagged peak across the valley. I gently kissed the nape of her neck, wrapping my arms around her waist, and leaned back to look at the sky. We were sat on the granite plateau—the rock still held a little heat from the sun's rays, but the evening air had an edge to it. 'Winter's truly on its way,' I murmured, holding her tight for warmth.

'Yes, but at this time of year . . . this place, it's enchanting.'

'There—it's gone,' I whispered, as the last arc of shimmering gold disappeared from sight behind one of the mountains. Then, 'Don't you think it seems quiet this evening? No birdsong.'

'Yes,' she agreed, before silence enveloped us once more. I listened to the sound of her breathing as darkness slowly drew in around us. 'Quiet down there too,' she said after a while. 'It's starting to really thin out. How many people left the commune today?'

'Oh, only two or three. I think they were German.'

'Right,' she murmured, turning into me slightly. 'They say we will get snow here this winter . . .' She paused. I sensed uncertainty in her voice when she spoke again, 'I may need to go back to Delhi soon, Ethan.'

My body seemed to jar involuntarily for a moment. 'Really?'

The slight movement of her hair on my chin betrayed the fact she was nodding, although darkness was shrouding the valley quickly now the sun had sunk below the horizon. 'I've been here nearly ten months, Ethan. I need to make sure the house is okay, see friends, check in with my aunt and uncle, that kind of thing. I can't just disappear off the face of the planet.'

I said nothing, instead drawing a packet of cigarettes from my pocket, then lighting one. The slight orange flare from the lighter's flame reflected from her glossy black hair for a moment. In silence, I considered the two options that seemed open to me: to stay at the commune and ask Lorna to come back, or to go with her to Delhi. I parsed each for some minutes, weighing up the potential reaction and consequences, and eventually I said, 'Lorna, if I stay to help Hal and Div over winter, will you come back once you've tidied things up in Delhi?'

There was a slight pause. Then, after a few moments, she reached up a hand and stroked my face. The skin on her fingers was slightly cold. 'Yes, I can,' she said. 'I would like that. But I think we need to talk.'

Again, I felt an unwanted surge of adrenalin grip me. What is it about her, I thought to myself, that just her words can evoke such a physical reaction in me?

'Talk about what?' I asked. As I spoke the words, I tried to sound nonchalant, but the question sounded strangled.

'Don't worry, Ethan.' She rested her head against my chest. I could feel her break into a smile. 'You sound worried, it's really nothing major.'

'Go on?'

'I do like being here in Shadow-Wall, but I also like stability, Ethan. We have nothing to aim for here. It's just treading water.'

'But you said you had nothing much to aim for in Delhi . . .?' I paused, then said slowly, 'Anyway, there may be something to aim for, you know?'

'What?'

I paused again, and we watched the first stars emerge from the black vault above us, silent in thought. Eventually I said, 'Ah, look, I like being here too. I feel kind of proud of this place. And I want to help

Hal and Div, they're our friends, and it's going to be tough going to get enough flutes produced these next few months with so few people here.' I paused again, then added, 'Also, we're making a little bit of money here, you know?'

Lorna sighed. Then she said slowly, 'You know that side of things has always made me uncomfortable, Ethan.'

'I know. But if we stay here and save what we make, it might be enough to start something up—a small business or something that we could do together.'

Lorna laughed softly. 'I don't think we'll ever get very rich staying here.'

There was a long pause. Eventually I said, 'Well, look. Either way, I think I need to stay and help Hal and Div. So why don't you go do your stuff in Delhi and then get back here as quick as you can? Then we can talk properly, make a plan for next year. Does that sound okay?'

Lorna planted a kiss on my shoulder. 'I suppose that's okay,' she agreed. 'Although I might be gone for two or three months at least—there are quite a few old friends I really need to see down south, in Madras and Goa, and I need to renew my passport. It's all going to take time.'

'Two or three months,' I repeated softly, considering whether I could face that long apart from her.

'It's okay if you stay,' she said. 'I do understand. And besides, what's a few months if we're to spend the rest of our lives together, right?'

*

How naïve we were. How naïve of us to regard life as some sort of blank canvas that we could paint as we wished, how naïve we were in our certainty of a happy future before us. We were, at that time, innocent to the fact that life is, in reality, indiscriminately cruel. Of course, we weren't to know what the future would hold, but whenever I look back, I see that conversation on the plateau as the point that I crossed the Rubicon. It really is as simple as that: I had a binary choice, two paths to choose from, and I know one was right, one was wrong. And I can pretend as much as I like that I wanted to help out Hal and Div, or that I didn't want to abandon them, or that I had some kind of emotional connection to Shadow-Wall that I didn't wish to break. But I would only be deceiving myself. For, by that point in time, I was fully aware of Shadow-Wall's potential to make a significant sum of money. And so there it is. A single moment in time, so straightforward to mark, that condemned my future so irrevocably. I should have left with Lorna; instead I stayed through greed.

*

Winter came slowly; first it manifested itself as an edge on the breeze that swirled down the valley, a cold moistness to the air, lower cloud that clung to the treetops. By late November, the temperature was close to freezing, and bitter winds peeled off the Himalayan plateau to the north. Each morning the ground was hardened by an overnight frost, and the heat of summer seemed a distant memory. Equally slowly, the size of our commune diminished. It was not a mass exodus, but rather a slow bleeding of the travellers and hippies from Shadow-Wall, with a few leaving each day like migratory birds seeking warmer climes.

'Fucking crazy year,' Hal observed, as the four of us sat cross-legged on the floor of his hut. Before him was around $22,000; it was the money we'd made from the flutes over the course of our time at Shadow-Wall, although much of it was from the past few months alone.

'Yeah,' I agreed. 'Couldn't have predicted things would end up like this.' I thought of my time in Delhi, of Scott and how he died before my very eyes, of the endless carefree summer in Shadow-Wall, of Lorna and what had grown between us, of the fact that we—Hal, Div, Lorna and I—had actually created a thriving, self-sustaining commune.

'So, when are you coming back, dude?' Hal asked Lorna. 'We need all the hands we can get here, you know.'

'I'm not sure,' she replied slowly, looking at me for a moment. 'I'll be gone at least a couple of months, maybe three, I think it rather depends on how I find things in Delhi. My affairs, I mean.'

Hal grunted. 'Well, dudes, it's time for us to hit the road to Kullu. A lot of flutes this month. You all packed, Lorna?'

She nodded, and the four of us got to our feet. Div walked to the door, opened it, and froze. 'Oh my god!' she exclaimed. 'It's snowing guys! I mean—*really* snowing!'

And so it was. Thick, heavy flakes that settled quickly on the frozen ground. Within minutes the world around us turned white. We whooped with the excitement of children, gathered snowballs to hurl at each other, slid through the pristine powder that now covered the clearing, grabbed handfuls of the stuff and threw it into the air. From the huts around us, others emerged and joined us in our childlike glee. And, for an hour or more we revelled in this novel arrival until the cold began to reach us. Then the four of us collapsed into a giggling heap in the centre of the clearing, the other inhabitants occasionally lobbing a snowball in our direction.

'I haven't seen snow for years,' Hal laughed.

Lorna, who'd started making a snow angel, sat up with a start. Her voice had a sudden urgency to it. 'Er, seriously guys, we better get going—we don't want to get snowed in.'

It was a good point. The rest of us sat up with equal suddenness—it was already a couple of inches deep.

'Yeah, let's go,' Hal agreed, looking up at the cascade of snow falling from the sky, 'let's go.'

With that, we walked to the edge of the clearing where a pile of two dozen or so large black trash bags, dusted in snow, were lashed to the four sleds.

'Well, that's one benefit of the snow,' Hal laughed, as he started to pull on the first sled. Since we'd first started using them a couple of months back, we'd found it extremely hard work dragging them over the hard, uneven ground. Now, the sleds glided effortlessly over the fresh snow.

It was an easy and enjoyable descent to the highway below. The track was steep in places, but we simply slid down those sections on our backsides. By the time we reached the metalled highway below, our clothing was soaked through, our faces and hands red from the cold, but our mood was happy nonetheless. The winding valley road was obscured by a thick, thick covering of snow, although a few furrows revealed the fact that at least some traffic had passed. In time, we managed to flag down a battered old minibus, large enough to take us all, our load of Krapi-Krapis included. We clambered on, stamping the snow from our trainers as we boarded, shivering from the cold.

29

JUBBAWY

'Lorna left for Delhi at that point?'

'Yeah,' I reply. 'Actually, we were snowed in for a couple of days in Kullu, she couldn't get a bus to Delhi, so the four of us stayed at some hotel, waiting for it to clear. But she left after that, yeah. Anyway, in some senses, her going kind of solved a problem for us. You see by then, all of our visas had expired, so we gave her a couple of thousand dollars and our passports to get it sorted out, she knew people who could get them renewed for us . . .' I hesitate. 'Well, you know, under the table.'

Jubbawy rolls his eyes, presumably in recognition of the corruption that runs, like traces of an illicit substance, through the veins of his country.

'It was really hard saying goodbye. I was pretty depressed at the thought of being away from her for so long, we were both crying when we said farewell. But . . .' I look at the ceiling, searching for the right word, 'but I was also quite *excited* about the next couple of months ahead.'

'Why so?'

I cast my mind back. 'I don't know. I felt we were on the cusp of something with Shadow-Wall. We were starting to make maybe $7,000 or $8,000 a month from the flutes. And we knew it could be a lot more, we knew it was *going to be* a lot more,' I pause. 'So yeah, I was kind of excited about that, about focusing on making it work for us.'

'I see.'

'Anyway, after she'd gone, well, the three of us decided to stay in Kullu for a while. We weren't sure if the track up to Shadow-Wall would be passable yet, even though the snow was starting to clear, so we spent that time making a plan.'

'A plan?'

'Yeah look, we'd delivered 7,000 flutes to Hemen on that trip, but he was complaining again, he wanted 10,000 the following month. It just wasn't possible, I think the . . .' I pause, then continue slowly, 'the *population* of Shadow-Wall had almost halved by then, so we needed to find some solutions.'

'Do elaborate.'

I think for a moment. 'Well, the first thing we agreed was to buy a jeep and a trailer. So that was kind of fun, we went to a used-car dealer in Kullu, ended up buying this second-hand Mahindra jeep. It was pretty old and battered, you know, but we got it for around $4,500. Then we went on a road trip.'

'What sort of *road-trip*?'

'We needed to grow the population of Shadow-Wall,' I shrug. 'That was the main way we could increase production. So we visited all of the tourist towns in the area, you know—Chamba, Dalhousie, Dharamshala . . . we went to all of them, finishing up in Manali.' I shake my head slowly. 'How ironic.'

'Ironic?'

'The etymology.'

Jubbawy looks at me for a moment, then nods. 'Yes, I suppose it is. Named after Manu—he went there to do penance.'

30

SHADOW-WALL, DECEMBER 1987

It was a pretty simple plan. We picked the fifteen largest tourist towns in the region, and went to each one in turn. According to the odometer on the Mahindra, we covered a couple of thousand kilometres on that trip. If we were technically working, which surely we were, it didn't feel like it—driving from town to town was exhilarating, the winding roads taking us through passes and valleys in the shadow of the towering snow-clad peaks of the Himalayas. The Mahindra's little engine would whine and groan as we climbed up to the various hilltop towns that dotted the state, the wheels spraying out arcs of gravel as we whizzed round the sharp bends.

The process was the same for each town we visited. We'd marked out all of the hotels and guesthouses listed in the 'budget accommodation' section of *Lonely Planet*, for these were the places we were most likely to find the hippies and travellers that we wished to attract to Shadow-Wall. And in five large boxes on the back seat of the jeep were thousands of small booklets. We'd spent nearly $2,000 getting them professionally printed in Kullu; each one was eight pages long, and included colour photos of Shadow-Wall in high summer, a description of the commune and what it was like to live there, a detailed map of how to get there, and various testimonials that we'd invented. Within the effusive passages we'd written about life at Shadow-Wall, we'd made sure to place a heavy emphasis on the fact that everything was provided for the commune-dwellers for free. For we were looking to attract the most parsimonious segment of travellers and hippies, those who were looking to make their money go that much further in India.

And so, in each hotel, guesthouse and hostel that we visited, we left piles of booklets in the common areas and on the reception desks, pinned them to whatever notice boards we could find, and left half-a-dozen or so in each coffee shop or bar that we visited to rest our feet after trudging around town. Although it sometimes raised quizzical looks from the proprietors and staff, more often than not no one cared about our marketing activities.

We ended our trip in Manali. From there, I tried to call Lorna, but I couldn't reach her despite spending most of the afternoon in the phone shop trying to get through. When I returned to the car park where we'd left the jeep, Hal was manhandling a goat into the backseat.

'Might come in useful for milk or something,' he called cheerily as I approached.

'Well you can go in the back,' I snorted, climbing into the driving seat.

Div joined me in the front, and Hal jumped in next to his goat, putting his arm around the creature. 'You know guys,' he shouted over the gunning engine, 'when we reach the trail, we're in for some serious labour?'

I nodded. 'You've packed the tents, right?'

'Yeah, I've got the tents dude. Let's go.'

With that we swung out of Manali, and headed back home.

It took us three days to clear a route up the mountainside that the jeep could handle. We had all the equipment we needed for the task—tents and firewood, spades and shovels, and axes and machetes to clear the bush—but it was hard, hard going nonetheless. The three of us painstakingly cleared metre by slow metre of trail, the tethered goat looking on indifferently as we hacked away at the rhododendrons and cleared mounds of half-frozen soil and rocks. When we finally made it to the top, we were exhausted. After distributing the supplies we'd brought up for the inhabitants who were sticking out the winter months, all three of us collapsed in our huts. I think we slept for sixteen hours that first night back at Shadow-Wall.

31

JUBBAWY

'This leaflet of which you speak, I'd like to see a copy,' Jubbawy says thoughtfully.

'They should be easy enough to come by,' I shrug. 'We ended up making that same kind of trip a few times, getting more printed and stuff.'

'I see.' Jubbawy pauses, then removes his glasses and examines the lenses. Satisfied, perhaps, that there is no dust on them, he replaces them and asks, 'The printing and distribution of the leaflets, that was rather mendacious, do you not think?'

I look down, and again pick absently at the scab where the cannula was inserted. The dried blood lifts a little, and a small trickle of clear fluid leaks out. I rub it away, considering the question. 'Was it?' I ask eventually. 'I mean, there was nothing we wrote that wasn't true.'

'But the purpose was to bring more people into your commune so that you might manufacture more flutes, no?'

I nod.

'And from what you say, the content of the leaflet actually referred to something that was, in reality, quite the opposite. You claimed it was a commune that shunned the concepts of capitalist society.'

I sigh. 'Yeah, but we gave them what they wanted. We delivered what *we promised*, I guess.'

'Yes, but it was a *guise*.'

'Perhaps,' I agree. I look back down at the scab on my wrist, and prod it gently with my finger to see if I can tease any more fluid out. 'But I really don't see that we did anything wrong. We provided the environment these people were looking for, we provided them with food and accommodation, and they paid us back in kind with carvings. I don't think anyone was unhappy with the arrangement. Call it "symbiosis" if you like.'

'No, Mr Hicks,' he retorts, 'as I said, I call it a guise. Regardless of whether what you included in the leaflet was ostensibly true, it's the *omission* that constitutes the lie in this case.'

Again I shrug. 'Whatever. Is it really that important?'

Jubbawy snorts. 'Well, for the people you tricked into coming to Shadow-Wall, I suspect in many cases it was *mortally* important.'

I can sense he is staring at me, even though I continue to examine my wrist. I say nothing.

'Anyway,' he says after some time, a hint of weariness in his voice, 'let's move on.'

'Sure,' I say. Finally, I look back at the policeman. 'Well our *guise*, as you seem to like to call it, was rather successful in the end.'

32

SHADOW-WALL, JANUARY 1988

It was overwhelming. We expected a few to trickle in initially, maybe a dozen or so in the first month if we were lucky. As it turned out, a lot more than that came. Sheets of drizzle were being whipped almost horizontally across the commune by fierce winds, and there was a numbing chill to the air, but still they came. It reminded me of when Hal, Div and I first arrived at Shadow-Wall—the weather was not much better then, and I wondered how all of these people felt, stumbling into such a desolate place, their clothing soaked through, their walking boots caked with thick mud.

The rain was relentless that first week, and a thick mist sunk down into the valley, obscuring the outlines of even the closest huts around the clearing. Yet, by the end of that week, the new arrivals had reached fifteen in number. As we would do with all of the newcomers that arrived at our commune, we firstly allocated huts, then provided them with a brief orientation session—where the latrines were located, where the stocks of firewood were kept, the best areas to collect fruit when it was in season, how we treated the water from the lake to make it drinkable. Only after they had settled in for a day or two would we explain about the flutes, how their production supported the commune, and how we expected everyone to make a contribution. We would only then start the formal induction for new arrivals—we would take them up the mountainside in order to show them where to harvest the bamboo, then we'd return to the clearing to train them how to fashion the Krapi-Krapis. We would patiently let them practise, watching them produce flute after flute while giving hints and advice as they did so, until we were satisfied with the standard of their carving. We also assigned various people with other duties—for digging out new latrines, for collecting firewood, for tending the chickens and the goat. Fortunately, Jamie was still with us, and he remained in charge of cooking duties, producing more than passable vegetable broths each night to help keep the bitter cold at bay.

Yet that first month back at Shadow-Wall following our road-trip was quite bleak in many ways. The weather was persistently foul, and it was hard to remain warm. Our rain-sodden clothes refused to dry in the cold damp air, and the drizzle would extinguish the fire overnight, leaving us shivering every morning until we could get it going again. Flute production was also challenging, with the tracks leading up to the bamboo on the hillside becoming churned and almost impassable. Our numb hands meant carving was slower than usual, torturous even. It was an unpleasant way to start the year there, and we all longed for the rain to start to clear, for spring to come. We spent most of our time around the fire in the daytime, sat there in plastic macs staring into the flames, talking or carving. Those who had seen our flyers and made the trip to Shadow-Wall must have wondered why they had come. For me, I wondered why they stayed. But they did, entranced perhaps by the ideology of a place that, many months later, would become their mass grave.

33

JUBBAWY

'Only about a dozen or so people had stayed up in the commune over winter,' I say. 'But it was pretty amazing, you know—after distributing the flyers, well, we had thirty or forty people turn up just in the first couple of weeks. We couldn't believe our luck, really.'

'Luck?' Jubbawy shakes his head slowly. 'Luck for whom exactly, Mr Hicks? Not for anyone coming to your commune.'

I sigh at the gibe. 'Well it was lucky for us in the context of *production*. When we met up with Hemen, he wanted a delivery of over 12,000 Krapi-Krapis the very next month. That was virtually impossible.' I shrug. 'We needed a lot of manpower to knock out that many carvings.'

'Manpower,' he repeats.

'Look, I know what happened in the end. Of course I do. I know all those people got killed. But we weren't to know that at the time, were we?'

'I am cognizant that you couldn't foresee the future, Mr Hicks. I am just rather intrigued by your phraseology.'

I shrug, then continue: 'And at the time, the more people that came the better as far as we were concerned.'

Jubbawy again remains silent. I wonder to myself what he is thinking right now. Does his mind stray at all? Does he think about what he's going to do when he gets home to his wife? What TV he's going to watch?

Does he think about where he's going to go on holiday next? Or does he just sit there with complete focus, analysing everything, dissecting sentences, searching for nuances and hidden meanings in my words, waiting for the inevitable mistakes?

'The important thing for us was producing enough each month to keep up with demand. And Hemen kept asking for more and more, so we knew we had to grow the commune to keep pace with that.'

'I see.'

'Anyway,' I continue, 'there were a lot of day-to-day issues to think about that came with the growth of our commune. Getting food up the hillside, sterilizing enough water to drink, ensuring we had enough tools to make the flutes, building new huts, all of that sort of stuff. So yeah, we were forced to be a lot more organized than we had been that previous year. We had to be.'

'Previous year,' Jubbawy repeats.

'Yeah,' I nod. 'Over a year had passed since we'd first arrived. Something happened to remind us of that, as it happens.'

*

I am sat alone near the lake when he enters the clearing, some hundred or so metres away. I am alone because Div and Hal are in Kullu. I should be with them, of course, but instead I am reading a book to pass the time before they return. My back is resting against a small silver fir, my right foot wedged up high on a large fallen branch. It's been two days since I twisted my ankle while making a descent from the plateau, and the joint remains puffy and swollen with fluid.

The man enters the clearing, and I know he's a new arrival, because they are so easy to mark—invariably they are carrying a rucksack. And so I stare for a few moments at the lone figure as he drops his bag, idly wondering to myself what nationality he might be. I then return to my book. A few seconds pass, and then something moves me to look back at the solitary figure—an unsettling sense of familiarity plays on my mind. Due to the distance, his features are impossible to discern. But the way he walks—a certain confident lope—is what triggers the sense of recognition.

'Oh no,' I murmur to myself.

'Miles,' I shout, hobbling into the windswept clearing. 'Wow, what a wonderful surprise. It's great seeing you again!' I say the greeting with a warmth that I do not feel.

'Hey, Ethan,' he nods. 'You've lost weight.'

I look at him; he's changed too. The long hair has been shaved completely, and the dome of his head is covered in a short black stubble. He has lost weight too since I last saw him, but it's his face that has changed the most; he has aged, I think to myself—perhaps five years in the space of one. His eyes are underlined by dark bags, and crow's feet line the skin near his temples. There are flecks of grey in the beard he now wears.

'So, what brings you back to Shadow-Wall?' I ask after a time. We are stood some metres apart still, as though some invisible force is repelling us from one another. I note my voice has an unintentional edge to it, for I do not know what he feels towards me.

'It's the anniversary of Scott's death,' he says simply.

'Yes, of course,' I nod, chewing slightly on my lip. 'Of course it is.'

There is a long pause, and he looks around the commune at some length; his eyes dart from side to side like a lizard's, taking in the new huts. 'This place has grown,' he grunts eventually.

'Yeah,' I nod, looking around. 'Yeah, it has.'

There's another pause, and then he reaches down to his rucksack. He pulls out a small cellophane-wrapped bunch of flowers, chrysanthemums perhaps. They are pink and white; the bouquet is a little crushed and misshapen from being in his bag. Then he looks at me. 'Let's go,' he says simply, 'and don't worry—I won't stay long.'

'Sure,' I say. I consider letting him go alone, for my injury presents itself as the most straightforward of excuses. But something compels me to go with him. Pity, or guilt—I'm not sure which.

We slowly make our way out of the clearing. Miles offers his arm to help me walk, but I politely decline. We say nothing more until we enter the forest. It stopped raining some hours ago, but the sound of the patter of water from the wet canopy fills the air. It is very cold.

'I'm sorry for what passed,' I say quietly, as we follow an overgrown path through the woodland. Our feet make no sound—there is a thick layer of pine needles and leaves underfoot. It smells very damp.

'Yeah,' is all he replies.

'Are you still angry with me?' I ask after a time. 'I wouldn't blame you at all if you are.'

'It is what it is,' he says with a shrug.

'Yeah.' Then, to make conversation more than anything else, 'Did you come far? You're still travelling in India, then?'

'I flew into Mumbai from Toronto three days ago,' he replies without tone. 'It's important to me to come and pay my respects, you know?'

'That's very good of you,' I say slowly.

We lapse into uneasy silence, saying nothing as we continue up the woodland path. Finally, we reach the grave. I have not been here in nearly a year. It is overgrown: creepers have engulfed the tombstone with their green tendrils so that the polished granite is barely visible. Where it is, yellow and red lichens have attached themselves to the stone.

'I'm sorry,' I mutter. 'We should have done more.'

Miles shrugs but says nothing. I look at his face. He is crying.

'I'll leave you in peace, then,' I say softly, turning on my heel and walking away.

*

'I never saw him again after that,' I say. 'I don't think he even stayed at Shadow-Wall that night, from what the other inhabitants said.'

'How wretched of you,' the policeman says flatly. 'How wretched of you to lead him to an empty grave.'

I say nothing but, even as I continue my account, the statement seems to hang in the air.

34

SHADOW-WALL, JANUARY 1988

Hal was clearly agitated. He was also pretty drunk. He paced around the narrow hut, stroking his beard with one hand, holding a bottle of Red Label in the other.

'So here's the January mid-month update,' he announced with a slight slur, waving his hand towards the open door, to the clearing beyond where a few dozen people were sitting around the fire. At least it had stopped raining for once. 'We've still got to carve over 8,000 flutes, and there's twelve working days left. Forty-nine people here, that's over fourteen a day to carve. Problem is that they're just too slow at carving.'

'They're new here, Hal. We sold them a relaxed, carefree, idyllic existence. We can't exactly walk round with a bullwhip.'

'Hmm. Well we can't stick with six flutes a day, that's for sure.'

'Hal, you only just put the quotas up at the start of the month. You can't do it again,' I ventured.

He lapsed back into silence for a while. I remained silent, watching him.

'I'm going to have to,' he resumed after a while. 'I'm going to increase the targets to ten a day, and we'll scrap weekends. Then if we keep getting a few people coming in each day over the next couple of weeks, that'll be . . .' He looked at the whiteboard he'd recently purchased in town, then scrawled out several columns of figures with a blue marker pen.

After a few corrections, interspersed with an abundance of swearing, he declared: 'Around 7,500, something like that. Maybe close enough to keep Hemen happy?'

'Hal, that's nearly a two-fold increase in what we're asking them to produce. And they'd be working every day . . .'

Hal took a pull of whisky, then wiped his lips on the shoulder of his t-shirt. 'Dude, we have no choice. I don't mind telling them, we'll announce a party or something at the end of the month, you know, to soften the blow or whatever.' He kicked at a cockroach that suddenly scuttled out from under the bed. 'Anyway, most of them are getting the hang of it, shouldn't take up more than eight or nine hours a day.' He looked at me and turned his palms to the ceiling, 'I mean, what the fuck else is there to do here?'

I shrugged. 'Okay, Hal, up to you.'

'Good, okay, now those were the numbers.' Hal took a long, long pull of whisky and gave a contented sigh. 'Now, here are *the* numbers.'

'More numbers?' I groaned. 'Really? Er, this is getting kind of boring, Hal.'

'Oh, this won't bore you, Ethan. So let's say we produce 11,500 Krapi-Krapis this month. That's around 14,000 bucks. A year of that's over $150,000, not bad for sure. But I want to run this by you . . .'

With that, he turned back to the whiteboard and hurriedly wiped it clean with an old rag. Then, for the next ten minutes or so, he jotted down more neat columns of figures, the occasional pull of whisky his only distraction. I smoked lazily as I watched him.

Finally, Hal emitted a low whistle. He put his hand to his head, clearly checking the workings for another couple of minutes, before whispering under his breath, 'Holy fuck.' He tapped the marker on his chin a few times, eventually nodding with satisfaction at his calculations. 'If we continue growing at this rate over time, say fifty new people a month, everyone carving ten flutes a day, seven days a week, and assuming twenty per cent of the people here leave in any given month, same workforce attrition as last year give or take . . .' He tapped the marker at the large blue numbers at the bottom of the whiteboard. 'That's a total revenue this year of $930,000. Fuck it, even with overheads, even if we don't get quite that many people coming in, we can bring in over three quarters of a million dollars here this year.'

I looked at the whiteboard for several minutes without speaking. I couldn't decipher how he'd arrived at the total, so in the end I just said: 'That's a lot of fucking money.'

But Hal wasn't listening any more. He was rubbing the whiteboard clean again, marker pen now wedged between his teeth. I got up and stretched.

'You off?' Hal mumbled, without bothering to remove the marker pen from his mouth.

'Yeah, I need to sweep out my hut, Lorna cut her hair in there this morning, would you believe?'

He grunted, then leaned down and picked up a single sheet of A4 paper from the bed. 'Here, before you go, take this.'

'What is it?' I asked.

'Updated P&L, dude.'

I took the page from him, rolled my eyes, and walked outside.

35

JUBBAWY

'It's interesting, you know,' I mutter. 'People can be pretty malleable.'

'Malleable?'

'Yeah. I guess because a lot of the inhabitants were new there, they kind of expected to be told what to do. Like if you're a guest in someone's house and they ask you to help with the washing up, you just get on and do it, right?'

'Washing up,' Jubbawy repeats slowly.

Ah, I think to myself. Of course. This high-caste Indian with his lofty police rank, he has people to do that sort of thing for him. He's probably never cleaned a plate in his life, I muse. 'Anyway,' I continue, 'no one really complained or anything, they just got on with it. And of course, anyone else who arrived after that, well, seventy flutes a week, that was the norm. Everyone else was doing it, so they just accepted it.'

'What sort of total volume of flutes are we talking here?' Jubbawy asks. The question is asked with genuine interest, I note.

'Towards the end, pretty big numbers. Nearly a 150,000 Krapis-Krapis a month.'

'There can't have been the demand for that many.'

I frown. 'What makes you say that?'

*

'30,000 flutes. That is what I am wanting, Mr Hal and Mr Ethan. 30,000 flutes by the end of February.'

We are sitting in the small, windowless office towards the rear of the low-rise concrete building that houses his shop. The last time I'd been inside, the room had contained little more than a desk and a few thick, yellowed purchase ledgers. Now it is transformed. Hemen is reclining in a plush leather armchair behind a vast mahogany desk, which is cluttered with telephones, a fax machine and piles of paperwork. An air-conditioning unit hums quietly in the background, wafting cool air over us. Behind Hemen's head is a giant Michelin map of the Indian subcontinent, dotted with hundreds of green pins.

He waves his hand behind him at the map. 'Look! I am badly needing more flutes—the whole country is wanting them since this damnable guidebook came out.'

'Do I really have to repeat myself?' Hal sighs, his voice weary. We'd been there nearly an hour already. 'We won't be far off. We're projecting 24,000 next month if another fifty people join us.' He taps his forefinger on the table to emphasize the point. '24,000, dude.'

Hemen drums his fingers on the desk, and a note of irritation has crept into his voice when he says: 'Don't be calling me "*dude*". And please be thinking more carefully about the consequences of your actions.'

'What consequences?' I ask.

Hemen folds his arms. 'Be thinking about it, my friends.' He picks up a Krapi-Krapi, casually examining it. Then he throws it on to the table with a clatter. 'This is being a piece of tat. It is cheap, tourist tat.' He glances disdainfully at the flute. 'I am accepting that the margin I am making on these things is most agreeable, *most* agreeable. But these things are not being that difficult to manufacture.'

'What are you saying?' Hal spits, half getting to his feet. 'Are you trying to say you're going to cut us out of the loop?'

Hemen holds up both hands, 'Not at all, not at all. Why would I? The price is fair, so I am having no strong reason to be changing supplier, with all of the inconvenience that is entailing, all of the potential disruption to the supply chain.' He pauses, then looks a little sadly at the Krapi-Krapi before him. 'But business is business, and if you cannot meet demand, I will, of course, have to consider looking elsewhere. How many times must

I be reminding you of the size of my family, the mouths I have to feed? If you cannot produce enough of these charming instruments, then that is, of course, creating a business issue for me.'

Hal starts to speak again, but Hemen puts a finger to his lips and says: 'I am giving you a chance, my friends. I assume you must be thinking I am simply sitting here all day, a parasitic middle-man, counting out the profit.' He smiles and adds, 'Well, I must admit that counting money is a most enjoyable activity for me, and certainly the last consignment of—' he looks down at one of the ledgers for a moment, leafing through the large pages, '11,612 instruments has made me a pretty penny. A very pretty penny, indeed. Yet you fell short of what I asked for, of course.' He looks at the ceiling for a moment and emits a long sigh. 'But perhaps I should be a little more open with you, my friends. You see, I am being rather more important to your success than you are perhaps very much understanding.' He bridges his fingers and looks at each of us intently.

'What do you mean?' Hal asks.

Hemen purses his lips. Then he reaches down below his desk, and withdraws an A4 Manila envelope. He slides it across to Hal. 'Open it,' he says. There is a slight edge to his voice I haven't heard before.

Hal opens the envelope. Inside is a picture. We both stare at it for a few moments—it is an image of an Indian man, lying spread-eagled in the street. At first glance, the eye is drawn to what looks like a red tilak, the smear of coloured paint that many Indian men wear as a religious mark, on his forehead. As I stare for a few more seconds, it becomes clear it is not. It is a neat, circular bullet-hole.

'What is this?' Hal asks hoarsely.

'You see, my friends,' Hemen continues, his eyes suddenly cold, 'these wonderful instruments are very easy to manufacture. Very easy to manufacture indeed. Unfortunately, in a country such as this, where counterfeiting is sadly so very commonplace, that creates a business issue for me.' He smiles weakly at each of us in turn, although it does nothing to soften his obsidian eyes. Then he waves a hand towards the photograph on his mahogany desk. 'As the gentleman in that picture would testify, were he still alive, I am most disliking of business issues. *Most* disliking.'

*

'We were pretty shocked,' I continue. 'I mean, someone had actually died because of our stupid carvings, you know?'

Jubbawy shrugs.

'Anyway,' I continue. 'It was then that I finally realized. It suddenly all made sense.'

'What made sense?'

'Our deal with Hemen—you know, the impossible targets, the money, how it had changed the commune, how *we'd* changed . . . and then someone getting killed. It suddenly occurred to me that we'd made a Faustian bargain.'

'A Faustian bargain,' Jubbawy repeats. Then he steeples his fingers and regards me. 'And will the devil carry *you* off to Hell, Mr Hicks?'

36

SHADOW-WALL, FEBRUARY 1988

'Hey, dude, do you want to join me a second?'

I looked over at Hal. He was sat under a large Himalayan cedar near the lake, an open notebook resting on his knees. One of the pages was covered in a series of calculations, the figures neatly set out into columns, with the occasional note scrawled in the margin. There was a book by his side, although I couldn't make out the title.

'What's up, Hal?' I said, slumping to the ground next to him.

'You think Hemen's target this month is impossible, right?'

I brushed an insect from my face. 'It looks that way. I just don't see how we can produce 30,000.' I paused. 'Maybe he's just looking for an excuse to dump us.'

Hal scratched at his neck. 'It sure is a big number,' he grunted.

'Yeah,' I agreed, craning my neck at his notebook, '30,000 is a *very* big number.'

He nodded. 'Yep. Actually, it's impossible for a cottage-industry like this. Only a properly equipped factory could hope to produce that number.'

'Right,' I agreed.

He picked up the book by his side and patted the cover with his hand. 'I've been reading this,' he said.

I looked at the red and white cover. It said, *Reengineering the Corporation: A Manifesto for Business Revolution.*

'Yeah,' Hal continued, 'only a proper factory could produce enough Krapi-Krapis each month, so that's what we need to transition to.'

'*Transition to?*' I laughed. 'What the fuck are you talking about?'

Hal's face was serious. 'We need to effect a paradigm shift, my friend. If we want to hit target, we need to reinvent this place.'

I raised an eyebrow at him, then shook my head. 'Shut up, Hal.'

'We cleared 12,000 bucks after overheads last month,' he continued. 'And we need to invest it. All of it.'

*

The crowd in the clearing grew quickly as word of our return from Kullu spread from hut to hut. As I parked up the jeep and trailer, I looked at the knot of people around us—they were mostly new faces, although I recognized a few people from the previous year. They were a younger bunch this time round, it seemed. Almost all were hippies or backpackers, marked as such primarily by their physical appearance—nose piercings, face studs, dreadlocked hair, tattooed limbs, henna-painted hands.

As Hal joined me and we began unloading the trailer, there were murmurs of interest as we hauled the chainsaws on to the ground by the fire. Then we unloaded the workbenches, and the lathes, then finally the circular saws and the cans of gasoline required to run them. A number of people came over and examined the new equipment, nodding appreciatively.

'My friends,' Hal called out to the inhabitants gathered around us once we had finished unloading. Instantly, a silence fell over the crowd. 'My friends, for some time now I've been thinking about ways we can improve Shadow-Wall, ways by which we can make your lives better.' He paused, scratching at the ground with his foot. 'Well, it's occurred to me that all of us would benefit from reducing the amount of time spent carving each day. I know it can be a little bit of a drag, and so I've made the decision to try and lighten this burden as much as possible.' He folded his arms, then nodded to himself again. 'So, my friends, before you on the ground are my gifts to you. Chainsaws to cut the bamboo, circular saws to cut it to size, and lathes to help fashion it.' He smiled, looking from face to face. 'I think you'll agree with me that our lives will *all* be a little bit easier from now on.'

*

And so Shadow-Wall started to morph into what amounted to a factory. It had to, simply in order to survive, but that was nothing more than a temporary stay of execution. From that point in time, the fate of the community we had built was sealed as surely as if we'd done nothing. It would never work because Shadow-Wall was becoming a paradox, a contradiction in terms—it was becoming a capitalist commune. Although we didn't know it then, our community was doomed.

37

JUBBAWY

'Weird, isn't it?'

'What's that?' Jubbawy asks.

'Eventually everything disintegrated because of greed.'

Jubbawy laughs.

'What?'

'I just find it remarkable how you perceive everything—you depersonalize it, transform it into something abstract. *You're* not responsible for the disintegration of the way of life in your commune, it is greed. You don't talk of individuals in your commune, you talk instead of a workforce. You seem to depersonalize *everything*, Mr Hicks.'

'Perhaps,' I nod. I pause and say hoarsely, 'Look, don't think for one moment that I consider myself divorced from what occurred, because I don't. But you must realize that there was a reason for everything I did, no matter how misguided that was! How was I to know that everything would fall apart? And *everything* fell apart, in the end . . .'

Jubbawy laces his fingers together in thought. 'Surely not everything, Mr Hicks. What about you and Lorna, for example? You didn't fall apart, did you?'

'Didn't we?' I gingerly run my finger over the bruising around my nose and say, 'I changed her . . . you don't understand what I'd turned her into by the end.' I can feel the slight smart of tears around the lids of my eyes. 'We would have fallen apart . . . we just didn't have the time.'

'You don't know that,' he offers.

'Don't you see?' I snap, annoyed by his glib, meaningless response. 'I corrupted her, for God's sake. She had this kind of caring innocence . . . I just tore that part of her personality out, replaced it with something else . . .'

Jubbawy says nothing.

'She knew, I suppose. She held me responsible for what happened to her.'

'Happened to her? In what sense?' Jubbawy asks.

'I suppose it is the innocent who provide the greatest scope for corruption,' I say quietly.

*

'It's so good to have you back,' I whisper to Lorna. Her head is resting on my lap as we sit on the plateau in the weak winter sun. She arches her back to look up at me.

'I'm sorry I was so long. There were a lot of things to take care of, and lots of people I needed to see.'

'Yeah, it's been too long,' I sigh, gently stroking her hair.

'Yes,' she says. I sense a note of reprimand in her voice as she continues: 'Actually, it all seems rather *different* to when I left. Shadow-Wall, I mean.'

I pause, then look south across the countless square miles of green forest that cling to the valley walls. It is silent save for a distant wail of a chainsaw somewhere to the east. 'Lorna, this year, it could change *everything*. It could secure our future?' I hadn't meant it as a question.

'I assume you are talking in financial terms.'

I pause, trying to figure out whether that is a rebuke. 'Look, you said yourself that your money was starting to run low. I'm the same. But this place . . .' I wave a hand down towards the commune. 'Lorna, it could actually set us up for life. Do you not see that?'

'Hmm.' Then she turns to face me. 'But is this what we really want, Ethan? When I first came here, all those many months ago, this place was an idyll. Over the summer, I genuinely saw a pride building in you for what you'd created. But now . . . this fixation on making money, doesn't it seem *wrong* to you? A *betrayal*, even?'

I consider my reply at some length, thinking about how I felt when Div had told me about Hal's fifteen years of hippie-living being bankrolled by some trust fund. 'But it will give us security,' I say eventually. 'A lot of security, actually. Isn't that important to you?'

Her cheeks flush slightly. 'But is it *right*, Ethan?'

I take her hands in mine, and look into her eyes. 'I don't know. I don't know. I am not sure it's wrong, though? I mean Hal's got a point.' I wave my hand towards the dozens of wooden huts in the clearing down below us. 'The people who come here, they come here for a reason, for an ideal. We can still give them that, Lorna. So I don't see that it's so wrong?'

She remains silent.

'Give it to the end of the year, Lorna. *Please*. Give it to the end of the year, then we can leave this place and start a life together elsewhere.'

Again Lorna says nothing, instead cupping her hand above her eyes and looking east towards the fast-rising sun. Eventually, she says: 'Okay, Ethan. I will do that for you. I will do that for you because I love you. I'll stay until the end of the year.' She turns to face me. 'But you need to make me a solemn promise that it will be no longer than that.'

'I promise,' I say, without hesitation. 'I promise.'

*

'People are malleable, like I say.'

'Lorna too, you mean?'

I say nothing. The question does not require affirmation, of course.

After a while Jubbawy, presumably realizing a response is not going to be forthcoming, asks: 'She knew what you were doing was wrong, didn't she?'

I nod.

'Did you think it was wrong?'

I look at him, and say truthfully, 'I'm really not sure. I suppose at the time I didn't think it was *wrong* to exploit our circumstances a little, to get something tangible from what we'd created. But . . .'

'But?' he prompts, as I lapse into silence.

'But I think we went a bit far, yeah. I mean the mechanization, the quotas, driving the inhabitants to produce more, stuff like that. We did go too far, and we lost sight of things, I guess.' Oh how we lost sight, I reflect.

'Do you feel a sense of guilt about that?'

He has no idea what guilt I feel. 'We did go too far, I do accept that,' I repeat with deliberate blandness.

38

SHADOW-WALL, MARCH 1988

We'd invested huge sums of money in the pursuit of more. The dozen Stihl chainsaws, the workbenches, the saws and other equipment. We spent a week felling trees and scrub around the path that led from Shadow-Wall up to the bamboo copses on the mountainside so that we could bring the jeep and trailer up there. As spring arrived, even more new arrivals came, but their first impression of our so-called idyll was the sight of Hal, me and other commune-dwellers hacking back budding rhododendrons and spruce trees to the scream of chainsaws.

Perhaps a little oddly, it remains one of my most vivid memories of Shadow-Wall. Throughout that spring, throughout the hot, hot summer that was to come, and for many months beyond, every morning the still calm of the commune was shattered by the eerie, stuttering high-pitched wail of the chainsaws; how the sound travelled through the valley. It was an alien sound, and it seemed to me to be some kind of metaphor for how things had changed. During the daytime, that sound was joined by a symphony of other noises; the whirring of circular saws, the hawing of the lathes, the brittle ping of bamboo on bamboo as another finished Krapi-Krapi was thrown on to one of the many piles that cluttered the glade. It was the heavy, mechanical sound of industry and it seemed to have no place in our mountainside commune.

However, the impact of the machinery was as immediate on our production as it was on the environment around us. And in a way, all of our lives improved. Previously, a flute might have taken an hour or so to complete from start to finish—yet soon enough most people were comfortably completing their daily quotas of ten flutes within five or six hours. So when Hal increased the targets to twelve flutes a day, nobody seemed to care that much.

*

'Twenty fucking per cent increase in production at the snap of my fingers,' he laughed, taking a pull on a bottle of Johnnie Walker Black Label. 'Do you know what the *value* of that is, dude?'

'No idea,' I replied. 'But they accepted it without question.'

'$7,000 a month,' he replied. He took another pull of the whisky, then held the bottle out to me. 'This stuff's much better,' he observed, 'much better.'

'Why?' I asked.

'No idea. Guess it's something to do with how long they distil it or whatever.'

'No, Hal, that's not what I mean. Why do they just roll over and take it when you increase the quotas to twelve per day?'

He looked at me and shrugged his shoulders. 'Dude, I don't understand these people. Really. I just don't understand them. It's fucked up, yeah?'

'Fucked up?'

'Well these people, these bums and hippies,' he said, shaking his head, 'they come here for some ideal, and now we've got them working for us like regular employees.' He held up his hand for a high-five. As I half-heartedly slapped his hand with mine, he laughed again, 'Fucking ironic. Go figure.'

I looked at him. How he had changed. His drive and determination was unsettling. But Hal had changed physically too. He had started to put on quite a bit of weight, his previously wiry frame now filling out around his torso, his face slightly puffy. The dark, tanned skin was pale from lack of exposure to the sun, and it was nothing to do with the winter we'd just endured; he spent most of the day in his hut, endlessly working through various figures—productivity, sales, overhead, margin, profit. His alcohol consumption had gone up too. That, and the extra insulation afforded by his bulk, presumably accounted for the heavy sweating that gave his pale face a constant sheen.

'You're drunk,' I said.

'I work better when I'm drunk,' he snapped back instantly. The irritation in his voice was clear.

'Sure you do, Hal,' I muttered. Then, to try and change the direction, 'We go to Kullu tomorrow then? What's the final number looking like being?'

'About 30,000, a little more. Just over target. It would've been more, too, if it wasn't for the manpower we expended on making the jeep trail up to the bamboo.'

I nodded, then got to my feet. 'Great job, Hal.' Then I turned and walked out into the spring sunshine.

39

JUBBAWY

'30,000 flutes,' I repeat. I light another cigarette. 'It was obscene, really.'

The policeman reclines back in his chair. He rests his chin on his balled fist, carefully studying my face. 'And you made how much money that month?' he asks, eventually.

'I don't know, $35,000 maybe? Me and Hal, when we got paid, we went a bit crazy. Bought quite a few things—a diesel generator, proper mattresses for the four of us to sleep on, even lighting for our huts. You know, we had the jeep and trailer by then, so we could bring up quite a lot of stuff.' I laugh, although the sound is hollow. 'Although we were fucking dumb sometimes.'

Jubbawy simply raises his eyebrows.

I put a hand in the air to apologize for the obscenity. 'So anyway, when we got back to the commune, Hal was all excited about setting up the lamps we'd bought, said it was straining his eyes when he did the accounts and stuff in poor light. Well, we started to run the generator, then realized we'd forgotten to buy extension leads and sockets to plug the lights into.' I shake my head. 'Quite funny, if you think about it.'

'Yes.' Jubbawy smiles, although it is clearly out of politeness, rather than reciprocated mirth.

I shrug and say nothing.

'$35,000 is certainly a great deal of money,' he ventures after a while.

I sigh. 'Well, by that stage, with the promise I'd made Lorna, the higher the better, as far as I was concerned, you know? I only had limited time to try and build up a decent amount of cash.' I pause, then continue, 'And it should have been so straightforward. It should have been so straightforward. We'd created the perfect business by then. We had a high-demand product, and we could produce it at virtually no cost. Nearly everything we made was pure margin.' I sigh, and add, 'but fate has to meddle, doesn't it?'

'How so?' the policeman prompts.

I sigh again. 'At the end March—well, early April, I guess—we delivered over 40,000 flutes to Hemen. But that's when the gods first started to turn against us.'

*

'Do you scoundrels really think you can be cheating me like this?' Hemen shouts. 'After all I have done for you?'

It is the first time we've been 'summoned' into Kullu by him, courtesy of an errand boy he sent to the commune. It will prove not to be the last. I have never seen him this angry before—spittle flies from his lips as he yells at us, his arms waving around his head as if he is trying to defend himself from a swarm of wasps.

'Calm down, dude,' Hal says. 'What are you talking about? We delivered more Krapi-Krapis than you asked for this month, yeah? So what's the problem?'

'What is being the problem?' he shrieks. 'What is being the problem? I will tell you what is being the problem.' With that, he reaches down by his desk, picks up a Krapi-Krapi, and flings it on to the table. 'That,' he says, his voice finally dropping in volume, 'is being the problem.'

I pick up the flute, and examine it. Hemen is still talking, but I am temporarily deafened by what I see. The carved bamboo is mottled with holes. In several of them, I can see a wriggling, white, translucent body. 'Jesus,' I mutter.

'So this is what we will be doing, my friends. You will be repaying me for the damaged stock I bought from you, and you will *without fail* be providing a double shipment next month. *Without fail.*' Hemen then claps his hands together, as if commanding a servant, and says, 'Now, come with me!'

*

'Termites. We lost tens of thousands of dollars because of some little bug, some little damned bug. And that was just the start of it.'

'The start of what?'

'I don't know. The start of a run of bad luck, maybe. The termites were just the beginning. Other stuff happened, albeit later in the year.'

'Well I don't wish to spoil your chronology, Mr Hicks,' he says, waving a hand as if to say 'continue'.

'So, after the dressing down he'd given us in his shop, Hemen took us outside. We followed him down these quiet back lanes behind his shop, and he led us to this old disused car park. Just cracked, broken concrete and street dogs picking at litter. And there, in the middle of this wasteland was the pile of termite-infested Krapi-Krapis which he'd dumped. Thousands upon thousands of them—it was metres high, you know? Then he just sloshed gasoline over the pile and lit it. The five of us just stood in silence and watched.'

'How very unfortunate,' Jubbawy says, his voice without any tone of feeling whatsoever.

'Well,' I shrug, 'it didn't end there.'

*

'I am hoping this will be a good lesson for you, my friends,' Hemen says as we watch the wooden flutes crack and flare in the flames that dance slightly in the late afternoon breeze; there is virtually no smoke, of course, just an intense heat that's so strong the five of us are forced to take a dozen steps back from the inferno. In the periphery of my vision, I see the street dogs scamper away in alarm.

'It's not like it's our fault,' Hal protests, shouting to be heard amidst a sudden crackling and popping of exploding wood. 'It's just one of those things.'

Hemen shakes his head. Also raising his voice to be heard, he says, 'Mr Hal, I find your constant excuse-making wearisome if I am speaking quite frankly, which I most certainly am.' He jabs his finger at Hal's chest and continues, 'Every month. Every month. Every month I have to chase and chase, push and push you to deliver what I need. Every. Single. Month.'

'And when have we not delivered?!' Hal protests. 'Sure, we've fallen a bit short on a couple of consignments, but nothing major!'

'Mr Hal, as a businessman I need to have partners of the utmost reliability. And, I'm sad to say, you have fallen short most grievously vis-à-vis my expectations this month.' He pauses, slowly shaking his head, 'So, my dearest friends, take this as your final warning. Let me be most crystal clear. The next time you fail to deliver the volume of flutes that I desire, our arrangement is over. Next month, you will deliver 80,000 flutes to me, and not one less.' He folds his arms, then spits towards the fire. 'If you deliver less, I shan't pay you a single penny. These stupid instruments are so very easily reproduced my friends, so very easily reproduced.'

*

'He was finally threatening to cut us out altogether.'

'I see.'

I shrug. 'I am not sure it came as a massive surprise to any of us, really. And we *had* screwed up that month.'

40

SHADOW-WALL, APRIL 1988

The four of us were very drunk. We sat in a row on the edge of Hal and Div's bed, silently passing a bottle of Black Label between us without speaking. On the floor, beneath our four pairs of dangling feet, was the sum total of our profits to date, a little over $40,000.

'There's something fucked up about refunding him,' Hal said after a while, still eyeing the depleted stacks of dollars and rupees.

'The Krapi-Krapis *were* ruined though,' I replied, 'it's not like he was lying about the termites.'

'And he did kind of make us what we are, I suppose,' Lorna added. 'I mean, he created all of this demand, god knows how.'

She was right, I mused. Hemen needed us, and we needed him. The little shopkeeper gave us the network and the demand for the flutes, while we supplied the product.

'Yeah, and without us *he'd* be nothing,' Hal spat. 'We invented the Krapi-Krapi, after all.'

'Yeah, but we did fuck up this month,' I said.

'Maybe we should just give up,' Div ventured.

'Well why did we buy all that insecticide to stop it happening again if we're going to throw in the towel?' I snapped back.

'And buying some sprayers and a few litres of pesticide is reason enough to *stay*?' Div challenged, her voice slightly slurred.

'We shouldn't have bought that generator,' Hal said. His voice sounded tired, strained. The words cracked slightly as he spoke.

'Yeah, well what about the jeep and the chainsaws and all the other stuff?' Div added. 'We spent way too much.'

Silence, except for a snap and a metallic scrape as Hal opened a fresh bottle of whisky.

'Anyway,' I sighed, 'there's no point us wallowing around in self-pity like this. Hemen wants 80,000 Krapi-Krapis this month. So what are we going to do?'

There was a long silence. It occurred to me then that the three of us were waiting for Hal to speak. Although nobody ever vocalized it, he had in fact become our leader.

I looked at him. His pale, sweat-streaked brow was creased in thought. He took a long, long pull on the bottle, then carefully screwed the lid back on. 'We need a town-hall,' he declared finally.

*

Hal's town-hall, as he dubbed it, was something of a disaster. Despite his stark warnings to the crowd that Shadow-Wall's very survival was at risk if we didn't deliver the 80,000 flutes the following month, nobody really got it. Of course they saw the piles and piles of Krapi-Krapis stacked at the edge of the clearing each month, but I do not think anyone truly grasped the inherent link between the industrial-scale outputs that were required and the commune's existence. For all the inhabitants of our commune could see, all that was needed each month for the place's survival was a few bags of rice and crates of tinned produce. Yet Hal was limited in what he could say, lest the artifice upon which Shadow-Wall had been sold to them might crumble. They weren't to know its survival was, in reality, underpinned by greed on a massive, massive scale.

In the end, there was a reluctant acquiescence, although it required considerable compromise on our part. We bought a multitude of additional tools and machinery, thus drastically cutting the waiting times to use the lathes and chainsaws—the inadequate amount of equipment we'd bought was one of the biggest complaints to come out of the town-hall. Lorna, Hal, Div and I also agreed to pitch in, joining the other commune-dwellers in the actual carving of the flutes. We even agreed to repurpose the generator, buying arc-lights that we ran off it to illuminate the clearing after dark, thus allowing people to carve into the night. And we made a solemn promise that the arduous targets that had to be hit by the end of April would never be repeated in months to come.

Still, many people complained, some were disgruntled enough to leave. Others failed to hit their target that month, either by design or because of their slow speed. Indeed, we were only saved by a continual steady flow of newcomers as the warmer weather came. And while these new arrivals must have felt surprise when they first arrived at our commune—surprise at the hum of industry from dawn until well after dusk, at the constant buzz of chainsaws, the pervasive smell of sawdust, the harsh illumination of the arc-lights—most ended up staying, bound perhaps by the fake ideology we had sold to them.

*

As the first light of the early May dawn filtered through the insect meshing on our window, I forced myself from the warmth of the bed I shared with Lorna, pulled on a pair of shorts and padded across the clearing to Hal and Div's hut. It was still cold outside in the early morning—a thin stratum of cloud laced the dark forest canopy, undisturbed by the gentle morning breeze. My toes, unprotected from the dew underfoot, were numb by the time I reached their hut. I shivered as I knocked cautiously on the door.

A minute passed. Then, a loud clank as the three deadlocks Hal had recently fitted slid back. His face appeared in the crack of the door. He rubbed his eyes, glancing briefly at his wristwatch. 'Bit early, dude.'

'There's a hell of a lot of flutes this month,' I shrugged. 'We need to get cracking.'

'Yeah,' he grunted, and disappeared into the darkness of his room. A minute later he returned, dressed in a pair of surfing shorts and a grubby yellow t-shirt.

We walked in silence to the edge of the clearing, where the flutes were stacked on to wooden pallets, lashed into place with a bright-green rope, the nylon already becoming frayed from use. The commune itself was perfectly silent—only two other people were up this early, their torsos poking out from the glassy surface of the lake; it was too far away to recognize their faces.

'I love this place when it's like this,' he said softly.

I looked around, grunting my assent. The sun had not yet fully cleared the dark horizon, but the mountains above us were already bathed in full sunlight, shimmering peaks of pink and gold. Away to the south, the valley that descended for thousands of feet below us was filled with mist. It looked as if you could just stride out on to the diaphanous white veil, across to the other side. The only sound was the fractious sound of water from the stream that fed our lake, and the occasional shrill call of a bird.

'It's changed though,' he commented thoughtfully.

I followed his gaze to edge of the clearing. Two dozen tall pyramids of flutes, each around two metres high, stood on their pedestal of sawdust. A waterproof plastic sheet, used to protect the chainsaws from the elements, crackled periodically in the morning breeze, and the jeep cast a vague, ugly shadow around our feet. Around us, all you could see were huts—they obscured everything. The forest and the rhododendrons that were flowering in a riot of colour may as well have not existed. A vague stench from the latrines hung in the air. Everything man-made here seemed wrong.

'Yeah,' I agreed through a yawn. Although summer would soon be on its way, this early in the morning my breath still condensed in front of my face as I spoke.

We reached the Mahindra. I wiped off a little dust that had accumulated in the vehicle's interior, then climbed in and turned the key, the plastic seat so cold that it made me gasp with surprise. The engine spluttered gently, then fired, shattering the silence. I revved the engine a couple of times, then reversed it so that the trailer was only a few feet from the nearest pallet.

'Ready to load?' I called, killing the engine and clambering out of the vehicle.

'Yep.' Hal bent down and grabbed one edge of the pallet. I took the other, and counted down from three. We hauled it on to the trailer with difficulty, then manhandled it to the far end.

We paused for a minute, catching our breath, not speaking.

'After three again . . .'

We dropped the second pallet into place, then pushed it until it sat flush against the first: two pyramids next to one another.

Hal leaned back against the jeep and lit a cigarette. Someone was walking up from the lake. 'Hey, you!' Hal called. 'Will you give us a hand?'

A wave, and we waited for the man to cover the fifty yards to the jeep, watching the clouds of our condensing breath slowly rise into the cool morning air. Across the valley, the mist was beginning to recede slightly—just the very tops of the trees were visible, like green islands in a motionless white sea. 'It really is quite a view, wouldn't you say?'

'Yes, it is, dude. Quite a view.'

We stood in silence, waiting for the man to reach us. Neither of us knew his name.

'Good morning,' I said, not sure whether to introduce myself. I had no idea how long he's been with us, so I decided against it.

He returned the greeting through chattering teeth. 'Hello, Ethan.' The accent was French.

'Will you help us get this pallet up?'

'Sure.'

The three of us lifted, and then flipped the third pallet over so that it nestled between the other two like a dog's tooth. A further pallet would go on top of the upturned base to make a stack of four, and the whole affair would then be lashed in place with ropes. In total the trailer would take one more such structure, a total of eight pallets—6,000 flutes. We'd need to make at least fourteen runs to Kullu—it would take us the best part of a week.

By late evening a few days later, we were richer by over $90,000. Hemen was appeased—for this month, at least. Hal and I celebrated with a bottle of Double Black Label at a bar near his shop.

'Cheers, dude,' Hal enthused, clattering his tumbler into mine. 'That was quite a month. Happy to see the back of April.'

I briefly returned his smile, then took a sip of whisky and looked around the bar, which was empty save for a table of Indian men who looked like they were having a drink after work. 'Cheers,' I muttered.

He screwed up his face. 'Something eating you?'

I shook my head. 'Nope, nothing eating me. It just seems a bit surreal—a couple of losers like us, and we're sat in a bar with a little under 100,000 bucks in a hold-all under the table.'

Hal let out an almighty laugh. 'Yeah, that's pretty fucking surreal,' he grinned. 'Pretty fucking surreal indeed, if you ask me.'

41

JUBBAWY

It got a lot more surreal than that, I think to myself.

'Mr Hicks?'

I look up. 'I'm sorry? I didn't catch that?'

Jubbawy frowns with impatience. 'I asked you if you wanted something to eat. You haven't eaten anything all day.'

'I am fine,' I say. But I am not fine, of course. My right hand still shakes in my lap, my empty stomach churns with dread, and the stitches on my face throb slightly in concert with the beating of my heart. But those are just outward, physical symptoms. They are of no consequence. What worries me is my head. It just doesn't feel quite right. It just doesn't feel quite right.

'Very well,' he says.

'We might have delivered to target that month, but it was a pretty close-run thing, you know? Every month we had to deliver, and every month became a struggle—demand just kept growing.' I emit an empty laugh. 'Hemen had even started exporting the Krapi-Krapis, you know? To Sri Lanka and Bangladesh.' I pinch the bridge of my nose between my fingers. 'I'm not sure I recall the exact number, I think he wanted 70,000 or something the following month. The 80,000 we'd just delivered, that was meant to be a double quota, two months' worth. So, it shows you the kind of growth we're talking about.'

'Indeed.'

'The only thing in our favour was that the commune was still growing daily.'

'How many people are we talking about?'

I think for a few moments. 'By May? 200, I guess? 220, perhaps?'

Jubbawy slowly lifts his hand to his face, placing a thumb on one temple, his forefinger on the other. After a considerable period of time, he says, 'Mr Hicks, we have recovered around 140 bodies now, including those of two children.' He slowly lowers his hand and looks into my eyes, 'How many more can we expect to find?'

'Well it's hard to be sure—' I start.

'Let me put it another way, then. How many people were there by the end, Mr Hicks?'

I pause, wondering what his reaction will be when I tell him. Then I say with a shrug, 'About 600, I guess.'

There is a clatter as the plastic folder he is holding falls to the floor.

I reach forward and pick up the packet of cigarettes. I take one out and light it. Then I drop my head and stare at my hands.

'Are you telling me,' he says, 'that all of these people . . . are they all *dead*?'

I take a drag. 'There were a lot of people there by the end, yeah.'

Jubbawy removes his glasses, and gently places them on the table. 'Mr Hicks, can I be very clear with you—this is absolutely not the time for exaggeration, nor fabrication for that matter? Do you understand that?'

I shrug. 'As I say . . . well, yeah, there were about 600 or so people there by the time . . . by the time the landslide hit. Yeah. About 600.' I give another shrug. 'Maybe 700, I guess. 750. Something like that.'

There is a long silence. Then he says very quietly, more to himself than to me, 'This is a disaster.'

I say nothing.

'So you are telling me we are going to find another . . .' he can barely say the number. '*What, another 600 bodies?*'

I say nothing, for the answer is already quite clear.

'Why didn't you tell me this before?' he demands.

'You never asked,' I reply simply.

'To be honest, Mr Hicks, given there were 127 bodies to deal with, my expectation was not that the number was going to be some kind of damned *fraction!*' He pauses, then looks at me; 'My god, didn't you think it might somehow be *relevant?*'

'I am sorry,' I mutter. 'This is all very stressful for me. I'm not really thinking straight.'

Jubbawy does not reply. Instead he gets up and leaves the room. He does not return for quite some time.

It is a welcome interlude for me. It gives me time to think, to get the positioning of things right, to evaluate what data I should provide to them, and what data I should omit. My account is a little like a house of cards, I reflect—it will only take one mistake, one slip, for everything to collapse. And we are slowly nearing the events of real importance. There are many weaknesses in the foundations upon which the artifice will need to be built. So much of what we did felt right at the time, of course. But what we did was wrong, I know that. And so there are a myriad of things I cannot tell my interviewer, and I must use this time productively. I must probe and test the account I intend to give. I must look for the inevitable weaknesses and errors, and correct them before Jubbawy returns.

I extinguish my cigarette and begin to think.

*

When Jubbawy re-enters the room with Inspector Shah, there is a notable change in his manner. There is a brusqueness now, an urgency. While it is a little unsettling, for the slow pace has suited me thus far, in a sense I welcome it. Because there is one element in all of this which is time-critical, and also completely beyond my control—and that is the autopsies. For when they come, it is surely over for me. I see no way out. But if I can somehow get to the end of my account, if they somehow keep buying into the concept that I am a victim in all of this, a lucky survivor, perhaps they will release me before any of the autopsies are complete; and then I can flee. It's a slender thread of hope, but I have little else to hang on to. I stare at the floor, trying to calm myself a little. It's moving, I note. The floor is undulating slightly, like its liquid.

'Let's proceed,' Jubbawy says tersely, returning to his chair.

'Sure,' I say. I take a sip of water, purposely using my steady left hand, and continue.

42

SHADOW-WALL, MAY 1988

I was lying with Lorna on the plateau, our heads over the edge of the hard stone, looking down at the forest canopy twenty metres below us. The heat of summer was beginning to seep into the valley; insects droned through the air around us, and the granite rock we lay on felt warm. Occasionally a branch would shake as a monkey leapt from tree to tree, and the sound of birdsong was all around us. Beyond and below the forest canopy, the commune was in full view, the clearing filled with miniature figures scurrying about their business. You could just make out a knot of activity where a clutch of new huts was being constructed—the wheeze of sawing and rhythmic reports of hammering shattered the silence.

'So full of people again,' she commented.

'It's been a really good month,' I agreed.

'It's come at a price, though,' she said slowly. 'This place, we've destroyed it.' She looked towards the decimated forest above us, then down at the clearing. 'The place has changed, Ethan.'

'Yeah,' I agreed, lighting a cigarette. 'It will grow back though.'

Lorna paused. 'And at what price for us, I wonder?'

'I hope none, Lorna.' I took a drag on the cigarette and added, 'look, I know you were never really comfortable with this, but it's nearly over. Just six more months or so and we can leave this place, start a new life. We'll have enough to set something up, a restaurant or something. We *need* the money, Lorna.'

'I know, I know,' she said softly. 'But I am glad this is coming to a close soon. It is time.'

I heard a rustling in the foliage behind us—the wind was picking up a little, and carried minute particles of dust that stung my face; a sign perhaps of the erosion on the hillside above us. 'I wonder what Hal and Div will do.'

'Who knows?' She looked west, to where the sun was lingering over the horizon, illuminating the snow-capped mountains with a pink and orange glow. Then she laughed and said, 'they will probably blow it all on drugs and alcohol.'

*

Another month passed. Lorna and I began spending increasing amounts of time up at the plateau; it was not the view that drew us there, I think, but rather an increasing isolation from commune life. We were, by that stage, decoupled from the day-to-day activities of the community. We didn't carve, nor help with menial tasks such as cooking or gathering fruit and firewood from the forest. Yet we were still somehow bound to stay at Shadow-Wall, and it left us listlessly waiting for the weeks and months to pass by. At one stage that summer, we had talked of taking a break from the commune, of trekking in another part of the Himalayas, or heading west to the Punjab for a while, but it seemed unfair to leave Hal and Div to manage things alone, and so we stayed.

It continued to grow, of course. Looking down upon Shadow-Wall from the plateau, it was easy enough to see. I could picture it like some time-lapse video—first, the density of huts increasing as more were crammed into the existing space in the clearing. Then, the point when the huts reached the ring of rhododendrons and cedars that encircled us. Finally, the felling of the trees and shrubs around us to make more space, the annexation of the very forest that had provided for us in so many ways.

Of course, that growth was accompanied by an ever-increasing output each month. And, in truth, that is why we stayed. It was the glue that bound us to Shadow-Wall. The money may have started as a trickle, but it soon enough became a stream, and then a river, and then a flood. It poured in each month, unimaginable sums.

*

'Here are your cigarettes, man,' Hal said, throwing me the carton of 200 Marlboro I'd requested.

'Are you okay? You look drunk.'

'I'm fine,' he said. He held up a half empty bottle of Johnnie Walker Green Label. 'Drink?'

'It's nine in the morning, Hal.'

He ignored me and took a swig. 'Hey, Lorna, I've something to show you guys!' he shouted as she walked past the open door to the hut. Her hair was wet from swimming, and had soaked the back of the white t-shirt she wore.

Lorna ducked into the hut. 'What is it, Hal?' She looked at the bottle of whisky and added, 'It's barely nine o'clock, Hal, isn't that a bit *early* to be drinking?'

'What's *with* you guys?' Hal moaned.

'Lorna's right, Hal,' I added. 'You should take better care of yourself. You're putting on tons of weight, you know?'

Hal looked down at his stomach, folds of fat clearly visible through the fabric of his t-shirt. He snorted, took another pull of whisky and said: 'Guys, I think we've all been kind of stressed recently with these targets going up so much each month. I reckon we all need to chill a little bit.' He slowly pulled himself up from the bed, and walked past us to a filing cabinet he'd recently bought in Kullu to store his accounts. I could smell the whisky on his breath as he passed. Then he slid open the bottom drawer, and pulled out an ornately carved teak box. 'So,' he continued, 'I've been shopping in town for us.' He walked back to the bed, placed the box on the mattress and opened it. Inside was an opium pipe, opium lamp and a large block of what was presumably the opium itself. 'Smoke, anyone?'

'Where did you get that from?' I asked, with genuine curiosity.

'Our shopkeeper friend,' Hal laughed, pinching off a small chunk of opium and starting to role it into a ball. 'Anyway, let's live a little. We've earned it.'

*

It was late June when the milestone came. It was an arbitrary milestone for sure, but one of some significance to us. I was sitting on Hal and Div's bed with Lorna, holding her hand as we smoked a little opium together. Hal was knelt on the floor, counting up the money from under the floorboards. He was also smoking, and drinking too. As I observed him, it seemed to me that everything he did was sequenced by his addictions—he'd start by counting the money, then take the opium pipe for half an hour, then start on the whisky, and then finally smoke a cigarette.

'It's been another good month,' he said, his voice dreamy.

'Yeah,' I nodded from the bed, feeling myself sinking deeper into his mattress. It felt softer than mine, and I briefly wondered if we'd somehow bought different brands in Kullu.

'Well, I'm done counting,' he declared, slumping back to the floor, the stacks of dollars and rupees all around him.

'How much?' Lorna breathed quietly, blowing a thin plume of smoke from between her lips.

'Well Termitegate was an unfortunate setback for sure,' he said with a shake of his head. 'But we've recovered it all, and then some.' He languidly waved an arm towards the pile of banknotes. 'If I've not miscounted, you're looking at a little over half-a-million US dollars in total.'

'Wow,' I exclaimed, taking the pipe from Lorna and wiping the mouthpiece clean.

'Yeah,' Hal nodded. He looked at the floorboards that were stacked vertically against the side of his hut. 'Actually, I think it might be time to buy a safe,' he said slowly.

43

JUBBAWY

'Half a million dollars,' Jubbawy repeats thoughtfully.

'Yeah.' I hang my head. Why did I tell him that? I'm just being glib, for Christ's sake.

'My god—' Jubbawy starts.

I don't say anything.

'My god.'

'Yes,' I concur after a time, filling the frosty silence that has fallen over the room. Neither of the policemen responds. I stare at my fingernails and wait.

'And where's all the money now?' he asks after a time.

I shrug. 'Up there, somewhere,' I lie, shaking my head. 'Under the mud, I suppose.'

The two policemen begin to converse. I take a match from the box, split the end with my teeth and use it to remove a little dirt that is embedded under one of my nails. It was indeed a lot of money, I reflect, too much to leave lying around really. God, how obsessed we became, especially Hal—he refused to leave the hut, even though it was hidden under the floorboards, behind the deadlocked doors. I can remember him sitting there on the floor, counting out the dollar bills like a kid with a piggy bank. He loved to count it, putting the banknotes into piles of the same denomination, flicking through each one with his finger, bundling them into $10,000 stacks. Then he'd just stare at the miniature green towers around him, stare for hours, before carefully placing them back in the hidden cavity.

'Mr Hicks, none of my team has come across any money at the site,' Inspector Shah states tonelessly. I note with surprise it is the first time I've heard him speak. His voice is thin, with a slight rasp.

I look at him and shrug. It seems like an odd thing to say—there is a lot more than money that they haven't come across, as Jubbawy very well knows. But the thought brings with it a wave of nausea.

Again, my two interviewers revert to Hindi. I wonder what they would think if I told them the truth, the true amount. They probably wouldn't believe me if I did.

Eventually, 'Your business was really rather successful, wasn't it?'

The question is rhetorical, but I answer nonetheless. 'It was just down to luck. Just happened, you know?'

'And now you have nothing, and everyone is dead.'

'Yes,' I nod slowly. 'Not really successful at all, if you think about it.'

'You must feel very bitter.'

'I don't really feel anything.' It's true—just emptiness.

'Half a million dollars,' Jubbawy repeats, pursing his lips.

'Does it matter?' I say. 'It's lost now.'

'We may find it,' interjects Inspector Shah. Then, 'Mightn't we?'

'I don't really care,' I reply. Then, after a pause, I say, 'Actually, I can tell you where some of it is, if you want.' I nod to myself. 'Not an inconsiderable sum, as it happens.'

44

SHADOW-WALL, JULY 1988

Evening was drawing near by the time we reached Kullu. A heavy mist clung to the town—caught by the late sun, it lent the town a strange orange hue. The townhouses that lined the main drag were barely discernible; only the pricks of light from the food vendors' hurricane lamps pierced the gloom. The thick, still air seemed to capture and hold the smells of cooking meat and fish in the cloying air.

'I'm hungry, dude,' Hal said as we parked up on the main drag and disembarked from the jeep. 'Why don't we find a restaurant and grab something to eat?'

'We're late already,' I responded. I looked at my watch, trying to make out the time in the half-light. 'He said six.'

'Not even time to fucking eat,' Hal spat. 'I don't know who he thinks he is. I mean sending his errand boy up to Shadow-Wall *again*?' He withdrew a crumpled letter from his jeans, and read with a sneer: '*Please be coming to my shop tomorrow at 6 p.m. Do not be being late.*' Hal shook his head. 'Don't be late? Like he's our fucking mother or something?'

'Well it can't be termites again,' I replied. 'The pesticide was a good idea of yours, Hal.'

He snorted. 'Well if we've not got time for dinner, let's grab some biscuits on the way. They sell Oreos in that mom and pop shop across the street.'

It took us a while to locate his store in the half-light. The shutters were down, and the building was shrouded in darkness. A sign hung on the wooden door. It said, simply, 'Shut'.

'Do you think he's here?' I asked.

Hal shrugged and knocked on the door. Perhaps, although there was no sound, we could sense movement inside—the two of us waited in silence for several minutes—yet neither of us bothered to knock again. Eventually, we heard the sound of bolts sliding back.

Hemen's errand-boy opened the door. He looked at us both in turn, then silently turned and walked inside, expecting us to follow. We did.

Inside, the store itself was unlit, the only illumination afforded by the orange glow from the doorway behind us. The large tiger carving was in the usual place; it seemed really quite grotesque in the amber light. At the far end of the room Hemen's office door was closed, but there was a thin stratum of yellow light at the base of the metal door.

The boy pointed to the room but said nothing.

Hal turned the handle and we entered. Hemen was seated behind his desk. However, he was not alone. Across the table sat a policeman, dressed in a light-khaki uniform. His shirt was stretched tight across an impressively large belly, and his head was large and bald. Thick rolls of fat meant the man had no discernible neck, head seeming to join shoulders directly. Obesity was not the only indicator of a prosperous existence—the stubby fingers on his hands were each adorned with large gold rings, some set with colourful stones.

'What the fuck is this?' Hal blurted. 'What the fuck? Police?'

'Welcome, my friends,' Hemen said, holding out both hands and pressing down on empty air to hush us. 'I would like you to meet Deputy Commissioner Saxena.'

The man acknowledged us merely by nodding his head at his lap. He did not look at us directly, nor did he speak.

Hal and I shuffled uncomfortably, both of us looking around for a chair. Hemen didn't seem to notice, and continued to speak as we stood.

'Deputy Commissioner Saxena is a highly, highly respected member of this community. Highly respected.' Hemen wrung his hands. 'He has overall responsibility for the policing of this entire state—he has many thousands of officers under his command.' He paused. The policeman said nothing, although he nodded, presumably in agreement with this description. Then Hemen looked at each of us in turn. If he registered the fear, the panic in our expressions, he didn't show it.

'Deputy Commissioner Saxena and I are close friends, as it happens. Very close friends. We grew up together in the same village, quite near to here, and went to the same school, would you believe?' He absently looked at the ceiling, as if trying to recall a memory. 'We were even in the same hockey team. Deputy Commissioner, I seem to remember our team remained unbeaten in 1954, unless I am very much mistaken indeed?'

The man grunted, then reached for the cup of black tea that sat before him on the table.

'How our paths have diverged since then,' Hemen continued with a sigh. 'Me, a humble shopkeeper struggling to make ends meet. Deputy Commissioner Saxena, one of the most esteemed and respected law enforcement officials in Northern India. It is peculiar how these things work out, don't you think?'

It was unclear for whom the question was intended. 'Yes, peculiar,' I said cautiously. The words came out as a rasp.

'Anyway,' Hemen continued, 'the Deputy Commissioner and I were catching up on old times a little earlier. He is a very clever man, much cleverer than I am.' Hemen studied the back of his hands. When he spoke next, his voice was a little slower. 'Take his memory, for example. Now, my esteemed friend is an extremely keen ornithologist. It is a great passion of his. Did you know he can name every species of bird indigenous to Himachal Pradesh? Can you believe that? He recited every single one to me this afternoon. My, it took so long we managed to finish four pots of tea, would you believe?'

Hal and I said nothing. My heart still thumped like a drum in my chest. Although the air-conditioned room was very cool, I could periodically feel beads of sweat streak down my face.

'And it's not just his memory that impressed me so greatly earlier this afternoon,' said Hemen, with a deferential nod of the head towards the policemen, 'Deputy Commissioner Saxena's knowledge of the criminal justice system in this country is most, most impressive. Yes, our conversation this afternoon was far-ranging, and certainly wasn't limited to his extensive avian knowledge—for example, I asked my friend what kind of prison sentence might be expected for an illegal immigrant who is prosecuted for running an unregistered business that employs overseas workers without work-permits, and which pays no tax whatsoever to the authorities.'

'Hold on a minute—' Hal started.

'It is a hypothetical question, of course,' Hemen interrupted, again shushing Hal with his hands. 'The Deputy Commissioner explained to me that I was describing a series of different criminal offences, each of which would be accompanied by a monetary fine and a period of incarceration. In isolation, perhaps such punishments may not seem so onerous. However, cumulatively, they are not insubstantial, I must say.'

'How could you?' Hal spat. 'After all we've done for you? This is how you repay us? By stabbing us in the fucking back?'

Hemen's face fell. Slowly, he put one hand to his chest. 'Mr Hal, your words wound me more than you think. But I still believe we have a very wonderful friendship, very wonderful indeed, even if you speak such things of me. I am sure it is the heat, today was unseasonably warm, even my wife commented the same a little earlier.'

'Twelve to fifteen years, and a fine of somewhere around twenty lakh.' It was the first time the policeman had spoken. The words were vocalized more as a wheeze than speech. He visibly needed to catch his breath after speaking.

'You see,' Hemen exclaimed happily, with a clap of his hands. 'Like I said, Deputy Commissioner Saxena is a very clever man indeed. Oh dear me, yes he is.' Hemen beamed at us.

Hal put a hand to his face and pinched the bridge of his nose. I just stared at the policeman.

'Now, of course the Deputy Commissioner runs a very tight ship, my friends. Oh yes, he is most intolerant of any impropriety taking place under his nose—most intolerant. Imagine, my friends, his very great consternation were he to learn of an illegal business, filled with illegal workers, on his very doorstep?' He shook his head slowly, then frowned. 'My friends, that would be a discovery with most serious implications, most serious.'

Hal's hand remained in place, his thumb and forefinger pressing on his nose. 'And?' he asked, simply. 'What are you asking from us?'

'Ah,' Hemen breathed. 'You young western people are so very direct, are you not? So very direct. No matter.' He paused, took a handkerchief from his pocket, and dabbed carefully at the corners of his mouth. 'Yes, let us think about the answer to that question. Well, the Deputy Commissioner is currently the very proud owner of a Toyota Landcruiser. Shall we consider the merits of that vehicle?'

'Yes, let's,' said Hal, a tone of annoyance creeping into his voice. Like me, he clearly sensed there was perhaps no foundation to the terror we had just endured. The policeman was merely a prop—although admittedly a very effective one—to increase the potency of the threat.

'A very fine vehicle, in my humble opinion,' Hemen continued. 'Reliable, relatively cheap to maintain, and of course it benefits from four-wheel drive—it is a car that is perhaps number one in its class for off-road driving.' Hemen paused. 'Now, I do not want to be so presumptuous as to maintain that I have any knowledge of the Deputy Commissioner's plans for this coming weekend. He may wish to simply relax with his family, or perhaps do a little shopping here in Kullu. But it strikes me that with such a robust and versatile vehicle, if he were to indulge in his passion for ornithology, he may choose to do so in the more remote areas of the state, perhaps even the rather inaccessible hills to the east of here.' Hemen looked at us with a grimace. 'But, my friends, let me ask you this: How very sad and upset would Deputy Commissioner Saxena be if his binoculars were to settle not on the buff-crested bustard, which I believe is a particular favourite of his, but on a species not indigenous to the country of India, a species that really didn't belong here at all?'

'That would be upsetting,' Hal said, his voice resigned now.

Hemen smiled. 'I am so glad you agree, my friends. So very, very glad.' He clapped his hands together in delight. 'Now, let us think this through a little more. If I may, can I ask you, Mr Hal and Mr Ethan, if you are familiar with the Mercedes 560 SEL?'

'It sounds expensive,' Hal said slowly.

'Oh, I am not thinking of the price, Mr Hal. You see, unless I am very much mistaken indeed, this is a vehicle that has not been designed for use on anything other than a very well-maintained highway. So you see, were Deputy Commissioner Saxena to change his automobile thus, there are certain areas around here where we can be very, very sure, *very sure indeed*, that he will not travel to when engaging in his ornithological pursuits.'

Hal stroked his chin but remained silent.

I said, 'So how much is one of those, then?'

*

'$200,000?!' Div yelled. 'Two hundred fucking thousand dollars?!'

'Hey, calm down,' Hal retorted. 'What did you expect us to say?'

'But that's nearly half of all our cash!'

'Yeah, I'm sorry,' Hal snapped. 'You're right. Let me just head back into town, hold my wrists out for him to handcuff, and then spend the next decade of my already rather pathetic little life in some Indian jail.' He kicked at a half-eaten pack of Oreos on the floor of his room. It slid across to the far wall, biscuits spilling out on the way.

'We'll get ants,' Div said.

'Jesus Christ!' Hal yelled. 'Ants! You're worried about fucking ants? A $200,000 bribe, and you're worried about fucking ants!'

45

JUBBAWY

There is a long pause. Then Jubbawy says slowly, 'The officer, you said his name was Deputy Commissioner Saxena. Are you *absolutely* sure that was who you met that night?'

I nod my head.

Jubbawy scribbles something on a notepad, and tears the page off with a slight shake of his head. He hands the note to Inspector Shah. 'Bring him in,' he says simply.

I sit across the table from Jubbawy. Neither of us speak for some time.

'You paid?'

'Of course we paid. We had no choice.' I pause, then add, 'It was a big, big blow, for sure. But in a way, it lanced a boil that had been nagging away at us. I mean, we were constantly anxious about getting caught, the place was just getting too big, too many people knew about it. We all worried that the day would come when we were discovered by the authorities. It was remote, yeah, but hell, it just needed a shepherd or a group of trekkers to wander past and the lid would have come off, so to speak.'

'$200,000,' Jubbawy repeats thoughtfully.

I say nothing, but the way he says the amount makes me wonder how much he gets paid.

'A big number,' I concur after a time, filling the silence that has fallen over the room. I stare at my fingernails. 'And therefore, a big setback.'

'Indeed.'

'Anyway,' I continue, 'the four of us, we started to feel a bit like Sisyphus, you know, the one who carried the boulder up the hill only for it to roll back down to the bottom again? Every time we got somewhere, started to make serious money, there was some kind of massive setback. It was like we were cursed. Do you believe in that stuff, in curses?'

'As I said before,' he responds slowly, 'what I believe or don't believe is of no importance.'

'Right . . .' I shake my head slowly. 'Well, I don't know what to believe, how to explain it. Whether it was God or a curse or fate or sheer damned bad luck.' Those unexpected losses still haunt me now, I reflect. Without them we'd have had enough to leave that place after the summer, to walk away from Hemen and his unfair demands that were backstopped by an equally iniquitous ultimatum. Instead we remained tied to Shadow-Wall, condemned to a path of doing whatever it took to slake Hemen's thirst for ever-greater numbers each month.

'Perhaps it was karma,' Jubbawy offers after a time.

I look at him. 'Perhaps it was,' I mutter. 'Anyway, I think we all started feeling the pressure, you know?'

'Pressure?'

'We had to meet these increasingly impossible targets each month, or it was the end—we'd leave with next to nothing. The bribe, the termites, the money we'd spent on machinery, it added up to an awful lot. So yeah, I guess we all felt this growing pressure to deliver a run of at least three, maybe even four or five, months to make a decent pile of cash to leave with. Otherwise those two years at Shadow-Wall would have been for virtually nothing, maybe 50,000 bucks each or something.' I shrug. 'We could have earned that much flipping burgers at McDonald's.'

The policeman snorts. 'And as for meeting targets that were, as you say, impossible to hit—how did you resolve that particular challenge, Mr Hicks?'

I pause, thinking for a moment, then decide to ignore the question. 'It was tough. The monsoon arrived, you see.'

46

SHADOW-WALL, JULY 1988

'Fucking rain,' Hal observed.

'Yeah,' Div said from the wicker armchair she'd recently bought. 'Fucking rain.'

We couldn't see it, because the door to Hal's hut was closed. But we could hear it beating down on the roof, endlessly. And it did seem truly endless—it had rained heavily, without pause, for three days now. The summer monsoon had arrived.

'It's killing our production too,' Hal nodded, slamming shut the accounts ledger he'd been working on.

'At least the jeep's going to be fixed soon,' I added.

The past week had certainly presented its share of problems. It had started with a minor landslide on the hillside above us—without the protection of the bamboo that we'd harvested, the slopes were exposed to the torrential rain that was carried up on the humid south-west winds. Discoloured streams had begun to slice through the mud, carving deep channels that exposed the dying roots of the bamboo. A huge slab of topsoil had become dislodged following a particularly heavy downpour and slid a hundred metres or so down towards Shadow-Wall. Then the jeep's engine had given up as Hal tried to drive up the trail—despite the four-wheel drive, the Mahindra's wheels had got snared in the heavy mud.

He'd revved it too hard in an effort to free the vehicle, the engine dying suddenly with a loud bang and the sound of metal scraping on metal from under the bonnet. Now we were waiting for several replacement parts to be sent to Kullu from Mumbai.

'Yeah, well if we don't hit target this month, the jeep's kind of moot, Ethan. And right now, it's sure looking like we're going to fall short. The problem is, the population's not growing any more.'

'Well then, let's hope the weather improves soon,' Div commented, scraping at a little mascara that had flaked from her lashes.

'You don't understand,' Hal spat. He paced over to the whiteboard that was nailed to the bamboo wall of his hut, and used an old rag to vigorously wipe off some figures and charts that he'd been working on. 'Look, Div,' he half-shouted, drawing a chart with a single black line shooting upwards, exponentially. 'This is the growth in the required output—going up, right?' He grabbed another marker pen, then drew a thick red line, declining. 'And this is the population of Shadow-Wall.' He threw the marker to the floor and kicked it away into the corner of the room. 'To hit target, we *have* to have population growth. Or the existing population *has* to produce more. It's that simple.'

'It's just the weather,' Div repeated.

'We're not going to hit target!' he yelled. 'Don't you understand? Hey, Ethan, are you listening to me, dude?'

I looked up from the book I was reading. 'Yeah I'm listening, Hal.' I looked at the whiteboard for a few moments, then added: 'To be honest, your decision to increase targets again last week wasn't the most popular.' I paused, then gave a shrug. 'A lot of people left when you brought in the fourteen-a-day rule.'

He clicked his tongue. 'Yeah. Well, we didn't have a choice, man. Didn't have a choice. We're well behind this month.'

'Whatever,' I replied, returning my attention to my book. 'I'm just saying it hasn't made you very popular, that's all.'

'I'm not here to be *popular*,' Hal retorted. 'I'm here to make money.'

47

JUBBAWY

'It's easier for a camel to pass through the eye of a needle than for a rich man to enter the kingdom of heaven . . .' I mutter, staring at the floor. It's still fucking moving, I think to myself.

'I'm sorry?'

'I like the saying,' I reply, steeling myself against the wave of nausea currently washing over me. 'It's apt.'

'Apt?'

'Greed. No one's immune.'

'Is that so?' It's a rebuttal, not a question. I ignore it and go to continue, but then there is a knock at the door. The sudden, alien sound makes me start. Jubbawy barks a command in Hindi, and the door opens. A policeman walks in, his uniform similar in design to my interviewer's. He salutes Jubbawy, then walks to the table and places down a thick red folder. He salutes once more, turns on his heel and leaves without speaking.

'Go on,' Jubbawy says with a wave of his hand. He does not look at me. Rather, he opens the file before him.

'Well Hal just didn't see it,' I say slowly, staring at the folder. 'People were fed up. We were very, very far removed from being a commune by that stage. It was a factory by then, and our inhabitants were not the sort of people who wanted to work in a factory. I mean most of them were hippies or whatever, you know? We weren't even paying them or anything.' I shrug. 'So no wonder they started to leave. We were absolutely haemorrhaging people during the monsoon, they were leaving much faster than we could replace them. We had to do something more. The question, of course, became what.'

*

We are sitting in Hal and Div's hut. Lorna is perched on the edge of the bed, I am slumped in the wicker chair, and Div is sitting cross-legged on the floor as Hal paces the room. The exchanged glances between us betray our shared sense of dismay. For the first time, many of the huts are empty. The whiteboard shows headcount is declining even more sharply.

'We're fucked,' Hal declares. He is smoking a cigarette, dragging on it every couple of seconds.

'I have an idea,' Lorna says, as she cleans the bowl of the opium pipe with a cotton bud. 'Why don't we pay them for each Krapi-Krapi they make?'

I sit up. 'Yes, why not? That will stop the attrition, and if we pay them . . . Well who knows, they might produce fifteen or twenty flutes a day or something? We could pay them, what, like a dollar a flute?'

'Yeah,' Div says dreamily, taking the pipe from Lorna. 'That would be fourteen bucks a day minimum, it will certainly appeal to them. Means they can earn a bit of extra money for travelling.'

'Pay them *a dollar a flute*?' Hal spits, the incredulity in his voice palpable. 'Are you guys fucking stupid? We only get a little more than a dollar a flute, you idiots. The only reason we make a profit on them is because there are no labour costs!'

'Sixty cents?' I offer.

'Jesus,' he hisses. 'What are you going to suggest next? That we throw in fucking healthcare, ten days annual leave and a pension plan?'

'I'm just trying to help, Hal.'

'We're not halving our fucking margin, dude.'

We relapse into brooding silence. Hal continues to pace the room.

'We have no choice,' Lorna says eventually. 'We need to do something to stop them leaving.'

*

'So you started remunerating them for their work?' Jubbawy asks.

I stare at the ashtray. Now I must begin a significant deviation from the truth. How honest and uncompromising I have been, I reflect, for I have not lied much up until now. I have told this policeman about the death of Scott through my incompetence, the drugs, the expired visas, the bribes. I have been like the castaway who throws scraps of food overboard in the hope that it somehow sates the circling sharks. And it will, most likely, prove to be a futile exercise. But now I have no choice except to lie.

'Yes,' I say, still staring at the ashtray. 'In the end we managed to convince Hal.'

I look briefly at Jubbawy to see his reaction to the fabrication, but he is still perusing the red file. He says nothing. I look back at the ashtray. The brown cigarette butts seem to be moving, as if agitated by an inaudible vibration. How very odd, I think to myself. I look away at the wall for a moment, then back to the ashtray. But still they move. I repeat the experiment three or four more times; the result is the same, however.

'Mr Hicks? Mr Hicks?'

His voice is raised, and I realize he must have been talking to me for several seconds.

'Sorry, what was that?' I ask.

'I just wondered if everything is okay, Mr Hicks. You are shaking.'

'Yes,' I manage, squeezing the bridge of my nose with my fingers. I have a splitting pain around my temples, and a strange noise in my ears, like the sound of gushing water. Odd. I hadn't noticed it before. 'Can you hear that?' I ask, suddenly.

'Hear what?'

'A noise, a kind of whooshing noise?'

Jubbawy tilts his head to one side, listening intently.

'No. Perhaps it is the air-conditioning?'

'Yes, that's probably it.'

'Why don't you have some water?'

'Yes, I think I will. Thanks.'

As I take a sip, Jubbawy says cautiously, 'Would like you to see a doctor?'

'Actually, I'd rather press on if it's all the same.'

'Well, shall we take a break?'

'No, really. I feel better after that,' I add, nodding at the glass of water. The whooshing isn't the air-conditioning, I think to myself. Surely they can hear it? From water pipes under the floor, perhaps.

'Are you sure?'

'I'm fine. Really. I'd just rather get this over and done with.'

'Over and done with,' he repeats thoughtfully. 'Yes, of course.' Something in his demeanour worries me, though.

'If I may?' I ask.

Jubbawy spreads his hands.

'Er . . . sorry—where was I?'

'You were talking about Hal agreeing to the remuneration of the inhabitants of Shadow-Wall. But allow me a brief digression, for I would like to ask you something, if I may?'

'Sure,' I say. I can feel the blood draining from my face as I speak.

Jubbawy nods slowly to himself, then refers once again to the red folder before him. After a pause, he slowly raises his eyes to meet mine. He is frowning. 'These are the initial autopsy reports. The first one is for the subject Jane Doe, as the Americans would have it. She carried no identification.'

I say nothing.

'Let me share this with you.' He carefully opens the folder, and withdraws a black and white photograph. He slides it slowly, purposefully, across the desk. As he does so, his eyes remain fixed on me.

When I look down, my only reaction to the image is to recoil, even though I don't recognize her. For some reason I was expecting the picture would be from the autopsy, a sanitized photograph from a mortuary slab where the victim has been cleaned and made presentable to the lens. But that is not the case. It was taken on the hillside. Only the upper half of the woman's torso is visible, the rest of her body is submerged in mud. To the side stand two Indian men, possibly paramedics, holding spades. Despite a slight blurring of the image, there is a lot of detail to her face, but it is her mouth that draws the attention of the eye. It is open, and filled with mud, and also some foliage. Leaves and twigs protrude from between her lips. Her eyes are open, but mostly caked in mud. Her hair is also matted with mud and twigs and leaves.

'Perhaps you know her?' Jubbawy offers eventually.

'I don't recall her, no,' I say. 'That's horrible,' I add, meaning it.

'Indeed.' He pauses, then withdraws a single sheet of white paper and places it on the table in front of him. There is a circular red stamp in the top right-hand corner. Below it, lines of type. 'Now, an analysis of the victim's blood revealed the following: Amytal, a barbiturate; Secobarbital, a barbiturate; Valium, a benzodiazepine.' He pauses, and frowns. 'Then we seem to have something of a laundry list of amphetamines—Dexedrine, Ritalin and MDMA.' Jubbawy removes his glasses and looks up from the embossed sheet of paper. 'Why is that?' he asks simply.

I remain silent. The blood is pumping so hard through my temples that I am unable to work out whether this is simply some kind of trick that Jubbawy is playing, or whether this is the end for me.

'Mr Hicks? Would you care to explain how it is that this woman had *six* different restricted drugs in her bloodstream? *Six*?'

It was always the case that this single thread would be enough to unravel the entire cloak of deceit. I look at the strip-light above my head, grasping for an answer, but the bright light stabs the back of my eyes, causing colourful imprints to dance before me each time it flickers. I can make some of them out, crimson and black kaleidoscopes, rotating slowly like a whirlpool; thin spindly black lines, like elongated fingers.

'Mr Hicks?'

I try to focus, and attempt to steady my breathing. With some effort, I manage: 'Look, I don't know what she took, what the others took, we couldn't control what people did there. We had a lot of travellers and hippies there, I suppose many of them did drugs. That wasn't really our concern, you know?'

'I see,' Jubbawy replies, but he doesn't sound particularly interested. Indeed, his countenance suggests mild boredom.

'We paid them seventy cents a flute in the end,' I offer, trying to change the direction of the conversation, and hoping that somehow by speaking I can camouflage my fear.

'Seventy cents,' he says slowly.

'Seventy cents,' I repeat. The words are becoming more difficult to form in my mind. We have been sitting here for hours, I reflect. My breathing feels shallow and rapid, and my mouth is dry from the extra air drawn through it.

Jubbawy says nothing. He looks at me differently now, I think to myself. There is more intensity to his eyes. It is, perhaps, how the cheated wife watches her husband in the company of other women. The policeman no longer trusts me. And it is tangible in his demeanour. From time to time he leafs through the file on the desk. I sit there, listening intently. Then that sound again. Whoosh, whoosh. Whoosh, whoosh.

I wait in vain for what must be several minutes, expecting a prompt or a probe from the policeman. When neither is forthcoming, I take a cigarette from the packet. There are now only three cigarettes that remain in the pack. When I go to light it, I see there are four matches left as well. Four matches for four cigarettes. It is as if by design, but it is nothing more than chance. What strange circumstances chance creates, I think to myself. How very odd that a simple encounter with a couple of bums in Delhi could have taken me on so strange a journey.

'Seventy cents,' I repeat, desperately wishing this silence away. I light the cigarette, forced to use my shaking right hand. Jubbawy stares at it as I hold the flaring match to its tip. I take a drag on the cigarette. Jubbawy sits there like a statue, saying nothing. Perhaps he senses the importance of events at this point. And if he does, he is very shrewd indeed. Because what happened next provides the causality that I imagine he is searching for. It provides a hook on which he can hang the blame. Perhaps he thinks the silence will somehow lead me to condemn myself through words. He may be right. I need to talk, to overcome this damned silence, to silence this strange 'whoosh, whoosh' sound deep within my head.

'We were really messed up by then,' I say, grasping at simple and inconsequential facts that I can articulate. 'Lorna as well; we were taking a lot of opium,' I add. 'It was all my fault. Like I wasn't satisfied with corrupting her morally. I had to corrupt her physically as well.' I shake my head and say: 'She'd told me she'd been a junkie once before, but there I was, taking all that shit with her in Shadow-Wall . . . what kind of a person does that make me?'

The words hang. Jubbawy clicks his tongue softly in thought. 'Yes,' he replies slowly. 'What kind of a person *does* that make you?'

I say nothing. I can feel the sting of tears in my eyes.

'Have some water if you are becoming upset,' he states flatly.

I wipe the tears away with my trembling hand. 'Yes, thank you,' I speak the words softly, yet they seem to ricochet off the bare walls.

Jubbawy's gaze is unflinching.

'I completely corrupted her,' I mutter, more to myself than to the policeman.

He shrugs to say he doesn't care.

I can feel myself flush, the stitches on my face tingling. 'It's important to me,' I sob. 'I really don't get why you are treating me like this.' I wave a hand at my smashed face. 'I am tired. I am *so* fucking tired. And my head fucking hurts.' I fold my arms. 'It's not fair,' I wail. 'I was caught in a fucking landslide and you see fit to treat me like *this*?'

Jubbawy stares at me for several seconds, studying my eyes. 'You are a liar,' he says.

I look up, disconcerted by the comment. 'I'm sorry?'

'You are a liar.'

'It's the truth.' I breathe deeply, for I seem unable to draw enough air in to sate my lungs. When I speak next it is a rasp, 'It is the truth.'

Jubbawy smiles, but it is a knowing smile. He doesn't break the silence that follows for several minutes, instead perusing the file once more, this time carelessly, as if he is familiar with its content. I light another cigarette with the half-smoked stub of my last, although it is not for want of nicotine. As I do so, I realize that the number of matches will no longer equal the number of cigarettes. Strangely, the thought fills me with a deep despair.

Eventually Jubbawy sets the red file down with careful precision, so it sits flush against the corner of the table. He absently taps his pen against his knuckles. 'We also have your medical report from the hospital, Mr Hicks. And to be honest, I find its contents rather puzzling. You see, according to the doctor who examined you, your injuries are inconsistent with those one might expect to sustain from a landslide.' He pauses, perhaps for effect. 'You broke two ribs, received several facial lacerations, incurred a little internal bruising . . . unpleasant injuries, yes, but in the circumstances, also rather odd. You see, if one compares the disposition of the other fatalities' injuries with your own, some quite remarkable differences become apparent.'

My heart is beating fast now, and I am conscious that I am dragging so frequently on my cigarette that its smouldering tip is almost half an inch in length.

'Let me elucidate.' He speaks sharply, reading from the file: 'Their bodies are covered in hundreds of scratches and abrasions. Their clothes are torn. The bruising to their bodies is extensive, not localized. The majority have broken arms and legs, because the extremities are more prone to be twisted and snapped in such a traumatic event.' He pauses again, then slaps the file shut. 'They have mud in their ears, in their eyes, in their noses, under their fingernails and in their mouths.' Jubbawy looks at me levelly. 'Can you offer an explanation as to why there was no mud under *your* fingernails, Mr Hicks?'

I can feel that the blood has drained completely from my face. I take a deep inhalation on the cigarette, and say hoarsely, 'As I said earlier, it's all a blur. I really can't remember a thing.'

'I see. Let me ask you this, then. Why are the seven bruises on and around your ribcage all identical in shape, then? Doesn't that seem a *little odd* to you?'

I automatically put my hand to my chest, then pull it away. 'I've told you already, I don't remember anything!'

'This assessment says that your injuries were inconsistent with those that would have been sustained due to the landslide. Why was there no mud in your hair, Mr Hicks?'

I say nothing. I stare, instead, at my trembling hand.

'Why were your clothes clean, Mr Hicks?'

Again, I say nothing.

Jubbawy slaps his hand on the table in rhythm to the words: 'Why was there no mud from the landslide on you, Mr Hicks?'

'I—am—a—victim! I come here to help, and you accuse me of lying!'

'Accuse you of lying? Well if you're telling the truth, Mr Hicks, I can only assume that as you lay barely conscious on a dirt track in the middle of nowhere, you somehow found the means to take a shower and launder your clothes. Is that what you're suggesting happened?'

'I want to leave. I'm not helping you any more.' I get to my feet and angrily push the chair away from me, 'I want to go now.'

'Sit down,' Jubbawy snaps.

'No. I want to go. Let me go—'

'Sit down,' he repeats. Then, more softly, 'Just sit down.'

I regard him for several seconds before wandering slowly over to the chair, as if the protraction is some kind of rebellious protest. Then I pick it up and return equally slowly to the table. 'This is unfair.'

'I'm going to ask you again what happened, and I want you to think very carefully about your answer.' He pauses and smiles slightly at me. 'The truth, this time.'

'It's like I said. I have nothing to add.'

He pauses, then refers again to the file before him. 'Well then, shall we look at another autopsy report, Mr Hicks? I find the results of great interest.' Another thin smile. 'Perhaps you will too?'

'What?' is all I say. Short sentences are easier, I reflect—they hide the quiver in my voice.

'Well, seven of the autopsies are now complete.' He shuffles the folder slightly, then looks at me over the top of his glasses. 'You see, we are rather spoilt for choice when it comes to corpses.'

I say nothing.

'This perplexes me, as it happens, so perhaps you can help me to understand. The second body we autopsied . . .' He looks at his notes. 'This time an unnamed male, estimated age eighteen to twenty years, height 172 centimetres.' Jubbawy looks up. 'Tests showed exactly the same combination of narcotics in his blood as the first autopsy. If you care to remember, that would be Dexedrine, Amytal, Secobarbital, Valium, MDMA and Ritalin.'

I remain silent. It amplifies the noise of the blood pounding through my temples.

'Would you care to help me understand how that could be?' Jubbawy asks.

'I don't know, like I said before, I guess drug-taking was pretty endemic—'

'And what I find odd is that the same narcotics were found in the autopsy of the third victim.' Again, he slaps his hand softly on the table in rhythm to the words as he continues: 'And the fourth. And the fifth.

And the sixth. And the seventh. All of them, Mr Hicks. *Every single one.*' He removes his glasses, then leans forward slightly to regard me. 'Seven autopsies, Mr Hicks. And the same result—for *every single one*. Dexedrine, Amytal, Secobarbital, Valium, MDMA and Ritalin.'

It was inevitable this would come to light. I can feel streaks of perspiration rolling down my head. I don't wipe my face as I don't wish to draw attention to the fact that I am sweating, although it can hardly escape his notice. What more can I say? Whichever way I look to turn this story, there are several inviolable truths that the structure of the fiction must accommodate. And these few pieces of the jigsaw are the key to everything—enough for Jubbawy to complete the puzzle, to work out the final picture. Denial is pointless. All I can do is try and shift the blame and see how this all turns out. My god, I think to myself, how did it end up like this? Now that he says it, the true horror of what we did to those people begins to form as a realization in my mind. I can no longer suppress it. The sweat rolls from my brow, streaking down my face, seeping into the sutured wounds. My chest is heaving as I try to suck sufficient air into my lungs, and there is my right hand, the trembling so severe that it leaps from my lap every few seconds. I look at the floor. It is still undulating, long lazy waves rippling across its surface. And the cigarette butts vibrate and buzz in the ashtray like angry bees. My god, I think to myself. I am truly, truly fucked. And all of this time I am trying to make sense of what we did; how it could have seemed somehow normal at the time. And it did. It seemed normal. And that is something I am simply unable to understand.

'It was Hal,' I rasp, eventually. 'He was obsessed about maximizing the profits . . . totally obsessed . . .' I pause. Jubbawy has started tapping his fingers on the desk, tap-tap-tap, tap-tap-tap. I look at his hand in surprise. It is making some kind of rhythm with the sound in my ear. Tap-tap-whoosh tap-tap. Tap-tap-whoosh tap-tap.

'Hal and I, we were in the woods, sat watching the logging,' I say eventually, hoping he'll stop that damned noise. 'We used to go up there sometimes, just to watch the others working . . .'

'Go on.'

'We went up there one afternoon, and nothing much was going on, so we sat down under a pine tree and smoked a cigarette before heading back. Hal leans back against the trunk, relaxing or whatever, then he just leaps forward and starts slapping at the back of his neck, saying something's bitten him. So we had a look, and there's this long column of ants scurrying up the bark of the tree, big black ants, and Hal just stood there transfixed by them.'

'Ants? Is this really of relevance, Mr Hicks?'

I sigh. 'Yeah,' I say. 'Very relevant, actually.'

Jubbawy says nothing. But he continues to tap his fingers on the table, tap, tap, tap, tap, tap.

48

SHADOW-WALL, AUGUST 1988

'Would you look at that,' Hal said.

'It's a load of fucking ants, Hal. What's the big deal?'

He slowly stroked his chin, then leaned in a little closer to watch. There were in fact two columns of ants—one moving up the trunk of the tree, a writhing black line that reached up ten or fifteen metres before disappearing out of sight. Another column descended, each ant carrying a small fragment of leaf in its mandibles.

'Look how organized they are,' he mused.

'Organized? Sure. They're just controlled by chemicals.'

'I know,' Hal said thoughtfully. 'No thinking, no complaining, just quietly getting on with the job.'

'They're just ants, Hal. That's what they do.'

'They are also perfectly efficient, wouldn't you say?' he said, scratching at his head.

I shrug. 'Let's head back. It'll be getting dark soon.'

'Sure. But I have an idea.'

'Oh?'

'Yeah.' He paused for a moment. 'There are two things we need to be able to hit target each month, Ethan. One is to find a way to stop people leaving so we can get back to positive population growth. The second is an increase in production from our workers.' He turned and looked at me. 'We need to go into town tomorrow, Ethan. We need to go get something.'

*

'This is fucking insane, Hal,' I yelled as we tore back along the winding mountain road, the windows of the jeep down, wind blowing through our hair. 'We can't do this, it's not right!'

'Aw, come on, Ethan, it's fine,' he shouted back. 'I just want to try it for a few days, see if it helps.'

'It's wrong,' I said, but the words were lost in the roar of the wind.

'Anyway,' he shouted, 'I'm talking about tiny amounts here. I just want to see if it has any impact on production, and if it doesn't, we'll stop straight away, okay?'

'It's illegal, Hal.'

He laughed. 'Fucking hell, Ethan, the whole commune is illegal. I'm just talking about a tiny bit—*tiny bit*—of the stuff. No one's going to know the difference, trust me.'

I turned my head, and looked in the back. Hal had bought eight large metal urns for tea and coffee in the morning. It was into these that he was intending to add the amphetamine Hemen had sourced for him.

'What if any of the children have it?' I yelled.

Hal looked at me briefly, then shook his head. 'Ethan, how many kids do you know that drink coffee, you fucking idiot?'

49

JUBBAWY

'I don't know why we allowed him to do it.' I fumble another cigarette from the pack and light it, my third in ten minutes perhaps. Now both hands are trembling, I note.

'What was the amphetamine called?'

I shrug, then massage my temples with the tips of my fingers as I form the lie in my mind. 'I honestly don't recall. I wasn't in the shop at the time when Hal got it from Hemen, I really don't know the name.'

'Earlier in your account you mentioned you were . . .' Jubbawy pauses, then picks up his notepad. He spends a minute or so thumbing through the pages. 'Ah,' he breathes eventually, 'that's right. You said you were a pharmacist's assistant, no?'

I look at the table. How very strange—I don't recall telling him that, I think to myself. 'What do you want me to say?' I ask after a time. 'I've told you already—I didn't go in with Hal, and I don't know what the drug was.'

'How incredible,' he says quietly.

'Look,' I say, trying to move the conversation on. 'It got out of hand pretty quickly. Production went up quite a bit at first, then people started to complain they couldn't sleep and stuff.' I shift slightly in my seat. 'So he started putting ground up Valium into the evening meal. He got Div to help Jamie make the soup every evening.'

'And the people there, they didn't notice this?' Jubbawy asks.

'No, no, look, we started with small quantities, really quite tiny quantities. And he told Jamie to make the soup really spicy, with chillies and shit—you know, so the kids wouldn't eat it?' The pain from my broken ribs is suddenly very intense and heightens my sense of nausea. 'So they got the amphetamine in the morning coffee or whatever to help with the productivity. And the tranquilizer in the evening meal, to help them sleep.'

Jubbawy says nothing, but the way he looks at me is unsettling. His expression is one of utter disgust, I reflect.

'At first, I don't think anyone noticed at all. Hal used to say something about it being no different to how they control passengers on commercial flights, you know, turning the cabin temperature up when they want people to sleep, making it cold when they want to wake people up for landing or whatever.'

Jubbawy pulls at his moustache slightly, but remains silent.

'He changed the commune's motto one last time, at the end,' I say hoarsely. 'Crave to carve.' My head is pounding now, and I am beginning to no longer care about what I say to the policeman. 'Anyway, when he saw it worked, when they started making more flutes, he increased the amount of amphetamine. Tried other stuff too. He did a lot of experimentation with the dosages and different chemicals and stuff.'

Jubbawy still says nothing, but I have to keep talking now. I have to keep talking.

'Of course it was wrong,' I mutter. 'Hal lost sight of reality.' I shrug.

'*Hal* lost sight of reality?' Jubbawy scoffs. 'Do you really think that you can decouple yourself from Hal's actions, even if your rather far-fetched claim to be some kind of onlooker to all of this is true? Do you not see your total complicity, Mr Hicks?'

I sigh, dismissing the comment with a wave of my hand. 'Perhaps. But we had disengaged by then, you know? Hal took over *everything*. He set targets, managed production, negotiated with Hemen, checked inventory, *everything*. So the three of us, Div, Lorna and I—we were, like . . . We were *redundant* by then, essentially.'

'Redundant,' he repeats.

'It was almost like we had nothing to do,' I add. 'We were like the audience to this dark play Hal was acting out.'

'Audience? How very convenient.'

'I am sorry if the word irritates you,' I say quietly, 'but we *were*. We didn't really have anything much to do, and the boredom created this kind of vacuum. We looked to fill it, however we could.'

'And how *did* you fill it?' he asks. He sounds tired.

I am tired too. I fumble another cigarette from the packet and light it. The mental effort of it all is becoming too much to bear. I go to put the extinguished match in the ashtray, and I am surprised to see a half-smoked cigarette burning away in there. I grind it out. Jubbawy observes me. He knows, I think to myself. He knows my fucking brain is fried by all of this. He sees the sweat drip from my nose. He sees my quivering hands every time I take them from my lap. He sees me flinch with pain when I shift in my chair. He knows I cannot cope with this any longer, with the endless questions, the hum of the air-conditioning, the fucking tapping of his pen, the whoosh-whoosh sound which I can hear but he cannot. He knows all that. But still he presses me.

'How did you fill it?' he repeats.

'Fill what?' I ask. I cannot recall what we are talking about.

'You said you were bored. That the boredom created a vacuum. How did you fill it?'

'I closed my eyes,' I shrug. I rub my temples, unsure what to say next. 'I finally realized exactly what we had created. I finally realized exactly what we had created, and I couldn't bear to look at it.' When I look at him, there are genuine tears tumbling down my face. 'I just couldn't bear to look any more.'

50

SHADOW-WALL, SEPTEMBER 1988

If we cared little for those around us, we cared even less about the physical environment in which we lived. And how it had changed. The lower part of the hillside above us was criss-crossed with the mud tracks that we'd carved out in order to access the bamboo with the jeep. Above it, the woodland on the higher slopes had been decimated, exposing rock and cracked, dry earth. The commune itself was now a sprawl of huts occupying an area of perhaps a hundred square metres. The smell of the latrines choked the air. The lake had changed, too—a rainbow slick of gasoline spread over its surface from the fumes of the two-stroke chainsaws and the diesel generator that now ran late into the night. Even the view across the valley was obscured—in recent days a thick, persistent mist had drifted down from the mountains above us. It was as if the gods were so offended by what we were doing to our commune that they would rather not have to watch.

The inhabitants didn't care by then either. The activity, sound, and even mood of the commune had become dichotomous. During the daytime, the workers frenetically harvested and carved, chattering away, their movements sharp and purposeful. But not long after dark, after soup had been served, it would fall eerily silent. The workers would trudge to their huts, dissipating from the clearing like shadows at dusk.

We did all we could to shut it out. Lorna and I spent most of our time in the prison that was our featureless hut, or on the plateau. Often Div joined us. We shut it out visually, but also mentally. Bottle upon bottle of whisky, endless cigarettes, pipe upon pipe of opium. Me, Lorna, Div. We had perhaps by then reached the stage where we were unable to live with what we had created, so we starved our minds of the oxygen of thought and waited, and waited, and waited for it to end.

*

'Production's good,' Hal beamed. He was stood before the whiteboard on the wall of his hut, holding a marker pen which he had used to chart output against time. The thick blue line was heading upwards, exponentially. He looked at the graph proudly. 'In fact, it's excellent.'

'How many have we carved this month?' Lorna asked dreamily.

'112,563 Krapi-Krapis,' he replied instantly.

'Wow,' I murmured, as I heated an opium pill in the pipe-bowl.

'We've got 700,000 bucks in cash now,' he continued.

Lorna looked at him and said, 'That's so much money.'

'Yep. We're making a mint, guys.' He waved the marker pen at us and added, 'Even with the landslides on the west face we've experienced this month, our output has risen hugely since the new . . . well, since the new approach has been implemented.'

'That's great,' Div murmured.

'Yeah,' Hal nodded to himself, looking at the board and not really hearing her. He scratched his head and added, 'Yeah, it is.'

51

JUBBAWY

I reach again for the packet of cigarettes. I am surprised to find it empty and scrunch the carton in my fist before depositing it in the ashtray. 'What a mess,' I mutter.

'What a mess indeed,' the policeman repeats. 'What a mess indeed.'

I look at him. 'I am sorry,' I say simply.

He regards me for a long period of time. Then he leans forward in his chair as if he is going to say something. He seems to think better of it, however, and sits back again, staring at his hands. 'What a mess indeed,' he repeats, almost to himself.

My god, I think to myself, if I could have one wish in my life, it would be to turn back time. Nothing else. And if I needed some kind of proof that my life is fucked, is that not it? That the only thing I wish for is that I could turn back time. I do not wish for happiness or riches or good health. I just want to turn back fucking time, to wake from this hideous dream. And I cannot.

'Is it possible to get some more cigarettes?' I pause, and add, 'if that's okay.'

'Sure,' he grunts.

We wait in silence. I stare around the featureless cell, at the white walls and two-way mirror and the humming lights. It feels as if I have been here forever. Perversely, it feels safe in here now, familiar. The thought of what awaits me beyond these walls is incomprehensible. How pathetic, I muse. This barren cell and this clever policeman are now the only anchors I have in my wretched life.

There is a knock on the door. It is loud and insistent. My interviewer barks something, and the door opens. A uniformed policeman enters the room, places a fresh packet of cigarettes and a box of matches on the table, hands Jubbawy a folder, then turns smartly on his heel and leaves. The file is buff, and judging from the width of the spine, contains little. Jubbawy asks me to continue my account but, as I speak, I again get the impression that his attention is elsewhere. He is scanning the pages of the file with intense interest, only occasionally glancing up at me as I talk.

I immediately reach for the new packet. I remove the shrink-wrap and pick up the box of matches. 'It was about that time that Lorna told me.'

'Told you what?' he asks, without looking up.

I am surprised to find myself crying again.

*

'I think I might be pregnant, Ethan.'

'What?'

'I'm pregnant, Ethan! I'm pregnant!'

I look at her for a moment, then set down the opium pipe. 'Well that's fantastic!' My face splits into a broad grin, I pick Lorna up and twirl her around the hut, before kissing her hard on the lips. 'That's just fantastic! Let's tell the others, make an announcement . . .'

'It's a little bit early for that, Ethan,' Lorna smiles, her face flushing with pleasure. 'I've only missed one period. But we haven't exactly been careful . . .'

'Well let's get a test in town! You could go and see a doctor there, then we'll know for sure.' I kiss her again, before curiosity gets the better of me and I eye her bare navel.

'It won't show yet,' she laughs.

'No, of course not.' I take a deep drag on the opium pipe, then through habit go to pass it to Lorna before pulling my hand back. 'Sorry, I wasn't thinking,' I say. I feel a kick of adrenaline begin to surge through my veins, fighting the opium high, clearing my head slightly. Perhaps my sudden sobriety stems from the gravity of her announcement, but for the first time in months I see Lorna's face, really see it. She looks drawn, her skin pale and blotchy, the tan long since faded. A red sore sits prominently above her thin lips, and her eyes, once lively and bright, are dulled. She is skinny too. The curves that I had found so attractive in Delhi have disappeared, the bony contours of her hips now protrude through the sarong she is wearing, her arms seemingly thin enough to snap. She looks like a junkie, and nothing more.

I sit on the bed, tap out the contents of the pipe and put it back in its box.

*

'I destroyed her,' I say, staring at the floor.

'Yes,' he agrees.

I can feel the sting of the saline tears as they seep once more into the stitches down my face. I close my eyes, but it just forces out more tears; I wonder to myself whether the droplets can somehow cleanse the wounds on my face.

'I can't believe I did that to her,' I sob.

He shrugs, then looks back down at the file.

'I can't believe I did that—'

Jubbawy raises a hand to silence me. Then he pulls his chair into the table, adjusts the file, cups his chin in his hands and proceeds to read in silence for some minutes. The only sound in the room is the occasional scrape as a page is turned. I observe him. His chest, the contours of which are visible under the tight-fitting uniform, rises and falls with perfect regularity. Yet his brow is furrowed. Sweat glistens on his head. Occasionally his tongue pokes cautiously from between his teeth to moisten his lips. He shakes his head slowly from side to side as he reads. I watch him for five minutes, ten minutes, longer. Then suddenly his entire body seems to freeze. It is as if he has been captured in a still photograph. His body is completely without motion. I realize I have stopped crying. For some curious reason, I feel a deep fear starting to grip me. I can sense bile rising up my oesophagus. For something inside me tells me this is the end.

'This is inexplicable,' he says finally. He starts to tap his pen on the desk. I physically flinch at the sound. Again, the beat falls quickly into tandem with the whooshing sound and the rattle of the air-conditioning unit. Tap-whoosh-rattle. Tap-whoosh-rattle. He taps the pen when he is thinking, I reflect. The thought adds to the overwhelming sense of foreboding I have.

Then the pen stops.

'Ah . . .' he says, the word carried on his exhalation of breath. He slowly looks up at me, his head cocked to one side again. He studies my face for several minutes. I stare back at him, not blinking. I seem to be able to feel the pulsing blood in every cell of my body as my heart beats.

'My god, Ethan, what *have* you done?' he asks. The impact of the sentence—the unexpected use of my first name, the presupposition of guilt in the question—its impact on me is so profound that I instantaneously vomit over the table. For I know he knows. He has worked it out, I think to myself. I don't know how, but he has worked out what happened. Streaks of watery bile run to the floor. I bend my head to my knees, and grab the back of my neck with my hands. Then I start to slap at the back of my head. It is a desperate effort to help me try and think straight, but my mind is addled with strange thoughts, my body hums with pumping blood, the stench of vomit fills my nostrils, and the sound of whooshing-humming-tapping noises fill my ears.

'I am so sorry,' I sob.

'Tell me,' he says.

'Lorna had nothing to do with it,' I rasp. Then, shouting, 'Lorna had nothing to do with it. We sent her home. You have to believe me. We sent her home. We sent her home.'

52

SHADOW-WALL, OCTOBER 1988

'Lorna, it's time for you to head back to Delhi. You need to get yourself cleaned up.'

'I want to stay here,' she whispered from the bed. She was on her side, drawing from the opium pipe again.

I sat next to her, and stroked her face. Lorna smiled at me. 'You've got to stop taking this stuff,' I said softly. 'Promise me you will.'

'I promise,' she said immediately, but I knew she didn't mean it.

'You need to go to Delhi tomorrow, the three of us will meet you there in a couple of months or so, okay?'

'Why can't you come?' she replied, looking concerned.

I paused. 'Look, Lorna, I'm not sure I completely trust Hal. With the money, I mean. We've invested too much time in this, I just don't know if he'll disappear with everything.'

'He *has* changed a lot,' she agreed.

'Yeah, well don't worry too much, Lorna. I just want to take care of our future.' I took the opium pipe from her, and placed it in the pocket of my shorts. 'Look, I've got rid of the rest of this shit, I threw it in the lake. It's for the best.'

'Oh . . .'

'Tomorrow, we'll pack your stuff, then I'll take you into Kullu, put you on the coach to Delhi. We'll meet you there before Christmas for sure.'

'Okay,' she breathed.

'Good. When we get to Delhi, we can sort ourselves out a bit, maybe get you a scan.'

'For the baby?'

'For the baby,' I agreed.

'I don't want to go without you,' she said suddenly, clutching my hand.

*

'It's only for a couple of months,' I said. 'Just a couple of months.'

Lorna and I spoke little as the jeep bounced and veered down the muddy path to the road. It was an odd feeling, her leaving the place that had been our home for nearly two years. There was a sense of a new beginning, but also of closure, of the sadness that goes with leaving the familiar. She cried a little, once we hit the metalled road to Kullu, and I steered the jeep with one hand, holding her with my other.

'How do you feel?' I asked, once we had picked up a little speed and the wind began to make our hair dance and flit across our faces.

'Empty. Odd. Coming off the damned opium, it's harder than I thought.'

'Are you feeling down?'

'It'll pass,' she murmured. I could hardly hear her over the wind. 'I'll deal with it.'

I looked at her, smiling. 'Just go straight to your place when you get back to Delhi. You've got your keys, right?'

She nodded, wiping her eyes.

'Get there, and just hang out. Sort yourself out, lock yourself away or whatever.'

'Where will we go?' she asked, after a while. 'After here, I mean. After India.'

'I don't know.' Her question made me think fleetingly of home, of how my parents would react to knowing they had a grandchild. I snorted, then shifted down a gear to overtake a black pickup truck, laden with chopped wood. Somehow, I knew it would disappoint them.

'I think I'd like to go to Singapore,' Lorna stated, a little more brightly. 'It's clean and organized and there'll be good schools and hospitals for our baby.'

'Your wish is my command,' I said, happy that her mood had lifted slightly. 'Are you going to be okay on the coach?'

'You said it had toilets,' she said. 'I've puked three times today already.'

'The man said it had toilets,' I nodded. 'And air-con.'

'Thanks Ethan,' she smiled, running her finger around my ear. 'I'm a bit of a mess right now, aren't I?'

'We both are,' I grunted. And it was true. Without opium, feelings of dark despair constantly ebbed and flowed through my mind.

She leaned over to my ear and whispered, 'I love you.'

The bus station was filled with the usual gathering of hawkers and weary travellers slumped on the hard, wooden seats, waiting for their buses to take them to wherever they were destined. The place had the fug of diesel fumes and cigarette smoke, and the nauseating odour of rotten litter. All around us stray dogs, their ribs protruding like bird cages, sniffed at each other or padded over to piles of trash, pawing at the collection of tin cans and plastic wrappers in the hope of finding some scrap of food. In the shadowy recesses of the terminal, I could make out the bodies of beggars, swathed in white as if they'd been prepared for burial, some asleep and others staring vacantly at me, hands stretching out of the gloom.

'You should get back,' Lorna urged. 'Before it gets dark. You can't drive up the trail at night, Ethan.'

'I'd rather wait with you,' I said. 'This place . . . it's kind of hideous.'

'You must go . . . Anyway, the coach will be here in less than an hour,' she protested.

'Really, I want to stay—'

'Go,' she whispered kindly.

'Are you sure? Are you sure you're going to be okay?'

'I've lived in India a very long time, Ethan. I'll be fine.' There were tears welling in her eyes.

'Sure,' I murmured, reluctantly getting to my feet. We stood in silence for a few moments, then I shrugged and said, 'So . . . see you in a couple of months, yeah?'

'Get out of here,' she smiled, wiping her arm across her eyes.

'Look at you,' I said without smiling, 'you've gone all blotchy.'

She laughed, sniffing at the same time, then wrapped her arms around my waist, looking up at me. 'Don't be too long, will you?'

'I'll see you soon, Lorna, and then the rest of our life starts.'

'I look forward to it.' She kissed me. It was to be the last time she did, although I was not to know it then.

'Two months, Lorna,' I said.

'Goodbye, Ethan.'

'Goodbye.'

I wiped my eyes, and held her tightly one last time. Then I turned away and walked outside to where the jeep was parked.

53

JUBBAWY

Jubbawy is staring at me. We are pausing for a few minutes as a maid has entered the room. I watch detachedly as she cleans up my vomit. First, she scrapes up what she can with a large roll of blue tissue paper, deposits it in a black bin-liner, and then proceeds to mop the floor. The smell of sick is slowly replaced by the smell of Dettol. Then she says something to Jubbawy. He nods, and lifts the various files from the table. She spends some time cleaning the surface. Finally, she picks up the bucket and the mop and the bin-liner, and leaves in silence. If only my life were so easy to clean, I think to myself.

'Tell me what happened up there.'

'I can't,' I say simply. I shrug and repeat hoarsely: 'I just can't.'

There is a long pause. Then Jubbawy speaks. 'Ethan, the facts are this. All of the adults that we have autopsied, they died from an overdose. *All of them.*'

I am unable to think straight. I do not know how to respond, so I just stare into space, at the undulating floor. Jubbawy leaves the silence unbroken. Whoosh, whoosh. Then I have a thought. It is the sound of a *butterfly* I can hear. The sound of a butterfly beating its wings. I feel a strange sense of elation that I have figured out what it is.

Jubbawy is still talking, I see his lips moving, but I can't hear the words. They simply pass by my ears, unheeded, drowned out by the sound of the butterfly. The insect doesn't rest against the wall, won't allow me to make out its colourful body against the white tiles. Instead it flaps around my head, tormenting me. Towards one ear, the noise increasing in volume, entering my head, invisible—yet each time I look there is nothing. I wonder if Jubbawy hears it, but my interviewer appears unperturbed. Doesn't he hear it? I have to ask. His composure troubles me.

'The butterfly?'

'Sorry?'

'The butterfly? You can't hear that?'

'I'm sorry, I'm not following you?'

'That whooshing. Can you not hear it?'

'Ethan, there is no *whooshing*.' Jubbawy looks irritated by my outburst, but he must hear it. He must. *I* can hear it, a few centimetres from my left ear now. I shake my head, and look around the room in confusion, trying to see where it is.

'Ethan, the adults died from an overdose. All of them. Not from the landslide.'

I have to talk. I have to fill this room with sound. I have to fill this fucking room with sound. But I have no response to the question. 'Sure,' I shrug, eventually. 'I know.'

'We have found the bodies of a number of the children now, Ethan. Two of the autopsies are complete. Strangely, the children *were* killed by the landslide.'

'Please stop this.' I can feel the suction of the damp t-shirt on my body as I lean forward. 'Please stop this.'

'Tell me, Ethan, tell me what happened.' The words are spoken in a conspiratorial whisper. He is inviting me to share the awful, awful truth. And now the butterfly is practically crawling inside my ear, the beating wings smashing a rhythm on my eardrum.

'I can't,' I whisper. My clothing feels drenched, my t-shirt clinging to my body, and my hands are shaking. I try to fumble another cigarette from the pack, almost panicking at the thought of this one expiring, but the red and gold carton is blurred, the colours suffusing into one another. 'Can we stop? I don't feel very well.'

'Oh, you don't feel very well?' he mimics, his eyes suddenly cold. 'There are an awful lot of grieving families that aren't feeling very well right now, so you must forgive me for my lack of sympathy, Mr Hicks. NOW TELL ME WHAT HAPPENED?!' he roars, slamming his fist on the desk.

'I can't breathe, I really can't breathe . . .'

'Tell me what really happened up there!' he yells. 'Why did the children die later, Ethan?!'

'Stop this,' I beg. 'Please stop shouting.'

'You weren't caught up in the landslide, were you?!' he barks.

'I want a lawyer!'

'What happened?!'

'I *want* a lawyer.'

Jubbawy leaps to his feet and strides round the table. He grabs me by the jaw and pulls my face to within an inch of his own. The pain makes my eyes smart. 'I am going to ask you one more time! *What really happened?*'

'Stop this,' I mumble through gritted teeth. 'Please stop this! I want a lawyer!'

He slowly draws his hand back, then slaps it hard across my face. My nose explodes over my t-shirt.

'You hit me . . .' I stammer, my head spinning slightly. I try to speak again, but Jubbawy is holding my jaw again now, my chest is heaving for breath and the blood is collecting in the back of my throat. I'm beginning to choke.

'Just raise your hand when you are ready to tell me,' he says calmly, slowly, as if time has no relevance.

I can't draw in air through my nose, and when I breathe through my teeth I can feel the blood enter my lungs, making me want to cough. But I can't, because there's no air to expel. I'm just gagging, trying to swallow and breathe at the same time. I know my eyes are bulging in my face, and the pulse in my neck is getting stronger as each second passes. If I don't do something soon, I'm going to fucking suffocate.

So this is it, I think to myself. How funny life is—I came to this country to escape my life, and now I am slowly having my life choked out of me by a policeman. And the butterfly flapped its wings, I muse, causing the hurricane on the other side of the world. Impossible to predict, and perhaps not even worth trying. Yes, I reflect—we will never know the consequences of our actions because the calculation is simply too complex to make, too many variables. We might as well not even try and shape our futures, for we are bound to fail.

I raise my hand.

'Good,' he says, releasing his grip. I splutter as I try and take in air. A little bubble of blood emerges from my mouth, speckling Jubbawy's glasses and face as it bursts. 'Good.'

It all seems so bizarre, him looking at me through a red mist of my own blood. It actually makes me laugh out loud.

54

SHADOW-WALL, NOVEMBER 1988

I knew something was up straight away. I had come to the plateau that evening to think things through, to make a plan for me and Lorna, when I saw Hal and Div some fifty yards from me. Despite the distance and the darkness, there was something to their urgency that alerted me—both were panting for breath, the rasps carried on the evening breeze. Yet still they half-ran, half-walked, so as to cover the ground more quickly.

'Fuck man,' Hal wheezed, putting his hands on his knees to help catch his breath. Then he slumped down next to me in a heap, his chest heaving with each pull of his lungs.

'Take it easy, Hal,' I said, taking a drag on my cigarette. 'What's up, for Christ's sake?'

'They're all getting sick,' Div said, her voice shaking. 'The soup's making them sick.'

I stared at her. 'Sick?'

'Yeah, like really sick.'

'Fucking hell,' Hal rasped. He looked at me, shaking his head. 'There's loads of them, out in the clearing. All of this fucking froth coming out their mouths and stuff, white froth.' He clasped his head in his hands. 'I think some of them are dead.'

'Jesus, Hal.'

'Fucking hell,' he repeated.

'What have you done, Hal?' I asked slowly.

'I don't know,' he muttered under his breath. 'I don't know.'

'What have you done, Hal!?' I shouted. Then I turned to him and grabbed his shoulders. 'What have you done!?'

'Jesus man, it was a mistake, yeah? I tried a few new things for the soup today, I thought it would be fine, just a minor modification . . .' He trailed away, then added: 'So much white froth, dude.'

'Jesus Christ, Hal,' I spat. 'What did they eat tonight? What was in it?'

Hal shook his head. 'Ethan. I think I went too far.' He hawked, then spat into the dust at his feet. 'Way too fucking far, to be honest.' He shook his head again, then said, 'Give me some of that whisky, will you?'

I passed him the bottle of Blue Label.

He grunted something I didn't catch, grabbed the bottle and then took a long, long swig. And so together we sat there drinking, me, Hal and Div, waiting for them all to die.

55

JUBBAWY

I feel so tired. My eyes ache and my vision is blurred. It is hard to focus on Jubbawy, and the butterfly is still beating in my ear, louder than before. This has all gone so wrong. I was never meant to tell them this. My interviewer has tricked me into confessing, but I can't even remember how he did it.

'Perhaps you would like to continue?'

The words echo all around the cell, bouncing from the walls, the sound coming from all directions. I look around, and realize how small the cell is, nothing more than a box. My reflection mocks me in the mirror. I look broken, drenched in a mixture of perspiration and my own blood, the rims of my eyes red and swollen. My hair looks limp and greasy, plastered to my pale face by the sweat, and I can see my chest heaving up and down, the air hissing through my teeth as I breathe.

'I'm sick,' I say to myself, watching my white lips moving to the words.

'Have some water,' Jubbawy says, but I don't turn around. Instead I stare at the mirror, past the ghastly image of myself. There is a dark shape I can discern behind the glass, like a shadow. It's someone behind the mirror, I think to myself—I can make out their silhouette. But they look like a devil, a hunched back and pointed face. I refocus on my own eyes, set into dark sockets, but the devil still flits playfully in my peripheral vision.

'No, I'll be all right,' I say. As I speak, the words are monotone, and the sound no longer corresponds to the movement of my pale lips, instead emerging fractionally later. I frown, confused by my own image.

'So continue, then,' he orders.

'It was like hell on earth,' I mutter.

'A hell that you had crafted,' Jubbawy counters.

The last trace of pity has gone, I reflect. But I cannot blame him for that. I shrug, and continue: 'It took them a long time to die, you know? And people were screaming, just screaming . . .' I sigh, then add: 'So we got very, very drunk. We drank until dawn came.' I shake my head, and stare at my hands. 'My god, the screams in the night. I won't ever forget that. A hundred screams. Five hundred screams, I don't know. They carried up to the plateau, carried all that distance. It was so fucked up . . . *So* fucked up . . .'

'*People*,' Jubbawy repeats. 'Not *workers*.'

I nod. '*People*.'

'Yes, *people*,' he repeats.

'You know, in the end it was too much. We could see them from the plateau when dawn finally broke, people still squirming on the ground, choking on their own vomit, dying from their own fucking vomit.' I look at Jubbawy. Tears roll down my cheeks, and it mixes with the blood on my chin, for I have just bitten through my own lip out of hatred for what I was part of. 'And we looked on as children saw their parents die slowly in front of them.' I start to sob out loud, then steady myself, holding Jubbawy's eye. 'And do you know what we did?' I am shouting now, but the anger is aimed at no one but me. 'Do you *know* what we did?'

Jubbawy simply shrugs.

'We ran away. We ran into the forest, me, Hal and Div. We ran into the fucking forest because we couldn't face watching them die.'

56

SHADOW-WALL, NOVEMBER 1988

The three of us huddled together on the ground, shivering from the brutal morning cold. The screams still carried up from the commune, helped by the thin winter air. Eventually they became less frequent, the density of sound decaying over time. By late morning, it was virtually silent. The still air was broken only by the sound of a deer barking from the woods to the east, and the occasional cry of a child far below us. None of us spoke. None of us looked at each other. Collectively, the three of us just stared at the ground. There was nothing to be said.

It must have been some time after midday before the silence was broken. Our teeth chattered and our bodies shook from the cold, despite the few weak rays from the sun. The air was still and had a bitter edge to it. I was surprised to see a butterfly flitting past. It landed on a nearby plant and I said: 'Shall we just let ourselves die here?' Looking back, there remains little doubt in my mind that that was what I wanted. No force could change that—not my love for Lorna, not our hardwired, innate desire to live, nothing.

But Div said, 'What about the children? We can't leave them.'

'What do you suggest?' I asked. As I spoke the words, I slowly hit the back of my head on the tree trunk against which I rested. 'Actually, this is your fucking mess, Hal,' I muttered. 'So what do *you* suggest?'

Hal lit a cigarette, but said nothing. He simply closed his eyes as if letting the words wash over him like water. We lapsed into silence. Div began crying, I started to bang my head more loudly against the tree trunk to block out the sound. A few minutes passed. Then Hal finally spoke. When he did, he was laughing. 'We met in a fucking rundown Chinese restaurant in Delhi. How did we end up here? Like this? In this situation? Fucking absurd, man.' He flicked the stub of his cigarette at the butterfly; it leapt from its resting place and flew erratically away into the forest.

'What about the children?' Div sobbed after a while.

'I can't deal with this,' I said. 'I just can't fucking deal with this.'

'Jesus Christ!' Hal snapped. 'Pull yourselves together.'

I looked at him. He was the only one not crying.

'Yeah,' I said, simply. 'So easy to say.'

Hal looked at me. 'Don't be so fucking weak,' he said.

'Fuck you,' I replied.

57

JUBBAWY

'We left mid-afternoon, left the wood. Walked down into the commune.'
'I see.'
'There were bodies everywhere.'
'Yes. Of course.'
'*Everywhere*. Like hanging out of doorways, in the clearing, down by the lake, in the huts . . .'
'A lot of people died, Ethan.'
'We held hands,' I say, laughing. But it is a hollow, hollow laugh.
'Held hands?'
'As we reached the commune, we held hands. Me and Div.'
'I see.'
'The kids were there.' I close my eyes, picturing them. 'Some of them were sat by the bodies of their parents, just crying, crying, crying.'
'That must have been very hard on you, Ethan.'
His voice is so soft. Compassionate. He understands me. Perhaps he is the only one who does. I feel a mix of warmth and adrenaline flow through me. 'It was.' I look up suddenly. 'What is your first name?'
'Jagpal.'
'It was very hard, Jagpal. Do you mind if I call you that?'
'Not in the slightest, Ethan. It's just fine.'

'There was a boy, I don't recall his name. Maybe six years old? He was with his mother.' I shrug. 'She was dead of course, lying on the ground, not far from the lake. He was crying, hitting her chest with his clenched hands.' I lick my tongue over the deep gouge my teeth have made in my lower lip, tasting the iron. 'He just kept saying over and over again, "Wake up, mummy, wake up, mummy, wake up, mummy . . ."'

'That is so sad,' Jagpal nods. 'So very, very sad.' He pauses, then adds: 'We know the children died about a week after the adults. Ethan, did you somehow create the landslide? To hide it all?'

I look at Jagpal and smile. 'Sure we did,' I say. 'Sure we did.'

'Was it Hal's idea?' he offers.

I nod, smudging away the tears with the palm of my hand.

'What happened, Ethan? Tell me. Please.'

58

SHADOW-WALL, NOVEMBER 1988

'I know I've created a bit of a mess, but I can fix it.' Hal took another swig of Blue Label, then folded his arms. 'I am going to fix the situation.'

'How?' Div sobbed. 'How can you ever, ever *fix* this situation Hal?'

'It's time for us to go, Hal,' I said. 'It's time for us to go, and we're taking the children with us. We need to face the consequences of what we've done here.'

He snorted, then took another pull of whisky. 'Easy for you to say, Ethan. You weren't the one who killed them all. I'm fucked if I'm going to prison.'

'We have to go, Hal. We can't just leave them here to die. We *can't*.'

'Nah,' he said with a shake of his head. 'Nah, we don't *need* to do anything, Ethan. We've got a million bucks sitting here, and you want to give all that up so you can go to prison? How's that going to help?'

'Oh, and what do you suggest then, Hal?' I spat. 'That we let those kids starve or freeze to death up here? Don't you think you've done enough fucking damage already?'

'Ethan, you're not listening to me. I am not going to fucking prison! I've spent two and a half fucking years in this place, two and a half years creating a business, driving profit. I am not throwing all that money away over a few fucking kids, do you understand?' There was an edge to his voice now. I looked at Div, but she was still crying, her head in her hands. Hal continued: 'Think about it, Ethan. We'll all go to prison. What happens then? Think about Lorna, dude—while you're rotting away behind bars somewhere, she'll find someone else.' He shrugged. 'It's inevitable, wouldn't you say?'

'Inevitable,' I repeated to myself slowly.

'You'll be behind bars and she'll be having it away with some—'

'So what are you suggesting?' I hissed.

He shook his head. 'Look, they will find this place sometime. And then it doesn't matter where we run, where we hide. They will find us, Ethan. They *will* find us.'

'So we're fucked either way.'

'Maybe not.' He grunted and shrugged his shoulders. 'We've burgled the house, and we weren't wearing gloves—now we need to get rid of our fingerprints.'

'Huh? What the fuck are you talking about, Hal?'

'I mean we need to erase this place from the fucking map. I mean completely erase it—like it never existed, dude.'

59

JUBBAWY

I run my hand over my broken ribs, then my face. 'Do you have the death penalty here?' I ask.

He says nothing, just purses his lips slightly.

'It doesn't matter either way,' I breathe. 'It doesn't fucking matter.'

Jagpal remains silent. My head spins with the silence. 'He knew *exactly* what he was doing,' I say. My voice sounds off—detached, robotic. 'I know his dad had some construction company, so maybe that was it . . . Anyway, it took Hemen three days to get the explosives. We had to pay a lot of money for them. A lot of money.'

'Did you tell him what they were for?' the policeman prompts. 'Hemen, I mean?'

I stare at Jagpal, but my eyes see nothing much at all now. Just whirling kaleidoscopes.

'We stayed in a hotel. The fucking commune was full of corpses.' I shake my head. 'At least it was cold. They hadn't really decomposed by the time we got back.'

'And the children?'

I try and look at Jagpal, but my vision has completely gone now. 'We actually locked them in one of the huts,' I murmur. 'Gave them food and water. *Why did we do that?*'

He again says nothing.

60

SHADOW-WALL, DECEMBER 1988

It was our last day in Shadow-Wall. The skies were perfectly clear, and the winter sun burned low in the sky. As the three of us trudged out towards the tree line, I stared at the ground under my feet, unable to look around at the bodies that littered the clearing. The fingers of my left hand were aching, the tendons straining under the weight of the heavy blue holdall. Sweat was rolling from my brow, down the side of my face, my tongue dry and swollen.

I turned to Div and asked, 'Did you bring any water?'

'No. You?'

'Why the fuck would I be asking if I had?'

'Shut up, you two,' Hal hissed.

We passed the furthest of the huts, and started up the trail through the woods, presently passing Scott's empty grave, overgrown with weeds and littered with deadwood. The headstone had sunk lopsidedly into the soil, so that it looked like it was about to keel over at any moment, the granite discoloured by lichen. The inscription was no longer legible. We moved on in silence, and as we slowly ascended, the woodland floor started to become noticeably lighter, the sun's rays filtering through the gaps left in the leafy canopy by the felled trees. All around us were severed stumps, the light-yellow ovals of wood contrasting against the dark floor of the forest, which was mottled in places by patches of rotting sawdust. It smelt very damp.

'Look!' Hal rasped, struggling slightly for breath. He pointed with the thick wooden staff he had found and was using to aid his ascent.

Both Div and I looked past his bloated body in the direction he was waving his stick. A couple of hundred yards west of the trail, I could make out a thick blanket of mud that must have been a recent landslide, the brown sludge piled up against the lowest parts of the tree-trunks like a snow-drift. The mudflow had collected hundreds of dead branches and twigs that protruded from the surface like spindly arms reaching out for help. I shivered and looked away.

'Do you think it's safe here?' Div asked.

No one bothered to answer, and we traversed a series of deep furrows carved out by the jeep's tyres. In the deepest and widest part of one, the rainwater from the previous week had formed a large muddy puddle that mocked us with our distorted reflections. Hal shattered the surface with his boot, then stopped to light a cigarette.

'You okay with that bag, dude?'

'Not really, it's fucking heavy,' I replied, lowering it carefully to the ground. One of the bags I was carrying had a few personal effects I'd shoved in; the other one, a heavy Adidas hold-all, contained the money. The sides bulged with the thick wads of banknotes. Hal and Div carried the explosives in day-packs on their backs. 'Give me a cigarette.'

'Sure,' he said, throwing me the pack. 'About another half-mile, then we'll be in the right area.'

We stood smoking in silence, taking in the decimated woodland around us, until Hal dropped his cigarette in the puddle with a hiss and signalled for us to continue. After walking for another few hundred metres or so, the scale of our manufacturing operation started to become evident. The area beyond the cedar forest, once covered in thick bamboo jungle, now resembled a muddy clearing, the ground a patchwork of footprints. The soil was studded with small stones and upturned bamboo bushes, long since dead.

'We'll get to the top of this clearing, then we can stop,' Hal said.

The loose soil and stones slid away from under our feet as we crossed the huge, devastated area, the scree scampering away behind us with a clatter. With only sky above our heads, we had an unimpeded view of the mountain above us, its grey, rugged granite peak hugged by pockets of late afternoon mist.

'Should've climbed it while we were here,' Hal commented eventually. 'Must be some view of the valley from up there.' No one said anything. Then he grunted and said, 'Anyway, this is it, man. This is the place—look at it . . . it's perfect.'

We were stood by a deep channel that ran parallel to the valley floor—were it not for its aspect, I would've assumed it was gouged by a stream. The incision was perhaps two metres deep, and meandered haphazardly for a couple of hundred metres until it disappeared into a lonely copse of lantanas.

'If we plant the explosives all the way along here, it'll take the whole slope down,' Hal said brightly. 'With that weight of mud coming down the hill, it should dislodge the soil on the lower slopes as well. I'll set the timer for three hours. It'll be dark, but I'd rather play it safe. We can watch from the plateau.'

*

It began with a low boom. I could feel a wave of pressurized air hit my face a few seconds later. Then, a low rumble that seemed, at first, to die on the slopes above us. The sound could easily have been a fleeting, distant roll of thunder. The sky was clear enough to make out the first watery evening stars, and the air lacked any humidity. Over to the west, where the sun had slipped behind the horizon perhaps an hour ago, a few lingering clouds were flecked with dull reds and purples, but dusk had already passed. Night always came quickly on the mountain.

I tilted my head to one side and listened intently. The crickets, concealed in the long grass around us, chattered to one another, seemingly oblivious to what was happening. Elsewhere, silence. A couple of seconds passed, and another rumble carried down on the breeze. It was, perhaps, a little louder this time.

'Do you think—?'

I put a finger to my lips. The rumble didn't die. Next to me, Hal took a sharp intake of breath.

'It's coming this way,' I said quietly, after a few moments.

It was possible to make out other noises. A sharp cracking, like fire consuming dry wood, cut through the air like rifle reports, accompanied by hundreds of tortured groans.

'Are we safe here?'

'Yes. I'm sure of it.'

The half moon, smudged by wispy cirrus, splashed an eerie, uncertain light over the clearing below us. Between the haphazard collection of huts, I could just about make out the shapes of the dead bodies. I thought of the children, locked in the hut. What must they be thinking? What torture they had been through.

'I'm hungry,' Hal said absently. 'That goat stew was kinda horrible, you know?'

'There's a pack of biscuits in that bag,' Div said.

The rumble was much louder now, and the crackling and groaning had picked up in tempo. I squinted at where I knew the forest to be, but it was indistinguishable against the dark mass of the mountain. In fact, if you could somehow shut out what was now becoming a violent roar, nothing would seem amiss. No movement, just perfect, tranquil stillness.

'What sort are they, Div? Are they Oreos?'

'No. I'm not sure what they're called—they're a bit like chocolate digestives.'

'Really?' There was a scrape of feet, shortly followed by a rustling.

The ground began to tremble slightly. I noticed that the crickets had stopped chirping.

'They're rather dry,' he commented.

'Yeah. But I like them.' Div had to raise her voice slightly to make herself heard.

The log on which I was sat began to roll as the rocky outcrop shuddered underneath us, and some sort of bird broke cover from the long grass in front of us, bursting into the sky with a squawk.

'Feels like the whole fucking mountain's moving,' he commented. Then he shook his head, pointed to his mouth, and said, 'These biscuits are awful, man. So dry. Can't even swallow. It feels like I've got a fucking sponge in my mouth.'

Below us was an intense roar of noise.

'Jesus,' Div shouted. 'What have we done?'

I turned sharply to face her. She said something more, I could make out the movement of her lips, but the thunderous noise drowned out the words.

'Yeah, what have we done?' I said, more to myself than to her.

When I turned back to look at Shadow-Wall, it was gone. Bizarrely, so was the lake. It was like a giant had taken a paintbrush and simply stroked it down the mountainside. As I turned back to the others from what was now a sterile, uncompromising blackness, Div was crying. Although she made no sound, I could see the wetness on her cheeks, illuminated by the feeble orange glow of her cigarette. Behind her, Hal was busy, noisily munching on biscuits.

'Fucking unbelievable,' he said.

'What?' I asked.

'We're fucking insane, Ethan, d'you know that?' He laughed. There was an edge to it, a hollow, empty laugh.

I was going to say something, then thought better of it, and instead looked back over what had been our home for the past two and a half years. For a while no one spoke, except the crickets, who tentatively resumed their idle, pointless conversations.

'Thank god this is over,' Div said eventually. 'Thank god.'

I shook my head slowly, my eyes still transfixed on the devastation below us. Without bothering to look at her, I asked, 'How will this ever be over, Div? How?'

'Don't be weak, Ethan,' Hal snapped. There was still an edge to his voice.

I turned to him. 'Fuck you, Hal. This is your fucking mess. All of it, all of it is down to you.' I rubbed my hand slowly over my face. 'Jesus, Hal. Where have you led us all?'

Hal snorted. 'Yeah, Ethan, I did *lead* us. That's right. I fucking turned this business into what it became. *I* did that, Ethan. *I* did.'

I shrugged, and got slowly to my feet. 'Whatever,' I muttered. I looked into Hal's eyes for a moment. They seemed to me to be entirely empty, detached. 'You've lost your soul, Hal.'

He said nothing.

'I guess this is it, then,' I continued. 'We all know we're not going to see each other again. So this is farewell.'

Div and Hal both remained silent.

'I'm going to go,' I said, 'I want to get off this fucking mountain right now.'

'It's too dark,' Hal said, looking at the sky. 'You should stay the night, leave at dawn.'

'Don't tell me what to do,' I hissed. 'I'm leaving now. I'm done with this, I'm done with you. Both of you.'

Hal snorted again, but said nothing, continuing to stare out into the darkness.

'Time to split the money now, Hal,' I said.

There was a pause. Then Hal said: 'Yeah, look Ethan, I've been meaning to discuss that with you.'

'Discuss what, Hal?' I spat. 'There's nothing to fucking discuss.'

'Yeah, I totally agree, dude,' he nodded. It was then that I half-glimpsed the wooden staff swinging through the dark night air, saw Hal's cold, unseeing eyes. Then I felt my face explode in pain.

61

JUBBAWY

'They betrayed me,' I sob.

'Hal and Div?' he asks, kindly.

I nod. 'Greed, it corrupted everything, everyone.'

'Of course. Of course it did, Ethan.'

'He beat me, he beat me till he thought I was dead,' I cry. 'I thought he was my fucking friend.'

'They took the money?'

I nod again. 'I don't know how long I was unconscious for . . .' My voice quivers as I speak the words.

'And when you came to . . . You walked off the mountain?'

I shrug, wiping the tears from my eyes with the back of my shaking hand. 'It took me a day.'

'You were lucky to make it down with the injuries you sustained.'

My sobbing is becoming uncontrollable now. 'Lucky?' I yell at the policeman. 'Lucky?'

He has no idea. He has no idea. Even through the swirling, addled mess of thoughts in my head, I have the lucidity to realize my life is utterly destroyed now—I know I will never see Lorna again, I know I will never even get to meet our fucking opium-baby. My sobs elide into a long kind of wail as an overwhelming dread grips me, the dread that comes from knowing that I'm entirely bereft of hope—there is nothing whatsoever to look forward to in my life now. There is simply nothing left to live for. And for what? For what? A fucking Adidas hold-all of dollar bills.

I lift my head back slowly, then smash it on to the surface of the table. Curiously, the sound it creates is more of a squelch than a thud. Perhaps I have split my forehead open, for there is blood everywhere. It starts to pool on the grey table-top, quickly filling the scars of Hindi graffiti so that the characters turn red one by one. I lift my head and slam it down once more; splashes of blood land on Jubbawy's folders. I smash my head again, and now my blood spatters the water jug; it runs down the plastic sides in red streaks. In my peripheral vision I can see the two policemen jumping to their feet. I slam my head once more, and the vibrating ashtray and bottles of pills are speckled with blood too. I can feel hands on me now, under my armpits, pulling me away. The chair falls to the floor with a clatter, and they drag me to the door. I turn and look at the cell. It's like they've butchered an animal in here, I think to myself. Once I am gone from here, they will probably just hose the blood away, down the black drain near the door.

62

NEW DELHI, APRIL 1990

They have told me that I will die in this place. I will die in *this place*. The irony is not lost on me—the differences between my cell and the interview room in which I condemned myself are few. The description of my surroundings is interesting only by its brevity; walls and a bed. There is not much more to add. And when I leave this place, it will be as a corpse. The judge made that clear. I know that I am here because I decayed morally. One day, as they wheel my corpse from this place, so shall begin the final decay. My body will start its decomposition. I will start to rot physically.

They say that I am sick. They give me medicine for my fucked-up head. They hold down my arms and push needles into my bruised veins and pump me full of chemicals that change who I am. They send a doctor into my cell a few times each week. I do not talk to her, for I have nothing left to say. She can try and assess me all she likes with her endless questionnaires and cognitive tests and abstract pictures and the electrodes she attaches to my head. No one can help me. Even she knows that. It is why I am writing this in crayon. They give me paper and a blue fucking *crayon* with which to write. They think I would try and kill myself if they gave me a pencil or a pen, think I would jab the instrument through my carotid artery if I had the chance, bleed out and die like Scott did. Yeah.

They are so fucking right. They are so fucking right. That is exactly what I would do.

And I *will* find a way—I just need to figure it out. In the meantime, I write in blue crayon and record this wretched legacy of mine. 724 people dead. That was the final number, apparently. Nearly a thousand ruined families, my photo on the front page of the *Washington Post* and *The Times* and *Le Monde* and *Der Spiegel* and whatever else, and scrawls of blue crayon over a few hundred pages of foolscap paper. What a wretched legacy indeed.

I know what I have done. I know what I have become. And the recognition of that is not just mine alone. My parents haven't come to see me—and I've been here for over sixteen months now. They will not come, this I know. And it matters little to me, to be honest. What matters to me is that Lorna will not come either. *She* will not come. So I have to pretend she doesn't know where I am. I have to pretend. I do understand this is not the reality. I do realize that I am like the drowning man, clinging to wreckage. But in this place, I need some wreckage to cling to—it keeps me sane, even if the police doctor contends that I am not.

And how that pretence manifests itself. In the late afternoon, an orderly comes and I'm allowed to take a walk in the garden for an hour. In truth, I care little for the hospital grounds. The lawn is scorched brown by the sun, and the few shrubs and plants that surround it are withered and dying. Dead bougainvillea cascades down the whitewashed perimeter walls, unmoved by any breeze. Even the large wrought-iron gates that are set into the far wall, and the razor wire that sits atop them, are scarred and mottled by rust. Everything here seems touched by death or decay. So I hate this place. And I cannot leave—I know what the point of the razor wire is, of course. I know why the walls are so high. The design is for people like me. *People like me.* But the one interesting feature of the hospital grounds is that you can see through the rusting iron gates out on to the street. The orderly told me it's Barakhamba Road, which isn't far from Lorna's house, only half a mile or so. And every day, for an hour, I sit alone on this wooden bench in the spiky shadows cast by a babul tree, and look out past the hospital walls. And every day, I pretend to myself that I'll see Lorna, taking a walk down to the shops or going to one of those cafés she likes near the park. I can picture it so clearly in my mind that it actually makes me cry each time I think of it—for some reason, the artifice of the thought in no way dilutes the emotion it conjures.

I have stared out through those gates every day for the last sixteen months. And I have learned to suppress the fact that it is not reality—for if I didn't, the wreckage would slip beneath the surface and I would surely drown. I know it is an illusion, that I am tricking my own mind. To me, that doesn't matter. And so it happens like this:

> She will be pushing a buggy, of course. I'll call out her name and she'll see me through the bars, smiling that smile that creases the skin around her eyes, flushes her cheeks. And the orderly will open the gates for me, and as I approach Lorna, I will see tears of happiness in her eyes, and then we will kiss and hold one another. I will clutch our baby close to my chest as we talk for a while, idle talk of going off to faraway places, of how it came to pass that we fell so in love with one another, of the endless metaphors and flirting that preceded '*us*', of the kisses we subsequently shared. We'll talk of *all* of the things that passed, of the simple happiness I always felt when I held her in my arms, of the comfort I felt as she wrapped her body around mine in bed, of the first time we made love, of all the times we made love after that . . . These were the things that were important to me, and yet perhaps she never knew exactly *how* important they were. Of course, I will tell her that, what she means to me. But it won't matter. Because we will talk of the little things too, and then she will know. Then she will know. We'll talk of the countless setting suns we watched together from the plateau, of the times we drank late into the night huddled together for warmth by the fire, of those seemingly endless summer afternoons when we wandered barefoot and hand in hand along the cool, pine-scented forest paths searching for fruit. These were the little things that meant everything to me, too. They did. They meant *everything*.
>
> And then the orderly will walk out on to the pavement to bid me farewell. I'll thank him for the kindness he has shown me, and he'll smile and tell me how beautiful Lorna looks. He will remind me how lucky I am to have her. He is right, of course. I always knew how lucky I was to have her.

And then we'll walk from this place, her hand in mine, down Barakhamba Road. Sticking pins in maps won't matter any more, for finally I will have found my purpose in life, finally I'll have found my direction. Yes, we will walk from this place, the three of us, a family. We will walk down Barakhamba Road, her hand in mine, squinting against the low, orange sun.

AFTERWORD

In May 1989, after a trial lasting two months, Ethan Hicks was convicted on 724 counts of murder and one count of manslaughter. He was sentenced to death by hanging. In December 1989, following his legal team's successful appeal to the Supreme Court of India, the sentence was commuted to life imprisonment on the grounds of diminished responsibility. In summation, however, the bench of five judges ruled that due to the grievous nature of his crimes, there would be no possibility of early release.

Despite one of the largest manhunts in India's history, Hal Fredericks and Div Mulvane were never apprehended. In June 1989, both were convicted *in absentia* on 724 counts of murder and sentenced to death by hanging. Although an article published in 1990 by an investigative journalist working for the *Times of India* claimed they were living in a remote village in northern Bangladesh, a police operation launched shortly after the publication of the story failed to locate them. However, local villagers did confirm a western couple matching their description had indeed lived there for some months.

In January 1991, Ethan Hicks was found hanged in his cell. No family or friends were reported to have attended his funeral. His body is now buried at Kashmere Gate Cemetery, New Delhi. The manuscript that he wrote while in prison, and upon which this book is based, can be viewed in Delhi's National Museum.

Lorna Roberts committed suicide in Delhi in September 1991. She was survived by one son.